# AT HOME IN HELLAS

# AT HOME IN HELLAS

## Life and Love in Ancient Greece

DAVID WESTON MARSHALL

LOMA PALOMA PRESS
Loma Paloma, Texas

ISBN-13: 978-0-9976866-0-9

*for Vicki*

# TABLE OF CONTENTS

# PREFACE

The world is well-aware of the astonishing impact of ancient Greek culture on western civilization, and the proliferation of that culture around the globe. Hellenic contributions are apparent in our social and economic systems, and in our political experimentations ranging from democracy to dictatorship.

Hellenes absorbed eastern lore and formed the foundations of our science, philosophy, spirituality, ethics, literature, art, architecture, music, theater, and athletics. Their mythology continues to infuse our popular culture. The material items they left behind form the core of our museums. Even our daily vocabulary, with words like *museum* from the Greek word *muse*, reveals our indebtedness to the world they created three thousand years ago.

Every school child knows the names of Achilles, Odysseus, Helen, Homer, Sophocles, Socrates, Plato, Aristotle, and other renowned persons of that vibrant civilization. But few know about the daily lives of the common people who worked and played, hoped and feared, lived and loved, much as we do today. Abundant information is available in the form of ancient literature and archeological evidence. But modern insight into lifeways is lacking.

The purpose of *At Home in Hellas* is to reveal the daily lives of the ancient Greeks by presenting a wealth of factual information in the framework of a lively fictional narrative. The narrative portrays the lives of Astrape (ä-strä'pē), his twin brother Bronte (brōn'tē), grandfather Pappos (pä'pōs), grandmother Ama (ä'mä), wife Tempe (tĕ'mpē), and grandson Pais (pās).

Their story emerges in the context of actual historical and cultural settings, and focuses on Athens and Attica during the Hellenic (Classical) Era, 495-350 BC. Ancient eyewitnesses who left written records are quoted in the text to provide the reader with an authentic feel for Hellenic thought and expression.

The narrative also features the tales of the forty-eight classical constellations, compiled from literature that spans nine hundred years from Homer (c. 750 BC) to Claudius Ptolemy (c. 150 AD). These timeless tales have captured the human imagination from prehistory to the present, and provide a compendium of Greek mythology, practical astronomy, philosophical speculation on the cosmos, and the fundamental moral beliefs of the Hellenes. Additional technical information, maps, charts, diagrams, and illustrations appear in the author's earlier non-fiction publication: *Ancient Skies* (W.W. Norton, 2018).

Readers who wish to dig deeper into the true historical context of *At Home in Hellas* may use the maps, endnotes, works cited, glossary, timeline, appendices, and index. These and color illustrations are also available at:

*https://davidwestonmarshall.com/at-home-in-hellas/*

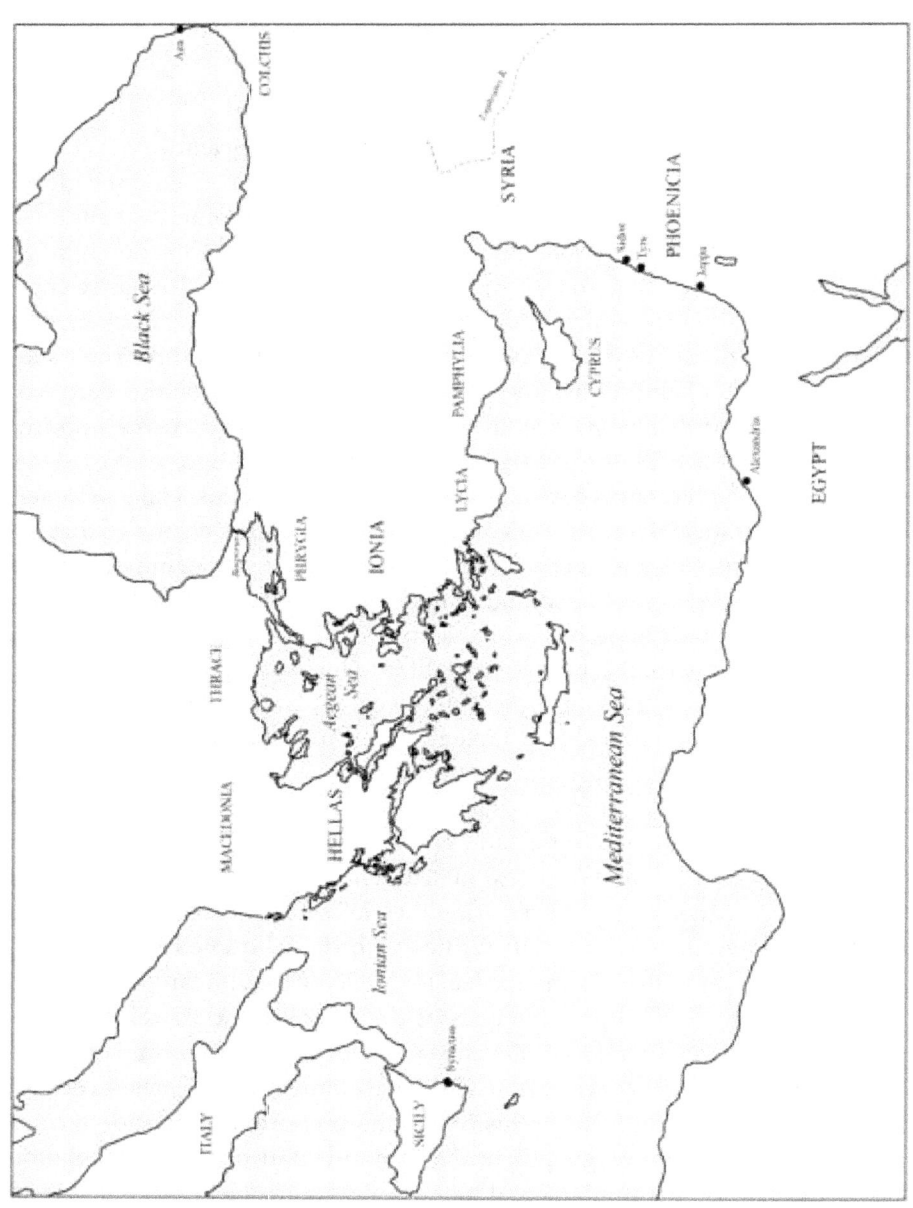

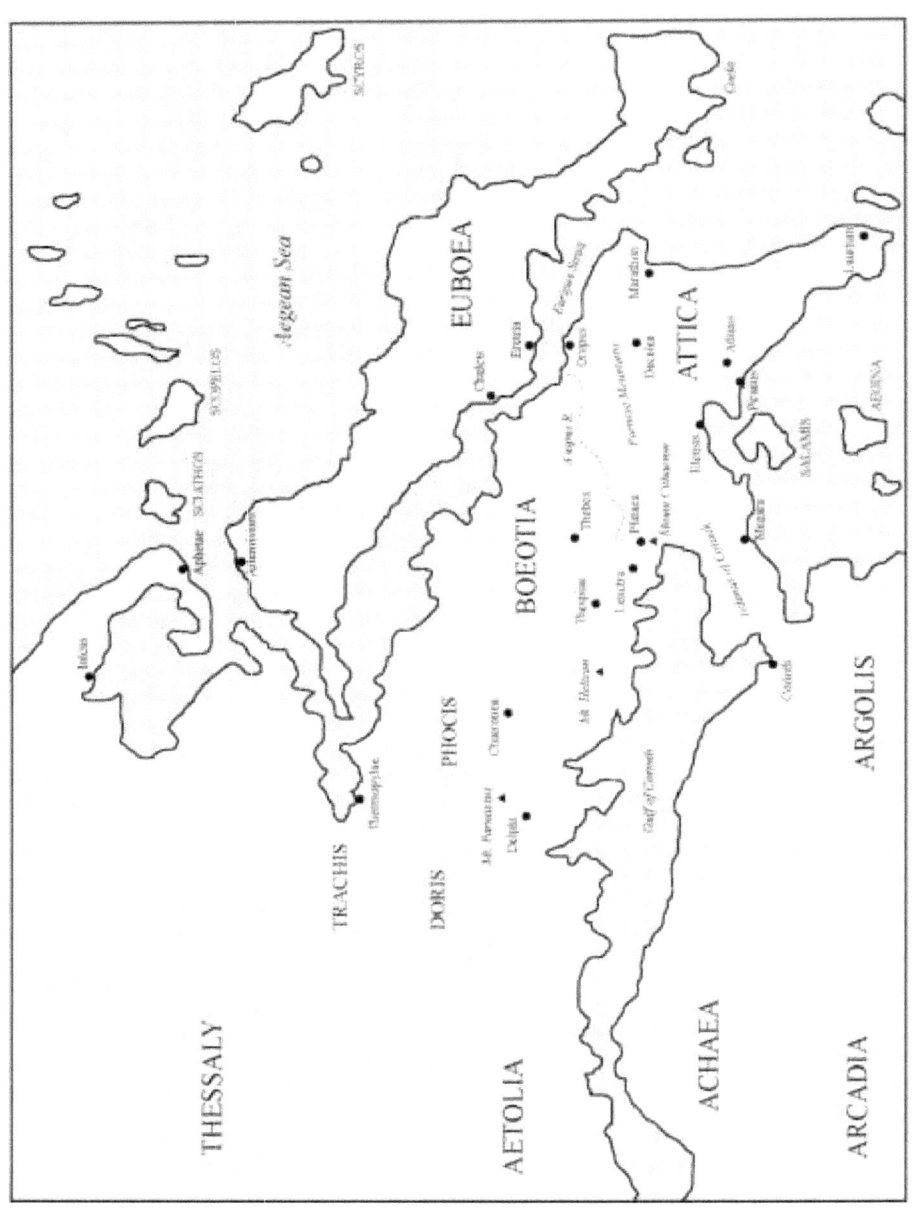

# Chapter 1.  A LOST LITTLE BOY

IN THE DREARY DARKNESS of a long winter night, while the world burrowed deep in sleep, I suddenly awoke and sat upright, shaken by the sound
of a mournful scream. My drowsy mind struggled to become alert. My ears
strained to hear. But silent moments suggested that the haunting cry was just
a dream.

I lay awake until the first purple hint of dawn on the eastern horizon forced
my phantom thoughts to flee. Then I rose to my feet with renewed spirit. Hefting a jug in each hand, I left the hut behind and tramped through dewy meadows toward a fresh, flowing spring to collect the daily draft of water.

As I reached a ridge, I paused for a moment, enchanted by the serene silence of the sleeping forest. I watched as the fading stars surrendered the sky
to *rosy-fingered Dawn*.[1] I peered among the trees as she slowly spread her light
to disperse the darkness and reveal nature's beauty.

The somber woodlands sprang to life with increasing clarity and color. The
melancholy hoot of the owl gave way to the cheerful song of the robin. And
when the sun finally peeked over the horizon, all the birds of field and forest
joined the joyful chorus.

A sense of satisfaction welled within as I descended toward the spring that
flowed through a deep hollow five hundred steps from home. Upon reaching
the foggy bottom, I heard the distant flutter of a flute, its notes wavering in
the damp morning air. From the tone and simple tune, I recognized Pais piping his humble piece of reed, though he remained hidden in the distance.

The tranquility of the morning, the fresh mist on my face, and the playful
sound of a five-year-old boy heralding the coming day, filled me with contentment. Pais was not one to dawdle indoors. An adventurous spirit drove
him into the surrounding hills to probe and explore with his closest companions—a flock of sheep and goats.

The only challenge came in convincing him that he was still too young to
shepherd alone out of sight of home. He was a headstrong boy with an independent heart. His personality, like that of most children, was becoming apparent at an early age.

I stooped to capture the cold spring water as it poured from a natural spout
of solid rock, worn smooth by centuries of constant flowing water. As the water filled the jug, some splashed to the ground and resumed the downhill

course. I glanced at the ground to save my sandals from the mud, then dropped the jug and jerked upright.

The wolf was back. I stared hard for a moment, frozen by the sight of a massive muddy track. The light filtered dimly through the willows by the spring. But my eyes did not deceive me.

The pawprint was too large for a jackal or fox. It was too large for the local dogs that roamed the woods in search of hares. It was even too large for most wolves. I shuddered while scanning the surrounding gloom.

Most wolves are not feared in backcountry Attica. Most are opportunists that remain aloof unless they spy a careless shepherd's straggling lamb. I have seen them stand at a respectful distance, assessing me with curiosity rather than malice as I walked alone in high meadows and forests. After vigilant moments, they vanished.

Dogs are thought to descend from wolves that, long ago, crept to campfires to beg for scraps from the hunt. But some wolves are not so sociable. They, like humans, sometimes produce malicious offspring of their own. This one descended from a frightening lineage of wolves familiar to local families for generations.

My grandfather had warned me to take heed of their features—a dark gray coat, a light gray mane, huge proportions, and a vicious disposition. Now, as a grandfather myself, I recall several scrapes with these rogues during my seventy-five years on earth. This wolf had haunted the wildwoods for years, long enough to learn the tricks of survival and evade hunters and their arsenal of traps.

Leaving the water jugs in the mud, I rushed from the thicket through barren grainfields in rapid retreat for home. From far behind, an ominous wail shattered the silence, like the scream in the night, and sent shivers up my spine. As my feet slipped forward over soggy furrows and stubble, I glanced behind toward the gloomy hollow but failed to see the beast that forced my flight.

I pressed on until close to home, then suddenly stopped, frozen in place, as a knot formed in my throat. The livestock pen with its crisscrossed logs stood before me. Each winter, we stacked the logs in a fallow field to allow the flock to nibble the stubble left from the harvest of grain. In return, the animals deposited a fertile layer of manure.

The pen provided protection during the night, but now it stood empty. The top logs had been lowered to free the fold. Pais had been impatient to wander the woods with his companions, and released them before my return. I called out for the boy, but my panicked shouts brought no response.

Hurrying to our hut, I burst through the door and babbled the story to Tempe. Without pause, she swiftly gathered a pouch of provisions, grabbed a goatskin of water, and rushed me out the door in search of our grandson.

I headed northwest at the fastest possible speed as if with a destination in mind. But, in truth, I only surmised which way Pais had wandered. Sheep and goats from surrounding farms had riddled the hills with cloven hoofprints, leaving no way to track one tiny flock in the early morning light.

The evening before, I had mentioned the mild winter weather that offered a chance for us to free the fold to graze the upland grasses. The southeast wind had blown steadily for seven days, bringing warmth to steal some chill from the air. Pais' excitement at the prospect should have served as a warning.

At the first farmstead, fate smiled faintly upon me as an old friend shouted from a doorway, telling me that a bleating drove had dashed up the trail, heard but unseen in the fog. I followed the direction, frustrated by my sluggish steps and longing for younger days when I could have gone triple the pace.

Now I shuffled along, hampered by aching joints and brittle bones. Not a billy or nanny, not a ram or ewe would be moving as slowly as me. I imagined the animals gaining greater distance with every jubilant jump and bound.

As the morning wore on, my legs wore out. The sun had now dispelled the fog, and I leaned on my staff in its radiant warmth to catch my breath before climbing a steeper trail through prickly scrub oak. Gritting my teeth, I shouldered the pouch and pushed upward. All that long afternoon, I struggled up the dwindling trace, following fresh droppings and desperately hoping that they marked the trail of our flock.

The path proved lonely. I met no shepherds coming or going. As much as I tried to dismiss the thought, I imagined a ravenous wolf stalking a lamb that was guarded by a child too young to defend either it or himself.

Toward evening, the faint strain of a flute caught my ears. The low, mellow tones sounded like those of a shepherd calming the fold, and revealed a somber mood. They did not resound like the excited trills heard at festivals and weddings, or the martial tunes of athletic games and military marches.

Leaving the trail that led up the mountain, I steered a steeper course through shifting scree and jagged rocks. At times, I crawled on tattered hands and knees and finally clawed my way atop a cliff. Poking my head above the rugged outcrop, I found myself face to face with an audience of curious sheep and goats—some white, some brown, some spotted white and brown, and all with quizzical stares as they chewed from side-to-side in slow unison. As I struggled to my feet and dusted scraped knees, the flock resumed nibbling and slowly withdrew without missing so much as a blade of grass.

At this elevation, the sea breeze buffeted my hair and cloak, and the salty smell mingled with the fresh fragrance of highland pine. Far below, the sea shone crystal blue under azure skies. A line of gray on the northern horizon revealed the coast of Euboea across the Strait of Euripus.

Above the whistle of wind in the trees, I heard the flute again, more clearly now as it reached me on the breeze. My attention turned to a twisted grove of ancient oaks clinging to a rocky precipice. As I approached, my attempt at stealth was betrayed by the crunch of dry winter grass. The flute fell silent.

A youthful face peeked from behind a gnarled oak. The child rushed to me with a smile of relief and held me in a lingering hug. For a moment, I felt too grateful and weary to scold him, but plopped down on a clump of grass to catch my breath. Pais settled beside me and together we silently sat, watching the white-capped waves break upon the sea.

A nibble of fig and a swallow of water revived me. At last, I turned to Pais and gave a soft but stern warning of the dangers of wolves. He heard once more how he should never wander without letting me know. After a period of respectful silence, Pais explained in a downcast tone that he only intended to free the flock from the pen and graze them near the homestead until I returned from the spring.

But the lead billy goat thought otherwise and left on a quick trot for the highlands with his charges chasing close behind. Pais had no choice but to follow and stay within sight. I understood, and well imagined how the old billy had quickly deduced the child's limited power over him, in the same way that a horse tests his rider to determine who is really in control.

As I whispered to him of the renegade wolf in the area, he sat upright, fearful for our safety and that of the fold. The day was late, and I decided we must remain for the night. To risk scattering the animals along the trail in the fading light might invite disaster. We quickly constructed a crude pen of brambles and brush, woven among the hoary trunks of the oaks.

As darkness descended, Pais pulled the last stubborn goat into the makeshift pen and fetched a final armful of kindling. After laboriously spinning a vertical stick atop a piece of pine, I succeeded in firing up a red-hot ember. We snuggled close and fed the flame.

A blazing campfire always lifts the spirits, with the security it provides from predators, its warmth on a cold night, the aroma of roasting meat, and the reassuring glow that plays on the faces of family huddled close. A thousand generations of ancestors hovered over their fires for the same reasons, and now we inherently long for the cozy comfort and soothing incense.

On cold nights we crouch by the blaze, trading tales and laughing at shooting sparks. Then one-by-one we slip into silence, mesmerized by the crackle and sputter, and the colorful, dancing flames. At last, we nestle near the glowing coals and drift to sleep.

As I sat, lost in thought, a rising breeze fanned the fire and caused the embers to glow and spark. Knocking down the kindling, I contented myself with rubbing sore toes and bemoaning my weary feet—the victims of too many ventures into rugged mountains and too many marches as a young man decked in bronze. Pais listened patiently as I told him again how the young and old are assigned light tasks together, like herding the flock; the young because their muscles require greater strength to push the plow, and the old because their frail limbs have failed them.

Boys might lack the strength of men, but are compensated by boundless energy, high hopes, and untarnished dreams. The elderly, with their glory days behind them, must seek satisfaction like Laertes, the father of Odysseus. In his final years, he delighted in tending a vineyard on the island of Ithaca while recounting youthful voyages to distant lands aboard the sturdy ship *Argo*.

Some do not fare so well. The old men of Athens, with no livelihood, remain dependent on eldest sons for leftover food, discarded clothing, and a dark corner to lay their blanket. In search of purpose, they spend their days attending gatherings of the Assembly, or volunteering to serve on juries so they can receive the tiny compensation of two obols a day. I am more fortunate to delight in the shepherd's life and the freedom and pleasure of spending my final years in the peaceful hills with family by my side.

Pais had begun to play the flute softly as I spoke. But now, in silence, we watched the darkening hues of sky and sea as the sun fell farther below the western horizon. Soon our sight became confined to the firelight that flitted among the branches above and cast a glow ten paces away. We detected movement in the darkness now, and saw or imagined gleaming eyes that appeared, disappeared, and reappeared at various points around the perimeter.

I urged Pais to vigilance. The odds remained in our favor that these skulking phantoms were common wolves with appetites for lambs, no doubt, but fearful of the dangerous circle of light.

Brown bears also roam these hills but rarely bother a shepherd's camp. They attack, instead, to defend their cubs or claim the carcass of a deer. Shepherds sometimes pipe the flute while walking warily through the woods to warn bears of their presence and give them time to lumber away.

Lion sightings are rare. Through many wandering years in the wild, I have never seen one. But Pappos recalled the terror that seized small villages in olden times. He told chilling tales of screaming victims dragged from their beds and into the brush. Yet even then, most lions stalked wilder regions like the mountain forests of Arcadia.

I resolved to remain on watchful guard through the long winter night, as I had many times in the past. The day's suspense would help to chase fatigue away, and to pass the time and discourage predators, I planned to talk aloud until dawn.

Pais burrowed deep in his cloak and pressed close to my side. Softly, he pleaded with me to tell the stories of the stars—the tales of old that my own grandfather had often told.

I remained silent for a time, reflecting on the shining stars and remembering dear old Pappos, who sat with my twin brother and me through long winter nights so many years ago. With deep emotion and reverent devotion, he told the ancient tales, carefully passing them down to us like precious pieces of pottery bestowed from one generation to the next. A wiseman once said that *the lessons of our childhood make a wonderful impression on our memories*.[2] Sure enough, Pappos' stories still resound within and inspire my conscious thought.

Pais peered from under his hood and patiently awaited an answer. At last, I revealed how Pappos had first recounted the stories to us when he was as old as I am now, and Bronte and I were only the age of Pais. He was our grandfather, but he called us his boys because he had lost his only son as we had lost our father, and he raised us as his own. Together we used to lay with the flock and listened close as the old man spoke, while our curious eyes searched the infinite skies.

We lived at the old homeplace then, on a hill that loomed above Euripus Strait, forty-eight stades southeast of Oropus.[3] Nearby, an ancient altar of rugged stone stood in a shady grove of oaks—a hallowed site where our family had searched their souls for untold ages. Pappos loved to pen the flock there at night, where the rocky bluff gave a brilliant view of the heavens above and the sparkling sea below.

On one unforgettable night, he tugged leafy twigs off an evergreen holm oak branch and braided them into a wreath. Holding the wreath aloft, he framed a cluster of stars and then another, telling the story of each constellation in turn. The memory of his gentle voice now stirred within me, and my mind returned to that place and time as I repeated his words aloud:

Fauna of ancient Greece included wild boars, lions, and deer, depicted on this vase painting. Ceramicus Archeological Museum, Athens. Photo by author.

# Chapter 2.  LESSONS OF LOVE AND DEVOTION

*Recalling the words of Pappos*

MY BOYS, ARE YOU AWARE that shepherds in their tattered tunics and ragged sandals are the most prosperous people of all? It is true, because we are free from the worries of the wealthy who forever fight to protect their fleeting possessions. We live in love, in the beauty of nature, and rejoice at night in the starry heavens.

Ages ago, Homer, the poet observed: *In the sky about the gleaming moon the stars shine clear when the air is windless, and into view come all mountain peaks and high headlands and glades, and from heaven breaks open the infinite air, and all the stars are seen, and the shepherd rejoices in his heart.*[4]

While the weary flock silently sleeps, we watch from dusk to dawn as thousands of shining stars rise in the east and roam westward through the night. We search the skies with eyes alert and soon perceive a starry parade in steady procession, traveling in family groups called constellations.

As we watch, we recall the ancient stories of the stars—the tales of old, of heroes and foes conveyed by the constellations. The stories urge us to live in harmony like the stars above. They teach us to walk in peace, as one, and avoid conceit, greed, and strife. They reveal the path to a complete and contented life.[5]

Now, my boys, peek through the wreath as I hold it high and notice a cluster of stars above the eastern horizon. Do you see two stars that gather close and outshine the others around them? These mark the hallowed heads of the TWINS, sons of Zeus named Castor and Polydeuces.[6] They stand side by side as constant companions with arms around each other's shoulders.

Through the trials and triumphs of life on earth, they remained devoted to each other and to all those around them. You, my twins, should always follow their example. Astrape, you must always stand by Bronte, and Bronte by Astrape. Beyond each other, your devotion should reach to family, friends, and strangers; to creatures of farm, field, and forest; to the woodland nymphs and immortal gods, and the mysterious source of all creation. In spirit, we are one, created to live in love.

Alongside the Twins, Castor and Polydeuces, other ancestral heroes shine as heavenly constellations. This is their eternal reward for earthly service to mortals and immortals alike. Long ago, an Athenian named Erechtheus gained the same lasting fame by seeking a life that was whole in body, mind, and soul. In his youth, all of Athens adored his athletic skills. He ran swifter of foot than any man and on horseback had no rivals. Still, Erechtheus searched inside for self-improvement, and relentlessly sought to gain greater speed.

First, he carefully matched his four fastest steeds. Then he trained them as a team to pull a two-wheeled cart of his own design. Together they rushed down dusty roads faster than man could fathom. Farmers with ox carts, slow as snails, gaped as the charioteer flew past with his hair and tunic billowing.

All the while, Erechtheus perfected the chariot's wheels and learned to manage the team on tight turns and rolling hills. Other athletes followed his lead and raced by his side like the rush of the wind. But none ever matched his valor or speed in the Panathenaic or Olympian Games.

Beyond being an athlete and clever inventor, Erechtheus became the most pious of men—a devoted disciple of the goddess Athena. He was the first to take a torch in hand and lead a procession under the stars to the limestone crest of the Acropolis. There he erected the first Athenian temple built in her honor.

Athena admired Erechtheus with fond affection, and he responded to her in kind. In this way, he reached the pinnacle of human potential. For we can only gain greatness through love and humble devotion to an ideal greater than ourselves. As an accomplished athlete and a wise and pious person, he achieved *arete*—excellence and virtue.[7] And he proved that *arete* never results in arrogance, but only in adoration.

At the end of his long and illustrious life, Erechtheus attained a reward in heaven. Here he shines in the night to show what mortals may become.[8] As a cluster of stars, he appears as the CHARIOTEER, standing tall and tugging the reins with the same powerful poise as the bronze statue in Delphi.[9]

Through the centuries, his children's children followed his example and built more temples to revere their beloved Athena. Sometimes they named the structures after Erechtheus to commemorate his devotion. The latest, the Erechtheum, rises on the Acropolis near the Parthenon, the temple of the maiden Athena.

The Erechtheum shelters the goddess' sacred olive tree, the same one she caused to sprout on the Acropolis long ago when first she pledged to protect Athens. The temple also houses an olive bough, carefully carved in Athena's immortal image.

As the craftsmen constructed the Erechtheum, they fashioned a set of six columns in the form of marble maidens to oversee the sacred tree. These maidens, the Caryatids, are priestesses of the goddess Carya—the guardian of walnut, hazelnut, and related fruit-bearing trees.[10] It was Carya who furnished these fruits to save our starving Achaean ancestors when times were hard, long before humans knew how to herd or farm. Now her maidens protect the olive, Athena's greatest gift to mortals.

In life, Erechtheus adored Athena for her many gifts and blessings. But he also loved all beings, great and small. As a constellation, he portrays gentle kindness by bearing on his left shoulder an old and feeble nanny GOAT named Almalthea. The Goat shines as one of the brightest stars in the sky because she, too, was known for her service to mortals and gods, and especially to Zeus.

When Zeus was newly born, his mother Rhea placed the tiny babe in a lonely cave on the isle of Crete. Here she hoped to hide him from his fearsome titan father, Cronus, who planned to destroy Zeus and the other infant gods he had sired. In this way, he sought to forestall the prophecy that one of them would one day depose him. Rhea, desperate to save her son, relinquished Zeus to the care of Almalthea to nurse and raise him in seclusion.

The nanny Goat dutifully adopted Zeus, not from fear, but from affection for the goddess Rhea. And so Almalthea suckled the infant god alongside her own twin Kids—her rambunctious baby goats. Soon she came to love him as her own. Zeus spent his childhood in Almalthea's cozy cave and grew to youth without the soft touch of his mother. But Almalthea cuddled and cared for him dearly and delighted to see him befriend the animals and nymphs around him.

Kindhearted Almalthea also raised an orphan goat beside her own twin Kids and the infant Zeus. She named him Aegoceros, meaning Goat Horn, because he loved to lock horns with the other goats, and push and play. The four grew up as brothers and remained friends for life. One can only imagine the adventures and escapades of the three young goats and the toddler god as they explored every mysterious nook and cranny of their cavernous home.

As they grew older, they ventured into the outside world to scramble atop boulders and splash across sparkling brooks. From morning to night, they played their favorite games and dared each other to perform reckless deeds, as boys will do. No doubt their poor nanny worried whenever they wandered from sight.

As the little foursome roamed the rocky shore one blustery day, Aegoceros, an excellent swimmer, dove into the spray and swam deep into the turquoise sea. After a long absence that caused his companions to anxiously wait and wonder, he suddenly bobbed to the surface. High above his head he held an exquisite conch shell that glistened like gold in the morning light.

No sooner had he splashed ashore on the pebble beach than he placed the seashell against his lips and blew a perfectly deafening trumpet blast. His wide-eyed partners jumped in alarm, then leapt and laughed in delight. Falling in line, they formed a procession, marching and shouting, and taking turns bugling until blue in the face. From that day forward, Aegoceros always kept his conch shell by his side, dangling from a cord.

The four friends enjoyed a carefree childhood, but all boys must grow up to assume the duties of adults. The time at last arrived for Zeus to claim his divine destiny—to rule over gods and titans as the prophecy foretold. Alongside him stood his constant companion, Aegoceros, who followed him into battle against Cronus and the titan host. The gods Hephaestus and Dionysus, riding on two Donkeys, also joined the march. And other deities, satyrs, and sympathetic supporters took up arms in a war between titans and gods.

After a long and weary journey, the army of Zeus discovered the dreaded lair of the titans, who remained unaware of their presence. Silently, Zeus and his band crept forward as close as they dared. In the final moment, near the mouth of the titan cave, Aegoceros put his lips to the conch shell and gave a mighty blast.

The deafening noise reverberated through the winding cavern and echoed around the surrounding hills, causing the two Donkeys to bray with all the strength of their lungs. The awful din so unnerved the titans that they dropped their weapons and fled in panic, never pausing to look behind them. Zeus and his faithful followers celebrated a great victory that night, although many battles remained to be fought.

The hero of the moment was Aegoceros, who Zeus, the god of sky and storm, now honored in grateful embrace. Many times, in battles to come, the simple goat turned the tide in favor of the gods. He did so not by the strength of the sword or by dazzling displays of daring, but with his favorite conch shell, a childhood toy, from the depths of the surging sea.

While the years passed and Zeus waxed strong as ruler of the gods, Almalthea, his nanny, waned in frail old age. When the day arrived that the nanny died, Zeus wept tears that showered down in heavy rains upon the earth.

To remember Almalthea from that moment on, he kept her soft and supple hide as a sign of her love and protection. In desperate times, he held it close and bore it in battle against his titan foes. The hide became his breastplate, the Aegis, his symbol of invincible strength. In grateful esteem, he gave the Goat a star of her own in the sky, where Erechtheus carefully carries her on his shoulder.

Zeus, being immortal, remained in his prime while most of his friends dwindled and died. Even his playmates, Almalthea's twin KIDS, followed behind their mother. Now they rest in Erechtheus' left hand, close beneath the nanny, and shine as two tiny, twinkling beams of light.

In the same way, Aegoceros came to the end of his days. High in heaven, his constellation, called GOAT HORN, honors him for bearing the bugle that won so many battles. It also applauds his aquatic skills and shows him swimming through the stars, as he once splashed in the Aegean Sea. But now he has a fish's tail to propel him as he holds his head and horns high above the surf.

The two DONKEYS, who assisted the gods as beasts of burden and helped to rout the titans, also share a prominent place above. Here they appear as two neighboring astral lights, riding eternally atop the head of the constellation called the CRAB. The Crab, as punishment for bad behavior, now serves the Donkeys as their beast of burden. To add to their reward, a heaping MANGER of golden straw rests within reach of their muzzles. At night, the straw shimmers in the distant sky as a hazy cluster of stars, with the hungry Donkeys nibbling from either side.[11]

Zeus and his friends and followers won the first fights with the titans. But the conflict turned against the gods when Gaea, who is Mother Earth and mother of the titans, brought forth her final offspring—the monster Typhon. The creature's enormous size, earth-shattering strength, and fiery breath made him the fiercest beast to ever be unleashed. Typhon rumbled forth from the bowels of the earth, determined to hunt down the deities and devour them one by one. Several fled in despair or disguised themselves as birds or fishes in order to take flight in the sky or find refuge in rivers and seas.

The goddess Aphrodite and her son, Eros, hid in the land of Syria. There they thought themselves safely beyond his reach. But as they dawdled dreamily down the bank of the River Euphrates one day, Typhon appeared without warning, as was his way. With a deafening roar, he burst from the earth and pursued them in volcanic fury. Pinned between fire and water, Aphrodite grabbed Eros in her arms and desperately dove for the depths of the river.

Aphrodite was born of the sea and easily adapted herself and her son to the water. In haste, they took the forms of fishes so they could breathe and swim in their new surroundings. To keep her son close by her side, she tied each end of a cord to their tails.

Fortunately for them, Typhon was a fiery fiend who despised the cold and quenching effects of water. He balked at the thought of pursuing them as they darted among the slippery rocks, through tangles and snags, and swam with the current to safety. Steaming and hissing in bitter rage, he angrily abandoned the chase. A comfortable distance downstream, Aphrodite and Eros emerged from their refuge and dried themselves in the springtime sun and balmy breeze.

In the years that followed, Syrians who resided along the river refused to eat fish because they respected the divine mother and child. Zeus, for his part, celebrated the close escape by designating stars to form the FISHES. High in the night sky, Aphrodite swims down the flowing stream of the Euphrates, still tied by a cord to Eros who dashes and darts to her left.

For further distinction, Zeus ordained that the sun should traverse their constellation in its annual passage across the sky. Now, every year, when the sun aligns with the Fishes, it marks the close of the cold and rainy season and heralds the emergence of lifegiving spring.

In later years, another fish of the swift Euphrates gained similar fame for saving Derceto, the daughter of Aphrodite. Derceto, in honor of her mother's escape from Typhon, had always favored the fishes of the river. At her temple in Bambyce near the banks of the Euphrates, she kept her favorite scaly friends in a sacred lake. Each day, she fed them as they gathered in schools and gaped above the surface.

One evening, as she leaned with food in hand far over the water, she lost her footing and slipped into the tranquil lake. Quick as a flash, the largest fish flicked his fins and darted beneath her sinking form. Rising to the surface, he laid her on the bank and saved Derceto from drowning.

Aphrodite, the grateful mother, rejoiced in the rescue and recognized the valiant deed by assigning the fish a place in the cosmos. Here, he is called the SOUTHERN FISH because of his position low in the southern sky. Like Aphrodite and Eros, he is praised by the Syrians, who honor the three by fashioning delicate fish designs of silver and gold.

The Southern Fish is adorned with one of the most dazzling stars in heaven, marking his gaping mouth beneath two tiny eyes.[12] As he swims across the celestial sphere, he opens wide to drink a draft of water poured as a pure libation by the constellation called Water Bearer.

Another wanderer of the watery deep, the Dolphin, received similar acclaim for his selfless service to a divine being. Poseidon, god of the sea, presided over all the dolphins and other creatures of his aquatic domain. But his powerful presence caused his minions to shudder and stay away. As a result, he remained quite lonely as he languished in his palatial undersea cave.

At last, he declared his longing desire to marry a modest nymph named Amphitrite. The coy sea-maiden was flustered and frightened by the affections of the powerful god. Straightaway, she fled far to the west where the waters of the Mediterranean Sea lap the shores near the Atlas Mountains.

Poseidon confided his feelings to his friend, the Dolphin, and convinced him of his genuine love for the girl. The Dolphin, fully assured of the god's good intentions, departed with haste through the salty sea to search for Amphitrite.

High and low he looked, not in wide open waters, nor on islands where sea folks gather, but in secret coves and sunken caverns far beyond the horizon. He knew the hideouts of the deep, every crack and chasm, every cave and coral reef. Time and again, as he swam beneath the waves and leaped above the surf, he scattered schools of fishes and slipped away from sinister sharks.

After searching for many days, the Dolphin discovered Amphitrite trembling in a tiny cave, surrounded by seahorses and starfishes — her only friends. With gentle words of encouragement, he assured the nymph of her suitor's love and convinced her to wed the god of the sea. Upon their long-awaited return, he presented the timid bride to Poseidon. The Dolphin then presided over the nuptials before a beaming, bubbling audience — a colorful array of the creatures of the sea.

On countless other occasions, the Dolphin and his kinsmen served humans equally well by guiding ships and saving floundering seamen. Even the Argonauts fondly recalled how *dolphins in calm weather leap up from the sea and circle a ship in schools as it speeds along, sometimes showing up in front, sometimes behind, sometimes alongside, and joy comes to the sailors.*[13]

For his service to Poseidon and fearless seafarers, the DOLPHIN earned an eternal home in the stars. There he leaps with elation and offers a sign of assurance at night for navigators traveling the trackless sea.

Mortal men like Erechtheus, and beasts of the earth, like Almalthea, the Kids, Aegoceros, and the Donkeys, faithfully served the divine deities. In similar manner, Syrians revered Aphrodite and Eros as the Fishes. And watery creatures, like the Southern Fish and the Dolphin, aided and honored the gods.

The birds of the air also displayed their devotion on many occasions. In fact, all of the deities have their favorite birds that faithfully serve them. The little owl is Athena's constant companion, as shown on the silver drachmas of the Athenians. Zeus' winged friend is the mighty Eagle.

As Zeus' campaign against the titans continued, the war clouds gathered. Lightning flashed in the stormy sky and rumbled in echoes of thunder. Beneath the terrible tempest, Zeus prepared his anxious army for battle. As he attempted to quell their fears and prompted them to perform valiant deeds, an enormous Eagle suddenly appeared like a rush of wind and alighted by Zeus' right side.

A spirited shout resounded through the ranks as the soldiers witnessed this favorable omen. Their hearts now swelled with courage, and they bolted forth to scatter the titan foe. As they hammered swords against shields, clinking and clanging in wrathful rage, the Eagle circled high above, offering inspiration.

At the end of the day, with the battle won, the Eagle returned to the god of sky and storm. Zeus raised the raptor high above his head, perched on his upraised fist, and declared him his friend from that day forward. In ages to come, the Eagle often proved his allegiance and favored Zeus with offerings. When Zeus called for a cupbearer, a person of grandeur and grace worthy to bear libations to the gods, the Eagle brought him Ganymede—*the fairest of mortal men*.[14] To the heights of Olympus he carried the youth, carefully cradled in his massive claws.

For this thoughtful deed, and to praise all his kind, Zeus immortalized the EAGLE, allowing him to soar in the nighttime sky in splendor for all to see. His breast is turned toward the earth, and he bears a bright star on his shoulders. Three neighboring astral lights mark the beak and upper wings and two adorn his tail. Tenderly clutched in his talons, six stars glow in the form of glorious GANYMEDE.

For his part, Ganymede, the son of King Tros—the eponymous founder of Troy, also appears in his own constellation because of his steadfast service to the gods. Here he is known through the ages as the WATER BEARER. Every night, from his right hand he pours a sparkling libation marked by a shimmering stream of stars.

The campaign against Cronus and the titans dragged on for months, and months turned into years, but the war only worsened. Heaven and Earth now quaked in fury. The seas slammed fiercely against the shores, and all of nature trembled.

To keep the army together in trying times, Zeus and the gods often affirmed their allegiance to one another by offering fragrant herbs on a sacred Incense Altar. In radiant robes they assembled, and in solemn procession they bore their blazing torches. One by one, they laid them on the altar's burning brazier and swore undying devotion to their cause.

Thus armed with fervor forged by oneness of mind, they sallied forth to destroy their foe. At last, ten tragic years of warfare ended. In dismal defeat, Cronus and the titans descended into the dungeon of Tartarus, into the darkest depths of the Earth.

That night, on the summit of shining Olympus, the deities delighted in triumph. Nike, the goddess of victory, resplendent in starlight, blessed the moment by pouring pure libations.[15] Then, Zeus raised the INCENSE ALTAR, with its rounded brazier and flying sparks, as a memorial in the sky.

There it glows as a reminder to immortals and mortals alike of the strength of sacred devotion. Now, all who see it in the sky are inspired to bow before altars in holy places and pray for success in worthy endeavors. Now they affirm allegiances with *incense and reverent vows, and libations, and the savor of sacrifice.*[16]

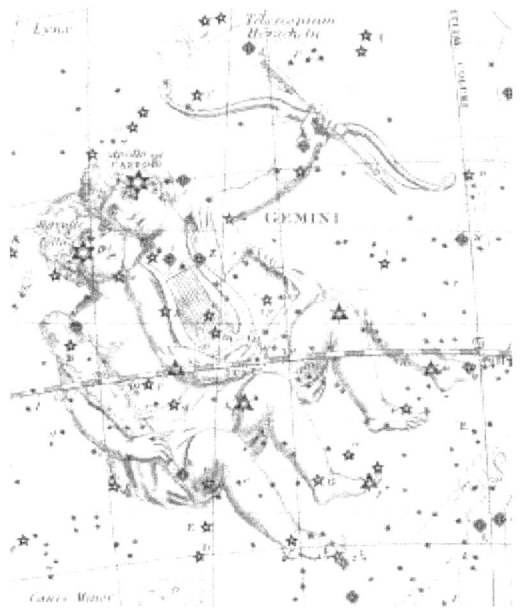

The Twins (Gemini), Castor and Polydeuces.
*Celestial Atlas* by Alexander Jamieson, 1822.

The Dioscuri—the twin brothers Castor and Polydeuces. Marble
relief, c. 500 BC. Archeological Museum, Sparta. Photo by author.

17

# Chapter 3.  BOYHOOD IN BACKCOUNTRY ATTICA

PAPPOS RECOUNTED MANY TALES that year during the cold months that lie between autumn plowing and spring pruning, as the three of us watched the flock under starry skies. His stories of the stars have followed me all my life, though desperate times have weighed me down with immediate worries that distracted me from the lessons learned.

The evergreen holm oak wreath that Pappos fashioned became dear to Bronte and me, and we often vied in competition to possess it. The winner wore it on his head as proudly as if he had won the Olympic pentathlon, while the somber loser planned and plotted to win it back. Between the two of us the wreath never left our possession.

Bronte and I remained playfully competitive and inseparable. We were twins and best friends. Whatever one did, the other tried to do better, whether in work or play. Pappos encouraged it. When he asked for the wreath to frame the constellations and tell the stories, he applauded the one who handed it over, while gently teasing the other. We fought and tussled as brothers will do, but if either was threatened with harm from bully or beast, our dual defense remained unshakeable.

During dark evenings at home, we gathered near the dim flicker of a lamp as Pappos told us other tales. With a smile, he described the stormy night of our birth and the pride that welled within him when he first held his grandsons. Then, with a forlorn face, he whispered of our mother who brought us into the world with the help of Ama and a midwife.

The two attendants had chanted the appropriate incantations for a healthy birth, and offered the proper apologies to the virgin goddess, Artemis, for having violated her code of chastity. But despite their constant care and compassion, mother faded away leaving Pappos and Ama broken-hearted.

Three months earlier, they had lost their only son to an enemy spear. Now, in deep despair, with their daughter-in-law gone, they faced old age alone and took up the task of raising newborn twins. They grieved aloud through the funerary and purification rites, and before they could rest, the rituals for the birth of babies began.

On our fifth day, a ceremony honored those who had assisted the birth. Pappos filled the father's role in the traditional running-around-the-hearth to welcome us into the family. He loved to tell how he carried Bronte in one arm and me in the other as we squalled in unison. Five days later, he presided over a solemn sacrifice and feast and gave us our names—Astrape and Bronte.

Oldest sons usually receive the paternal grandfather's name. But Pappos chose to name us for the curious circumstance of our birth. On that stormy night, I was born first, quickly and quietly, while Bronte followed afterward, slowly and loudly, like the lightning followed by thunder for which Pappos named us.[17] Bronte often teased me about my name, saying I was a sharp pain to the eyes. I retorted that he was a dull pain to the ears.

Pappos had seen seventy years when we came into the world. Ama had seen fifty-five. To help with the burden of newborn babies, they hired a wet nurse and paid her with grain which they could ill-afford to give away. Their hunger kept us fed.

Each day, Ama swaddled us snuggly in clean cloth and laid us side by side in a basket. When we grew old enough to pick and pull at each other, she fashioned another basket to keep us apart. On each, she hung an amulet to ward off illness, bad luck, and the evil eye. As toddlers, we wore the amulets around our necks even when we ran otherwise naked.

She filled our home with songs from her childhood and regaled us with stories of gods and heroes. She spoke of wolves and monsters that snatched naughty children in the night, and of Gorgo, the most dreaded of ghouls.[18] More often, Ama told cheerful animal tales that conveyed moral lessons handed down by the poet Aesop.

At an early age, we recited lines from Homer and Hesiod, having heard our grandparents quote them on countless occasions. Pappos revealed how our distant ancestors throughout the ages had passed stories to their children, word for word, until men like Homer and Hesiod learned to write them down. He and Ama considered rote memory important for preserving our history, culture, and ethics. Under their guidance, recitations became competitive events for Bronte and me that often resulted in the passing of the coveted wreath.

When left to ourselves, we loved to race through grainfields, wrestle in the soft plowed earth, throw clods, play chase, climb trees, or swing on a rope that hung enticingly low from a branch. We challenged each other to games of toss using acorns, hazelnuts, or braided rings of willow shoots.

A favorite pastime involved throwing dice made from knucklebones—the astragali, or ankle bones, of deer. Pappos provided these when he came home from a hunt. We tossed the bones in the air and tried to catch them on the back of the hand. Or we scattered them on the ground and tallied points based on the sides that faced upward.

Ama remarked that we looked like Eros and Ganymede playing dice with knucklebones. She said that Bronte, like cunning Eros, apparently knew some secret trick because he always seemed to win.[19] She also declared that people receive answers from the gods based on the roll of a knucklebone. Pappos only chuckled.

Pappos sometimes made us toys, like a tortoise-shell rattle, a carved wooden top to spin, or a little ball stitched from animal hide. We loved to toss the ball to each other, or throw it at each other, depending on the mood. Most of our toys were of our own making, like crude human and animal figures of clay, little carts or chariots that we pulled with strings, boats made of bark, and miniature farmsteads with baked-mud houses, twig fences, fields, creeks, and trails.

We also played with dogs, lambs, kids, and ducks. In the city, Athenians tamed weasels as pets and claimed they chased rats away. But Ama thought of weasels as pests. She believed they brought bad luck as well as killing chickens and causing other mischief.

Backcountry Attica was a boy's paradise with hills to climb, creeks to swim, woods to roam, and seashores that washed up shells and other treasures. We considered ourselves as rich as kings until schoolmates in Oropus pointed out our poverty. Even so, we rarely knew hunger or lacked true necessities.

We lived in simple contentment, much as Tempe and I do today, and much like other families with homesteads scattered along the rugged border of Attica and Boeotia. Pappos had built our hut many years before from bricks of mud and straw formed in wooden molds and baked in the sun. Every few years, we scurried like swallows, plastering walls with a fresh coat of mud and replacing clay tiles on the roof.[20]

We lived outdoors in the daytime, finding refuge in the shade of a tree on hot summer days or under the south-facing porch in wet or cold weather. On winter nights, we huddled at the hearth on reed mats that covered the packed-earth floor. We warmed ourselves near glowing coals while repairing tools, sharpening knives, or carving wooden spoons. We fashioned clay into cups, saucers, pots, pans, grills, water jugs, food jars, braziers, and oil lamps to replace those that had broken. All the while we passed the time with familiar stories and songs.

Starting and stoking fires remained an important childhood chore. On fair days, we played in the woods and dragged home fallen limbs that ranged in size from kindling to timber. After breaking branches into smaller pieces, we stacked them according to size in a lean-to under a tight thatch of straw. We searched for combustible tinder in the fibrous inner bark of a tree or the feathery stalk of a reed. A lidded jar inside the hut protected the vital tinder from moisture.

When Ama called for a fire, we gladly obeyed with thoughts of cooked food and cozy warmth. First, we fetched a smoldering ember saved from the previous fire in a covered bowl near the hearth. We gently blew on the ashes to find the glow and retrieve it with a stick.

If the ember was cold, we bundled up and walked four stades to borrow a live one from our closest neighbor. When all else failed, Pappos resorted to fire sticks.[21] First, he placed a notched piece of softwood on the ground. Then, he stood a hardwood stick upright in the notch and twirled it between his palms while pressing downward. The friction soon produced smoke and finally sparked an ember.

We quickly cradled the glowing coal in a tiny bundle of tinder, then blew as soft as a whisper until smoke billowed and burst into flame. Now we set the bundle outside on the ground, or under the porch if the weather was wet, and added kindling in increasing sizes to build a blazing fire.

How we enjoyed the warmth on a chilly day while waiting for the oak to burn down to coals! At last, we scooped the coals into a clay brazier, carried them inside, and triumphantly dumped them onto the hearth under Ama's approving gaze. By this time, the food was prepared for cooking.

Ama would scoot close to the fire, warming her tiny hands while placing morsels on pans, grills, or spits to sizzle over hot coals. The coals produced little smoke. But if haze hovered near the ceiling or began to burn our eyes, we opened tiny windows under the eaves or moved roof tiles to allow a breeze to whisk the smoke away.

Our hearth was a simple layer of rocks piled a half-foot high and shaped into a square of two-foot-lengths-by-two near the inner wall. For a portable hearth, we used the brazier and sometimes set a pot on top for cooking. Some families simply piled their coals on the bare floor or used a clay-lined pit.

We fared better than many. In addition to the hearth and brazier, our main room held a small table and stools. A clay basin rested on the table for washing hands, or on the floor for bathing. A backed chair in the corner awaited Ama or Pappos. The basin and one of the pots had been passed down from previous generations. We shaped the other ceramics ourselves and hardened them out-side in a brush-covered fire.

Our valued possessions sat sheltered in the main room. We tied the boat's mast, yardarm, and furled sail to the rafters. The rudder hung high on the wall near the hearth. We suspended the lyre from a peg on the opposite wall. Our reed flutes remained always with us.

The smaller room served as a bedroom and storage. It held a log-framed bed laced with rawhide webbing that sagged under our weight and that of pelts and woolen blankets used for cover. Ama's spindle hung on the wall while her loom remained on the covered porch.

In one corner of the room, she hoarded baskets of cloth and unspun wool. In another sat a chamber pot to be used only in the worst weather and emptied into an outdoor latrine. The latrine also served as a dump for things not thrown on the compost pile. Every few years we dug another.

Ama firmly believed in cleanliness of body, mind, and soul. She insisted, with shears in hand, that our hair remain at moderate length, not bald like a slave or long like a Spartan. She urged us to bathe in the sea every few days and scrub with sand from the beach.

Only on the coldest days did we opt to use the basin and bathe by the fire. It seemed much simpler to dip in the surf than to haul water from the spring, heat it over the hearth, and dump it on the field after bathing. Our chores al-ready compelled us to fetch water for drinking, cooking, and Ama's bath. She, like most women, insisted on bathing more modestly from a basin.

In later years, when in Athens or aboard a ship, I would be forced by pro-priety to also bathe in a basin. But I refused to waste fuel by warming water. Nor did I resort to the public baths in Athens, with their needless expense and ceaseless gossip.

As toddlers, we ran naked or bundled ourselves in little blankets when weather turned cool. But at the age of three, Ama dressed us in homespun tunics, called chitons, that reached to the knees. She taught us how to wrap these simple pieces of rectangular wool around our left sides and pin them at both shoulders.

A rawhide string around the waist secured the cloth and held the garment closed. On cold days, we draped wool blankets on top. How proud we were to finally wear big-boy clothing!

The chiton allowed ample room for running, jumping, and climbing. Later, we wore it for herding and plowing without having to burden our hands with the task of holding the cloth in place. In the city, citizens who rarely work are easy to discern. Their fashionable, free-flowing dress requires the continual use of a hand or two to keep it in proper position.

Chitons remained our constant companions. We wore them during the day and slept in them at night with belts removed. We also bathed with them and scrubbed them along with ourselves in the surf.

When we first began to herd the flock, we added sandals to our attire but only wore them in rugged country. Pappos taught us to make and repair them with a sole of thick leather and a rawhide thong. We attached the middle of a thong to the front of each sole and drew both ends between the first two toes before threading them side to side and tying them around the ankles.

As we grew older and spent more time in dreary weather in fields and forests, Ama replaced our small blankets with rectangular wool himations. She showed us how to drape one end over the left shoulder, run the remainder across the front and under the right arm, then across the back and over the left shoulder to end in front. In foul weather, the extra cloth provided a hood, and the whole himation served as a bedroll. For extra protection from snow and rain, we laid brush and leaves on the soggy ground, rolled up in our himations, and pulled a deer hide on top.

Many farmers wore hats, but we never had them as children. A hat caused the brow to sweat, blew away in the wind, or got knocked off by a branch during herding and hunting. Without hats, our faces tanned as brown as hazelnuts. Ama considered women's hats excessive, worn more for fashion than practical use. She also dismissed jewelry as mere vanity.

She and Pappos lived simply in their traditional way. They followed a code of ethics handed down for centuries that even predated Homer and Hesiod. They lamented the moral lapse that followed the Hellenic defeat of the Persians, when succeeding generations learned to live in luxury.

They looked back with nostalgia to a golden age and revered the words of the two great sages—Homer and Hesiod. They carefully heeded Hesiod's instructions to *make holy sacrifice to the immortal gods in a hallowed and pure manner* and *seek propitiation with libations and burnt offerings.*[22]

Every meal, no matter how meager, began with a ritual ceremony. First came the washing of hands in the basin on the table. Then, a simple libation sufficed for meals at morning and noon.

The evening meal stood as the main event of the day and required greater supplication to bless the olives, figs, onions, garlic, sweet peas, or chickpeas wrapped in barley flatbread. The ceremony took only a moment but seemed endless to two hungry boys.

On special occasions, with guests present and meat served, the ritual became more elaborate. Pappos recalled the example of Eumaeus, Odysseus' faithful herdsman, who showed proper devotion toward gods and men, including strangers. As the story goes, Eumaeus did not realize that the impoverished beggar at his door was his long lost master, King Odysseus. Still, he embraced him in perfect kindness and served him the best cut of meat while bowing in reverence to the gods.[23]

Pappos followed his lead. He addressed the gods with hands upraised in grateful praise and reminded them of his ever-faithful devotion. He implored them for divine protection of crops and herds, and the health of his family.

He poured a libation of water or wine near the hearth and sprinkled barley grain on the coals. To this he added a small but choice piece of meat to burn as a solemn sacrifice. Often, he apologized to the gods for the size of the portion and explained that it came from a poor man of humble means.

Ama now took up the task of cooking. If meat was available from the hunt or the flock, she slid it onto spits or laid it on a grill. Soon it sizzled and we devoured it like ravenous beasts, prompting her to scold us for gobbling like Boeotians.

With every scrap consumed, Pappos sprinkled thyme or sage on the dying coals as a final sacrifice. He opened a roof tile to clear the room of smoke, and to allow the gods to savor the smell of meat, barley, and herbs. Then we rested in contentment as Pappos lightly stroked the lyre and sang a hymn. He often called on us, or our visitors, if we had them, to recite favorite poems, sing cherished songs, or recount stories from long ago.

Meals marked hallowed occasions, and other moments also called for reverence. Early in the morning, before dawn brought light to the eastern horizon, we followed the example of Pappos as he followed the example of Hesiod — washing our hands and faces and offering morning prayers. Pappos concluded with a small libation poured before the rising sun.

During the day, in the course of work or play, we washed our hands upon reaching a stream and prayed before wading across. For divine spirits inhabit water sources, whether spring, stream, river, lake, or ocean.[24]

Clay toys, classical era. Archeological
Museum, Corinth. Photo by author.

Swallows in flight. Fresco, 1600-1500 BC, from Akrotiri
on the island of Thera (Santorini), National Archeological
Museum, Athens. Photo by author.

25

# Chapter 4.  AN EDUCATION IN THE WILD

AMA ALWAYS REMAINED ALERT to a divine presence that might appear in any form at any time, like the whisper of wind through the leaves or a flitting sparrow at the door. She also interpreted dreams, believing that the subconscious mind drew a person closer to the divine spirit.

She trusted the pronouncements of the Oracle at Delphi—the mysterious maiden, Pythia, who enters a trance and speaks on behalf of Apollo, the god of the sun. The Oracle offers advice to rulers and peasants alike. But we lived far from Delphi, so Ama resorted to drawing black and white beans from a jar to help her make crucial decisions.

She truly believed that a divine spirit inspired the outcome. Many other Hellenes held firmly to the same convictions, and even our civic leaders in Athens sometimes relied on beans to ascertain the will of the gods. Pappos only grumbled that the gods made beans for eating.

While always seeking to understand the divine will, Ama was also vigilant in warding off evil. She spat when a person spoke blasphemy toward the gods. And if it happened to be Bronte or me, she followed up with a stinging swat of the willow switch.

One neighbor of ours seemed to have ample time on his hands to visit the surrounding farmsteads and share the local gossip while begging to borrow barley and wine. Ama always sighed when she saw him coming, and his vulgar tongue kept her spitting and frowning long after he disappeared around the bend.

Even so, Ama had a gentle and peaceful soul that cradled us in comfort. The divine protection she invoked was more for our sake than hers, and she offered continual assurance of how much she loved us. She took the task of raising and protecting us to heart. She instilled in us reverence for all things divine, and gratitude for our meager bounty. By her example, we embraced a work ethic that mixed six-parts labor with one-part leisure.

From the time we could walk, she urged us to remain alert and observant in the world around us—to enjoy it, revere it, and call on it for survival. We barely recognized a distinction between work and play as we gathered from nature's abundance. On tottering feet, we explored the vast world near home. We discovered the lean-to, the grainfield, the livestock pen, and finally the meadows and woods beyond.

Every dawn promised a new adventure and every dusk saw us return with amazing treasures. We proudly displayed our tiny bundles that surely provided for our family's every need. Ama patiently taught us that certain items, like sticks for kindling and edible nuts, were held in higher practical esteem than colorful leaves or delicate seashells.

Our wanderings led us to sunny hillocks and dark caves. We explored lush meadows where we would later graze the flock, and mossy trees that provided shade for a nap. We learned to recognize birds by their songs and distinguish sparkling creeks by their taste. Soon we discovered the best places to find wild berries, fruits, herbs, tubers, figs, hazelnuts, walnuts, and chestnuts.

In bad years, when crops failed and natural provisions like fruits and nuts were in short supply, we had to compete with wildlife for acorns. Ama made them edible by shelling, roasting, and grinding them into meal which she formed into tiny loaves for baking. From the acorn shells and husks she extracted tannin to cure deerskins, goatskins, and sheepskins. As we grudgingly munched our meager fare, she reminded us of our remote ancestors who dwelled long ago in the rugged mountains of Arcadia. They relied on acorns as staple food in the distant past, *even before the moon existed*.[25]

In those days, people survived off the wild plants they gathered and the animals they hunted. They found simple contentment in the bounty around them. Later they learned to grow crops and improve them by sowing seeds from the healthiest plants.[26]

They had little need for trade, which makes a person dependent on others. Instead, their self-sufficiency secured their independence. Even today, backcountry folks rely on the bountiful earth more than on commerce. Pappos claimed that we were the remnant of a golden age, before the decline of humankind into a world of commercial greed and strife.

As Bronte and I grew older we became better foragers and brought home snared birds and captured hares. We learned to cut willow shoots with the proper bend for Ama to weave into baskets. We learned to harvest river reeds with the right texture for sleeping mats.

We gathered fallen limbs to be shaped into lumber or chopped into firewood. When we found a sturdy piece of oak, we set it aside for carving into furniture or handles for tools. If we came upon a fallen pine, we dug into the sappy stump and cut out heartwood for torches.

As our backs grew stronger our burdens became heavier. We started each day with the primary chore of hauling water from the spring. If the spring ran dry in the drought of a brutal summer, we resorted to water scooped from a muddy creek or pond. But we accepted life's pains with its pleasures.

Robbing beehives brought both. When we spied bees in the forest, we followed them in search of the hive. But the bees flew home in a perfect straight line while we stumbled over boulders and stumps. We waded creeks and climbed cliffs while they laughed and left us behind.

But we noted their route and waited for more bees to lead us to the hive. If luck remained with us, we found a crack in a rock or a hollow tree that swarmed with bees. Now we tossed the knucklebones to determine who won the dubious right to slip slowly forward and poke a smoking evergreen bough in the hole to calm them down. The winner received a mixed blessing of bee stings and Ama's praise, while we all shared the reward of golden honey.

One day, when we were still quite young, Pappos smiled, nodded toward the livestock pen, and asked us to release the flock. With eyes wide in excitement, Bronte and I glanced at each other and bolted over the furrows, kicking up dirt as we ran. This was the moment we had anticipated, the moment when Pappos introduced us to the shepherd's life.

He taught us how to protect the animals from predators, to lead them to fresh water, and to remain alert while the goats rushed ahead to browse leaves and the sheep lingered behind to graze grass. The flock was our most valuable asset—our source of wool, mohair, clothing, bedding, milk, cheese, and meat. Other assets included the fertile field, the leafy vineyard, and an ancient grove of olive trees.

Pappos followed us in our first years as shepherds. He was now too old to plow or hoe, and we were still too young. With regret, he hired a neighbor to farm the land for a share of the crop. As Pappos shuffled behind us through wild meadows and woodlands, he appeared happy to return to the task of his youth.

Our waking time came earlier now. Long before light, we jumped to our feet, washed our hands and faces, tied on belts and sandals, devoured a breakfast of barley porridge and figs, fetched the water, and still had time to release the fold by sunup. On our way out the door, Ama tucked barley bread in our packs for a mid-day snack.

With a knapsack slung from one shoulder, a staff in the opposite hand, and a flute hanging by a string from the neck, we vanished into the morning mist to release the milling sheep and goats. Together we lowered logs on one side of the pen and allowed the drove to jump free. At each quarter of the moon, we dismantled the pen completely and moved it to a new location so the animals could graze new stubble and fertilize the next patch of fallow field.

Pappos let half the field lie fallow each year while the flock enriched the soil. This brought better crops year after year. He told us of farmers who failed to pen their sheep and goats in the field and planted their seeds in the same field year after year, hoping for a larger crop. While they might produce more for a year or two, the soil became exhausted, and the harvest soon declined.[27]

Pappos kept a close count of the sheep and goats and limited the fold to twenty adults, mostly nannies and ewes in equal numbers. More livestock than that proved hard to control and pen at night in the grainfield or distant pastures. And loose livestock invited deadly predators. Culling the herd became a festive event because it meant fresh meat on the fire. Or it brought the chance to drive stock to Oropus for bartering.

The meat, when we had it, often came from a lamb or kid. We also savored venison, hare, fowl, and fish. Feral pigs that ran half-wild in the surrounding woods provided us with pork. They lived on acorns and tubers and sometimes grazed our grainfield.

Pigs proved hard to handle. They seemed to have a stubborn streak that made them bolt and run in the wrong direction. But we enticed them with grain into a stout pen of heavy logs and fattened them on stalks and scraps of food. On a cold winter day, when meat was slow to spoil, Pappos and friends from neighboring farmsteads gathered to butcher and share the pork.

Oxen and donkeys cost more than we could afford. But we often borrowed a neighbor's pair for threshing and plowing. When freed from the harness, they fended for themselves, foraging on what they could find. We had to watch them closely or tether them to a tree. If not, they roamed too close underfoot, nosing about the hut and sheds, or slipping into the woods and out of sight.

But the flock remained our priority. We guarded it from dawn to dusk and sometimes through the night. When on the move in the morning light, we followed the animals into the gloom, out of sight of our happy home, and far from the soothing smell of woodsmoke. The mystical hills and lowlands became our second abode.

Pappos, as persistent as a schoolmaster, seized every chance to teach us the names of plants and animals and explain their traits and uses. Holm oaks and deciduous oaks stood supreme over the forest. We revered their hoary age and sacred reputation, and gathered the timber, firewood, and acorns they provided.

We also valued the fragrance of pine and juniper, the fruit of walnuts and hazelnuts, the bounty of apple and pear trees, the shade of the sycamore figs, and the dancing willows near the spring. We esteemed every grove of trees for the provision and pleasure they offered and respected them as the haunts of dryads and spirits.

Sometimes the dryads seemed to reveal their presence with a creak or groan among the spreading branches of oaks. In a similar way, the oreads of the mountain crags caught our attention with little landslides, and the naiads of the streams beckoned to us with mysterious splashes and unexplained ripples. Wild animals haunted the woods as well and took refuge in the shade of trees and hollows. But the wildest beasts and mischievous spirits roamed the mountain crags of Arcadia, far to the south.

When we grazed the fold within twenty stades of home, we hurried to be back by dark. Farther away, we pitched a hasty camp and braced ourselves for a long and watchful night. To protect the sheep and goats, we fashioned makeshift pens of branches and brush or found refuge in one of the stone corrals built by shepherds in ages past.

Within the cold confines of the ruined ring of stones, we lay awake and imagined great events that happened here long ago. In our mind's eye we watched a valiant herdsman defend his drove from a hungry lion. We witnessed a band of Hellenes fighting a fearful Persian host and forcing it to flee.

Finally, we fell silent and still under the calming gaze of Hesperos—the evening star.[28] Hesperos is the shepherds' star—the brilliant light once praised by the poetess Sappho as the *fairest of all stars*; the star that reunites *everything that shining Dawn scattered*. She said of Hesperos: *You bring the sheep, you bring the goat, you bring back the child to its mother*.[29]

We slept soundly through the remaining night until dawn gently urged us to open our eyes. After scanning the landscape for dangers, we released the sheep and goats. If they seemed contented to graze the meadow and showed no desire to wander away, we slipped into the shadowy forest and entered the mystical world of woodland creatures. We watched their behavior and over time, we learned their ways. With familiarity came respect for their skills of survival and the food they provided.

Pappos taught us early how to catch hares by chasing them into a bush and clubbing them as they darted out. Some people used nets, but the cost was beyond our modest means. Homemade traps helped us collect quail, thrushes, and partridges for the cook pot. We also practiced with bows and arrows in hopes of bagging a duck, goose, or deer.

In high mountain pastures, we sometimes spied wild goats peering curiously at our flock from the crags above us. But they always stood at high alert and scampered away at the slightest movement, scaling impossibly steep cliffs. They remained far beyond our hunting skills, as did the wild boars of the valleys with their lightning reflexes and sharp tusks.

During days away from the fold, we wandered the seashore where fishing offered another means of provision and entertainment. We simply walked the beach for most of what we gathered, bagging mollusks and wading into the surf to fish. Sometimes we rowed Pappos' boat into a calm inlet and dropped lines with weighted and baited hooks in promising places. Serious fishermen use nets as well as lines and hooks. But we made do with homemade basket traps lowered into calm pools of water.

Later, we learned to launch the boat into the surf, row it straight and true through approaching waves, and hoist a sail when the wind was right. Pappos showed us how to work the sail in rhythm with the turn of the rudder. He taught us to read the winds on the water and compensate for their constant variations of direction and speed.

We also learned to prepare the boat for winter storage according to Hesiod's instructions: *Draw up your boat onto the land and prop it up with stones, surrounding it on all sides, so that they can resist the strength of the winds that blow moist, and draw out the bilge-plug, so that Zeus' rain does not rot it. Lay up all the gear well prepared in your house after you have folded the sea-crossing boat's wings [sails] in good order; and hang up the well-worked rudder above the smoke.*[30]

One of our early excursions alone, without Pappos, taught us a hard-learned lesson. After launching the boat from the beach and rowing through the surf, we decided to save our strength and take advantage of a gentle breeze blowing northwestward up Euripus Strait. We released the halyard and watched the sail billow beautifully as the boat lurched forward with increasing speed. In that moment, we felt the great sensation that every sailor enjoys when his well-trimmed vessel swiftly skims the surface of the sea.

How proud and confident we felt! Heeding Pappos' warnings, we remained ever watchful for ripples that might suggest a shift of wind, a change of current, or a rock beneath the surface. The sight of unfamiliar shorelines, beaches, bluffs, and woodlands filled us with pleasure as we slipped swiftly past. When we came to the village of Oropus, with its bustling port and proud assortment of boats moored at the docks, we marveled at how effortlessly our sail had rushed us to this place in a fraction of the time required to walk.

We soon lost sight of the town altogether and reluctantly agreed to tack about and head for home. With the yardarm and sail lowered and furled, we slipped the oars into place and turned the bow southeastward. After several strokes, we realized our mistake.

The fresh breeze that had hurried us forward now became our loathsome bane. We traded turns at oars and rudder, straining to make headway against the wind and waves. We worried aloud at the prospect of making landfall at night on some lonely shore. But after the sun fell below the horizon, the winds slackened, and we spied Oropus in the twilight.

Weary beyond words, we struggled toward shore, reached the dock, and rowed the boat into an empty slip. A smiling stranger, a guard of the port, saw our plight and pulled our trembling bodies from the boat. We watched on wobbly legs as he stored our oars, mast, sail, and rigging in a nearby hut that he called home.

As darkness descended, we gathered our strength, gritted our teeth, and marched the forty-eight stades toward home. Well into the night, we came at last to our dear old door. The mood of Pappos and Ama quickly passed from relief to anger to amusement as we relayed our story and dragged our exhausted bodies to bed.

The next morning, Pappos made a point of waking us well before light. With him by our side, we trudged back to Oropus. Upon reaching the docks, we greeted the friendly stranger with humble gratitude. After handing him a gift of grain, we gathered our rigging, launched our boat, and waved farewell. With the wind against us, the three of us took turns rowing close to the coast until, much relieved, we sighted our own familiar cove.

Some mistakes teach lifelong lessons and are never repeated. This was one. In later years, on the few occasions that we traded by boat in Oropus, we carefully gauged the wind and calculated the return trip. Sometimes our crops yielded rare abundance, or leisure time allowed us to fashion extra pottery or clothing. If our surplus became more than we could tote on our backs, we hauled our bounty in several trips to the beach and loaded the boat for transport to market, but never on days when the wind blew strong away from home.[31]

Wild Goat. Vase painting, 660-500 BC. Archeological Museum, Island of Rhodes, Greece. Photo by author.

# Chapter 5. A NEW WAY OF LEARNING

AT AGE SIX, SCHOOL INTERRUPTED our childhood paradise of field, forest, and seashore. We suddenly fell subject to a different kind of instruction and discipline. But we soon began to realize the pleasures of learning from verbal lessons and written scrolls, and our curiosity of the world of writing now rivaled our wonder of the natural world.

Learning became a new adventure. We had no notion of the expectations of the Athenian polis, which deemed that the boys of Athens and Attica should receive an education in order to participate in a democratic system.[32] The polis also urged rural citizens to become more active in the political and judicial life of the local deme, tribe, or polis.

Day after day, we jostled and played for forty-eight stades as we followed the coastal road to Oropus. Our teacher lived in a hut no larger than ours, which served as our classroom when weather was cold or rainy. But most of the time we gathered close to the mossy trunk of a shady oak with birds chirping in their own world above us. The teacher instructed the children of a dozen families from the town and surrounding farms, and we carried bags of barley to pay our part.

He taught us the curious method of communicating through written inscriptions, one letter at a time, with a sharpened piece of reed called a stylus and a wax tablet upon which we made our marks. At first, we had more fun forcing our friends to jump with a poke of the pointed reed. But soon we learned that the teacher frowned on frivolity and carried a willow switch. By the end of the month, we sat silent and still and tended to our work. Even so, I seemed to spend more time smoothing out my mistakes with the blunt end of the stylus than writing with the end that was sharp.

Each student also had a straight piece of wood to keep written lines from wandering. These writing tools remained in our classroom when we parted for home at the end of the day. The teacher also showed us other ways of writing. He kept a supply of powdered ink, which he mixed with water to demonstrate how adults write on papyrus or pottery shards.

He also had a small collection of tattered scrolls bequeathed to him by a former schoolmaster. From these, we learned to read and recite selected quotes from Homer and Hesiod. Bronte and I had ample time to practice recitation on the way home from school, and Pappos and Ama always expected an evening performance of what we had learned that day. I was surprised to discover how many of these ancient lines our grandparents already knew, and how many passages they had engrained in our minds before we entered school.

When we complained about the tedium of memorizing by rote, they sided with the teacher and exclaimed that the works of Homer and Hesiod offered a valuable exercise for the mind and preserved our traditions and way of life. Homer himself had emphasized the need for a broadened mind and the ability to see *both before and after*, meaning the past as well as the future.[33]

Pappos and Ama declared that Hesiod should also serve as an inspiration because he was a backcountry farmer and shepherd, like us. He lived three centuries earlier in the neighboring province of Boeotia. Yet his intellect and wisdom withstood the tempests of time and his teachings survived as essential learning throughout the Hellenic world.[34]

At school, exercises in writing and spelling kept pace with memorization of famous sayings. Our teacher often pulled out his cherished scrolls and scanned them for words appropriate to our level of learning, then read them one at a time as we tried to write them. The first to write the word neatly and correctly gained acclaim from the teacher and envy from the classmates.

Once we had mastered the alphabet and how to spell words, we attempted reading aloud and writing full sentences. By the second year, we launched into simple addition and subtraction, and by the third we graduated to the complexities of multiplication. For this, we counted our fingers to work most problems.

We learned that six obols equal one drachma, which is the unskilled laborers six-day wage. We learned that one hundred drachmas equal one mina, and sixty minas equal one talent. As I labored at calculations, I doubted that any amount beyond the drachma would ever apply to our lives as farmers.

Regardless of the hopes of the polis, some classmates could not continue in school beyond the first few years. Their parents could ill afford to pay the tuition and needed all hands on the farm. Many sons of Attica were barely literate, and few women could read or write. But students from families of better means often remained until the age of eighteen, especially in Athens.

Our teacher illustrated the problem of illiteracy and ignorance by telling us about an incident in Athens some seventy years earlier. A political leader had rallied citizens against his rival—a famous and honorable man known as Aristides the Just. According to common practice, the Athenian Assembly annually asked all citizens if there was any troublesome individual who should be forced into exile that year. In response, the crowd gathered to cast their votes by writing the unfortunate person's name on a pottery shard.

One of the men, who could neither read nor write, was among those who had been goaded to vote against Aristides. As he elbowed through the crowd, he bumped into Aristides not knowing who he was and asked him to write the name *Aristides* on a shard for him so he could cast his vote. When Aristides asked the citizen why he disliked this man, he responded that he knew nothing about him, but was tired of hearing him called *the Just*.

Aristides never changed his expression but quietly wrote his own name on the shard and handed it back to the man. The tallied votes sent Aristides into exile. Such is the cost of an uninformed populace that is easily manipulated and whipped into a frenzy by people in power.

In the fourth year of school, we gladly began the study of musical instruments. Bronte and I, and most of our classmates, had piped the flute since before we could remember. But now we learned new melodies, as well as the complexities of proper fingering, breathing, and volume control.

As we became adept, our teacher showed us how to trill and staccato. He taught us to make slight changes of timbre with the shape of the mouth to produce bright or mellow tones. We also learned the theoretical value of music and its role as a primary component of our mental and spiritual existence. Our teacher quoted Pythagoras, who declared that music aligned with the harmonious balance of the universe.

Many years later, I listened as another philosopher, Plato, reiterated the point. He said that music *is granted to us for the sake of harmony... which has motions akin to the revolutions of our souls*. The Muses did not bring us music *with a view to irrational pleasure, which is deemed to be the purpose of it in our day, but... to correct any discord which may have arisen in the courses of the soul*. The pleasure that music provides is *a higher sort of delight, being an imitation of divine harmony*.[35] As such, continued the philosopher, the study of music should not be dismissed from the schools by business-minded civic leaders in Athens who consider it an impractical pursuit because it fails to put money in their pockets.

Musical instruments originated, after all, as gifts from the gods for the purpose of maintaining a joyous balance in the universe and in our personal lives. The drum, or tympanum, came from Rhea, the mother of Zeus, whose enthusiastic followers, the Corybantes, accompanied her through all the lands with drumbeats and joyful shouts.[36] The flute, or aulos, was the invention of Euterpe, the Muse of musical instruments and granddaughter of Rhea. The lyre, or cithara, came to us from Hermes, the messenger god and grandson of Rhea, who as a precocious child fashioned the instrument from a tortoise shell and sacred cattle horns. Thus, the ancestral instruments that create such marvelous sounds, whether by means of flowing air, or vibrations of hide or string, are bestowed on us as blessings from the gods.

With this divine and lofty thought in mind, our teacher taught the fundamentals of the flute and showed us how to pluck the seven stringed lyre to accompany singing and poetry. He insisted that we follow a proper series of notes and not vary from the conventional standard. He believed that if it was good enough for the bards of old, it was good enough for us. But in private, Bronte and I practiced many variations in the manner of innovative performers at musical contests.

Drums had no place in the classroom. We played them instead as toys. Despite their divine origins, many considered them too closely associated with hedonistic ceremonies to gain entrance into the moral curriculum.

The flute, on the other hand, had practical as well as spiritual applications. Flutists played at family events, religious processions, dramatic performances, athletic contests, and military marches. Those who excelled at its use could even compete for prizes. But most of us played the flute for entertainment at home during long winter evenings. Or we piped to provide a rhythm for gathering the harvest, or calming nervous flocks, or chasing away loneliness during nights spent under the stars.

Most backcountry folks made their own flutes. Pappos carved ours from river reeds by cutting stalks to a measured length, carefully boring finger holes, and sometimes attaching a sliver of vibrating reed as a mouthpiece. At times, he assembled flutes in pairs and tuned them to harmonic intervals by inserting wax stoppers to achieve the proper pitch. His flutes proved as good as those in Oropus.

One of the more talented craftsmen in Oropus used his spare time to fashion lyres when work at the docks was slow. Often, we watched with fascination as he made a lyre in the traditional way, from a large tortoise shell or other bowl-shaped object. He stretched a skin over the hollow, then attached two horns or pieces of wood. To this he added a crosspiece and a stout bridge of holm oak that held the seven sinews in place. He traded the lyres at market for bags of grain and olives.

Music, reading, writing, math, and memorization of the classics made up only a few of the subjects of our curriculum. The teacher introduced the word *arete*, which he defined as personal excellence, goodness, and virtue. *Arete* embodies the appropriate pursuit of life to its full physical, mental, and spiritual potential.

In the physical sense, *arete* means beauty, athleticism, and strength. In the mental sense it involves the attainment of knowledge and wisdom, which lead to the spiritual qualities of virtue, goodness, self-restraint, and justice. He stressed that beauty is found far beyond facial and bodily features: *For he that is beautiful is beautiful as far as appearances go, while he that is good will consequently also be beautiful.*[37]

He declared that, ideally, an individual should achieve a balance of physical, mental and spiritual pursuits rather than excelling in one at the expense of the other two. To achieve the proper proportion, a person should follow the two-part advice inscribed on the wall of Apollo's temple at Delphi.

The first says *Know thyself!* That is, be introspective, knowing your own strengths and weaknesses so that you can work toward improvement. The second says *Nothing in excess!* That is, maintain a moderate and harmonious balance in all things.[38]

In later life I came to treasure the wisdom of that humble country teacher. His thoughts compared in many ways to the great philosophers of our day. As a child, I had accorded him too little credit.

Even with our love of learning, time spent in the classroom became tedious day after day. Sometimes we stayed at home to help with the harvest. Or we visited neighboring farms for kinship feasts marking births, weddings, and funerals. Family gatherings offered diversions, but religious festivals became the most exhilarating events in our lives.

This proved especially true with the two annual celebrations in Athens. While toiling in the field or classroom, our minds anticipated the events to come. Our lives followed the seasonal cycles of planting and harvest, but also the schedule of festivals. Pappos and Ama made every effort to attend them, barring unforeseen illness.

The Athenian festivals offered the height of excitement. Crowds paraded through streets with laughter and song. Elaborate processionals congregated at important shrines. Musicians, thespians, and athletes gathered for competitions.

For two country boys, this offered an otherworldly experience. The Panathenaea took place on two summer days following the grain harvest, climaxing in a triumphant march through the city amid *the sweet-sounding pipe and cithara… and the sound of castanets.* Above the din of instruments, *maidens sang clearly a holy song, and a marvelous echo reached the sky.*[39]

Toward the end, the jubilant crowd clambered atop the Acropolis to bedeck the dazzling statue of Athena in an embroidered robe made especially for the occasion. Nearby stood stately *altars smoking with incense* that spread the rich aroma of *myrrh and cassia and frankincense.*[40] Solemn priests in sacred apparel sacrificed hecatombs of bawling cattle on the altar and distributed the meat to throngs of famished followers.

In spring, we attended the Dionysia with its droves of strangers from foreign lands. They mingled peacefully among the Athenian crowds and flocked to the hillside amphitheater on the south side of the Acropolis. From several stades away, we could hear the chorus singing and the flutes piping throughout the day. Often, we paused to listen to enthusiastic outbursts of shouts and applause, and the thunderous stamping of feet.

Our anticipation of these annual events proved almost as fun as the festivals themselves. For two days we traveled by foot to Athens, letting Ama set a slow pace. We carried provisions and slept beneath the stars along the way. The occasional inns we passed only lodged the wealthy, but that mattered little to us. We knew the outdoor life and often reposed on the ground. We also felt at home tramping on paths of dirt that turned to mud in the slightest rain.

Bridges did not exist outside of Athens, so we forded every river and stream while warily watching when rain clouds formed in the mountains. Heavy rains in those rugged heights sometimes sent flash floods that swept away livestock and unwary wanderers. Some coastal folks avoided the roads altogether, preferring to sail their small boats close along the shore. As we trudged the well-worn trails, other like-minded families joined from numerous footpaths that finally converged into one main route.

Along the way, we admired the extent of country that stretched from our northern coastline through mountains and foothills to the fertile tablelands of the interior. Small farmsteads began to appear closer and closer together until they joined each other with no intervening woodlands. Large estates came into view, owned by wealthy Athenians who possessed extensive vineyards, olive orchards, and herds of magnificent horses. Pappos muttered at the blatant display saying, maybe they can keep it and maybe they cannot. He had seen mounting debts and multiple heirs cause estates like these to splinter.

Anticipation grew as the burgeoning band of Attic families approached the capital city. We now descended onto the coastal plain where thousands of people crowded together like bees in a hive to inhabit Athens and the bustling port of Piraeus. As the Acropolis arose in the distance, we shouted aloud in celebration. Ignoring our weary limbs and feet, we quickened the pace until reaching the winding streets of the city.

For a few days, we enjoyed the endless merriment among the dizzying crowds and pageantry. But soon we became as anxious to return to our home as we had been to leave it. Once again, we packed our bundles and slung them over our shoulders. In two days, we arrived back at our dear old door in exhaustion and contentment. After checking our flocks and possessions, and finding nothing amiss, we collapsed on our blankets and slept soundly in the welcoming silence.

For the next several days, we babbled about the festival—how amazing it was, the best ever, we would always agree. Then we began to look forward to the next with greater expectations. Bronte and I soon realized that the journey weighed heavier each year on Pappos and Ama. We worried that each upcoming trip might be their last.

At the age of eight, we urged Pappos to let us manage the flock without him. After all, we had been shepherding for a few years now. Pappos pondered long and hard but finally had to agree.

He felt confident that we could keep the sheep and goats from harm and survive with them in the forests, meadows, and mountains. Pappos was now seventy-eight and barely able to ascend the steeper trails. But we knew he would miss the shepherd's life.

By the following year, Pappos and Ama could no longer help us carry the water or keep up the homestead. A neighboring farmer agreed to plow the field, but Pappos could not expect him to take on the other chores. Nor could we afford to share more of our meager supply of grain.

Bronte and I talked, thought, and finally concluded that we should divide the labors among us. One would tend the flock for three days while the other farmed and maintained the homestead. Then we would trade duties. During plowing, planting, harvest, and threshing, we would pen the sheep and goats, and toil together to complete the heaviest tasks.

The arrangement worked well, though a deep feeling of loneliness weighed upon us when we were apart. From the day of our birth, Bronte and I had remained together and close to family. Although we loved the life of the herdsman, we both preferred to work at home and enjoy our evenings spent together with Pappos and Ama.

With the coming of spring, the six-month span of shepherding began. We argued about who should have the privilege of remaining at home and who should follow the flock for three lonely days in the wild.[41] As usual, a toss of the knucklebones resolved the issue. And as usual, Bronte managed to win. With a grumble, I draped a himation over my shoulders and flung a flute around my neck. Grabbing a staff and knapsack, I headed westward with the fold toward the hazy valleys and hills.

The first day passed without problems as the eager sheep and goats nibbled the new spring grass. At evening, I drove the thirsty animals to a nearby mountain stream. As I bent to fill a goatskin flask, I noticed wolf tracks along the bank, but that was not uncommon. Still, I took precautions that night and penned the fold in a stone enclosure that stood nearby in ruins.

The long night safely turned into day and eased my troubled mind. But the following night, the pack of wolves pressed close and caused the sheep and goats to panic. I kept myself awake by marching around the enclosure and piping martial tunes to muster courage.

When dawn arrived at last, the wolves had disappeared. During the day, I took quick naps but mostly remained alert while gathering firewood in anticipation of their return. At midnight, the pack appeared and probed closer around the perimeter.

Most refused to venture within the campfire's range of light. But one large wolf searched tirelessly for a chance to dart toward the pen. I yelled and threw firebrands to chase him away.

He withdrew each time and stood aloof, then snarled in defiance and attacked from another direction. As he came into view in the flickering light, my heart sank low at the sight of his dark gray coat and light gray mane. He was one of the fiendish lineage of wolves described by Pappos. His gleaming, hate-filled eyes burned a lasting image in my mind that haunts my dreams to this day.

I quickly tossed more wood on the fire and prayed the supply would hold until morning. The standoff seemed to last forever, but finally the pack moved away. I could hear them whining and howling as they consoled themselves by chasing prey along the streambed four stades away. I did not sleep but huddled near the fire finding comfort in the stars. Soon, Pappos' stories came back to me, and his reassuring voice resounded in my mind:

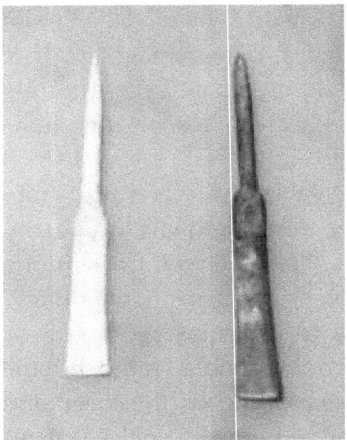

Styluses with sharp ends for etching wax tablets, and flat ends for erasing etches by smoothing them out. Reed, 5th-4th century BC. Archeological Museum, Corinth. Photo be author.

Apollo with his tortoise shell cithara (lyre). Vase painting, c. 470 BC. Archeological Museum, Delphi, Greece. Photo by author.

# Chapter 6. THE VALUE OF VIRTUE

*Recalling the words of Pappos*

ZEUS, THE GOD OF SKY AND STORM, wielded the awesome power of lightning and thunder. Into battle he bore his jagged bolts and hurled them with fury at his foes. With this weapon, he led the Olympian deities and faithful mortals to vanquish the titan host. Now Zeus ruled unrivaled over earth and sky.

The victory of the gods brought happiness and harmony to humans. People dwelled in peaceful repose with neighbors and with nature. They cherished the flora and fauna that thrived around them. They remained respectful, fair and just, in close accord with all creation. In return, they found their needs fully met.

They lived according to the words of Hesiod, who said: *Those who do not turn aside from justice at all; their city blooms and the people in it flower. For them, Peace, the nurse of the young, is on the earth, and far-seeing Zeus never marks out painful war; nor does famine attend straight-judging men. For these, the earth bears the means of life in abundance.*[42]

During this golden age, Astraea—the starry goddess of purity, peace, and plenty—lived her immortal life among the childlike mortals she loved. From an ancient lineage she descended, being the luminous daughter of Astraeus and Eos, the god of Dusk and the goddess of Dawn.

Astraeus and Eos also brought forth other *shining stars with which the sky is crowned.* Among them is Phosphoros, the morning star, who rises radiantly above the eastern horizon, heralding the approach of her mother, Dawn. Their other children include the buffeting breezes: Boreas, the north wind; Notos, the south wind; Zephyros, the west wind; and Euros, the east wind.[43] Unlike their serene and stately sisters, the blustering brothers roam, ever restless, rushing about, pushing against one another to dominate the direction of the wind. Rarely do they rest for long in quiet and calm.

But Astraea's manner is always soft and sweet—the pleasant personification of peace. In the golden age, she found the simple innocence of humans charming and endearing. She gently whispered to village elders, *ever urging on them judgments kinder to the people.* And peace prevailed, *for not yet in that age had men knowledge of hateful strife, or carping contention, or din of battle, but a simple life they lived... The oxen and the plow... abundantly supplied their every need.*[44]

As a heavenly constellation, Astraea glows in the sky as a MAIDEN in virtuous youth. Beautiful in her benevolence, she carries a bright star named EAR OF GRAIN in her left hand as an emblem of agrarian bounty. On her right wing rests a beam of light called HERALD OF THE VINTAGE. This is the star that annually rises on the eastern horizon as a sign for farmers to hasten to the vineyards and harvest the ripening grapes.[45] In her right hand she raises a palm leaf as a symbol of peace on Earth. Adorned with these, the greatest of earthly gifts, Astraea the Maiden shines on high as the everlasting sign of divine love for humankind.

In those golden days, other gods and goddesses also granted blessings to earthly beings. Even the centaurs—those galloping, gamboling creatures, half-man and half-horse—received divine gifts from immortal gods. Much like mankind, centaurs ranged in character from worthy to worthless. But two among them are always held in highest esteem, as high as any human. One of these centaurs was Crotos, the son of Eupheme.

Eupheme, a gentle and mild-mannered centaur, served as nanny to the nine maiden Muses, daughters of Zeus, who resided on the heights of Mount Helicon. On the day that Eupheme gave birth to Crotos in a shady glade near the Hippocrene Spring, the nine divine sisters helped with the delivery. The girls giggled in mirthful delight as the tiny centaur, newly born, rose to his feet and wobbled forth on four spindly legs. In time, he found his balance and began to buck and play.

The sisters fell in love with the little fellow right away. Adopting him as a brother, they doted on Crotos from that day forward. Through the years, the young centaur benefitted from their blessings of constant encouragement and kind instruction. Unlike most centaurs, he enjoyed a civilized, cultivated life in their care.

Crotos soon advanced in childhood skills. He reveled in racing with woodland friends. He laughed while clambering up rocky peaks. He excelled in notching a feathered arrow in the string of his recurved bow, drawing it back, and sending it swiftly in flight to knock acorns or leaves off holm oak trees.

As Crotos grew older, the Muses immersed him in learning. His knowledge of the universe broadened in time and space through the study of history and astronomy. With the talented Muses as tutors, his love of the arts also flourished. Their divine duty, after all, was to share the arts of poetry, music, dance, and drama, in addition to serving as patronesses of history and astronomy.[46]

From their inspiration, Crotos bloomed into a brilliant and bold musician. He developed the method of emphatically marking the rhythm of songs and stories with claps of hands and stamps of feet. He also showed how to follow performances with grateful applause, formed by faster claps of the hands.

For these innovations, the nine divine maidens lavished grateful praise. The rhythmic beats brought their epic tales and music to life for listeners. The applause allowed audiences to respond in joyful ovation.

Often, when the Muses performed their livelier songs or stories, Crotos could not contain himself but joined with a spirited dance. Taking his olive-branch wreath from his head, he tossed it on the ground. Then, he merrily pawed and pranced around it and jumped with leaps and bounds.[47]

The Muses and the two centaurs, mother and son, lived joyful lives together and became as one. All the while, Crotos' pious devotion to the nine divine sisters and their father Zeus grew stronger through the years. But alas, each passing day saw the centaurs growing old and gray.

At last, the immortal Muses, forever young, watched with heavy hearts as Eupheme and Crotos fell into feeble age and passed away. When Crotos breathed his last, the grieving girls asked Zeus to make a place for him, their fondest friend, in heaven. And so, among the stars, he continues to roam as though rambling through the forest.

He carries a recurved bow clutched tight in the left hand and drawn back by the right. His wreath of olive leaves lies on the ground before him. Crotos' constellation is called the ARCHER. His wreath is called the SOUTHERN WREATH, because of its location low in the southern sky, beside his prancing hooves.

Another centaur, Chiron, achieved the same acclaim for his piety and compassion. Like Crotos, he shared none of the savage traits that characterized so many of his kind. Instead, he remained steadfast in mind and spirit.

Chiron surpassed all others in the knowledge of botany and medicine and excelled in celestial lore and music. He shared this wealth of wisdom as a mentor to several students who rose to become lofty pillars of learning and leadership. One of these students was far-famed Jason.

When Jason was only an infant, his wicked uncle, the king of Iolcus in Thessaly, plotted to kill him in his cradle to prevent, one day, his possible bid for the throne. Chiron pitied the innocent child and hid him in his cavern home on the heights of Mount Pelion. There he raised him as a son, imparting his knowledge and lore.

By Jason's side, the child Asclepius practiced the healing arts. Asclepius was one of the centaur's gifted students, and Chiron freely imparted to him a command of the curative properties of plants. When it came time to set studies aside and rush outside to play, the boys, Jason and Asclepius, loved to wander the woods together.

Through towering firs and shady glades, they climbed to the heights of Mount Pelion. The farther they roamed, the less they feared the deep and dreary forest that surrounded their mountain home. Along the way, they watched for bees that led them to wild honey trees. And they learned to recognize useful plants to add to Chiron's herbarium.

Some years later, when the boys left their childhood cave as men, Asclepius chose to journey with Jason and his adventurous band of Argonauts. As a valued member of the crew, Asclepius served as ship's physician on the voyage to distant Colchis. At Chiron's behest, Jason also invited Orpheus, the famed musician, to join the quest.

Chiron supported the Argonauts' valiant endeavor from start to end. He offered prayers as the men prepared to sail their ship, the *Argo*, into unfamiliar waters. Then, when the crew raised the anchors and heaved the ship into the surf, Chiron descended to the sandy shore below Mount Pelion. With an impassioned plea to the gods for the safety of his sons, he waved farewell and, with a smile, wished them a swift return.[48] What became of them, we will later learn.

Over the years, rumors of Chiron's wisdom spread far and wide, and many men sought his sage advice. Often, they searched the forested slopes to find the shady pathway to his cave. Heracles, son of Zeus, knew the trail quite well and frequently came to request the centaur's counsel.[49]

Once, as the two enjoyed a lively conversation in Chiron's cave, a poisoned arrow, tipped with the venomous blood of Hydra, suddenly slipped from Heracles' quiver and punctured Chiron's lower leg. Chiron collapsed and fell into a coma. In horror, the mighty hero, suddenly helpless, held his centaur friend and watched as he closed his eyes and slipped away.

As earthbound mortals mourned the tragic loss, the gods gathered and agreed to honor Chiron in the eternal sky. His constellation, simply called the CENTAUR, stands tall on four legs and walks with a stately gait through the celestial sphere. In his hand he holds a WILD ANIMAL, a savage stalker of his forest home, which most perceive as a wolf in the shimmering sky. The stars show Chiron clasping the hind feet of the beast in his right hand. In the left, he carries a thyrsus—a staff adorned with leafy vines and pinecones—in devotion to Dionysus, the god who likewise loves to wander through wooded mountains.

Crotos and Chiron both gained endless praise from immortals and men. Both embodied the qualities that Hellenes most admire—skill at arms and in the arts; valor devoid of vanity; an adventurous and enlightened spirit; knowledge and wisdom; compassion and piety. They portrayed the essence of *arete*. Appropriately, the two appear in the sky as they approach, in reverence, the Incense Altar of the gods. In proper display of their personalities, Chiron is shown in solemn procession and Crotos in joyful dance.

Crotos and Chiron lived their lives during glorious times for mortals. But every golden age must come to an end, and centuries sometimes lapse before another begins. The collapse began when mortals, male and female, young and old, fell into the folly of conceit. They came to consider themselves the center of all creation. In blind lust to rule the world, they soon lost sight of their oneness with nature and the spiritual essence within and around them.

The beauty of Astraea's divine blessings—purity, peace, and plenty— dimmed in a fog of ingratitude. The goddess found herself alone, ignored as if invisible, without the laughter and love of her earthly children. Weeping at their woeful deeds and the dreadful consequence sure to come, she fell into deep despair. Sobbing in soulful lament, she left the world behind and ascended into heaven with a broken heart.

Without her peaceful presence, human greed for power and possessions brought the horror of hatred and war among them. And so began the sordid age of the restless workers of bronze, *who were the first to forge the sword... and the first to eat of the flesh of the plowing-ox.*[50] Without a divine beacon and a moral ethos as their guide, they turned on each other like wolves, *and they slaughtered with the bronze.*[51]

The kingdoms in Hellas and Asia now warred with one another from one side of the Aegean Sea to the other. Some blame the Phoenicians or Persians of Asia for instigating these wars of old.[52] Others accuse the Hellenes.

Herodotus, the historian, recorded a Persian account that said a crew of Phoenician sailors arrived at Argos one day. Here, they bartered their goods for olive oil and purple wine, and the painted pottery of Hellas. After several days of successful trade, the sailors prepared to depart.

As they rigged the ship and coiled the lines, they suddenly grabbed several girls of Argos who had come to the docks to shop. Before there was time to react, the Phoenician crew caught a freshening breeze, a favorable wind from the west, and fled far over the eastern horizon. One of the mournful, captive maidens was none other than Io, the princess of Argos. Her father, the king, was furious and demanded revenge for his daughter's abduction.

In swift response, a Hellenic merchant ship sailed across the Aegean Sea and moored at the Phoenician port of Tyre, on the Asian coast. Upon completing their commerce, the crew seized Europa, a princess of Tyre, in retaliation for Io. Soon afterward, another crew of Hellenes, trading at the eastern city of Aea in Colchis, absconded with the Asian princess, Medea.

Hellenic versions of this story vary. They say that Medea fled from Aea of her own accord and returned to Hellas with Jason and the Argonauts. They further insist that it was Zeus, the adulterous god, who captured Europa and Io.

The Hellenic account says that Zeus, upon resting his gaze on beautiful Io, pursued and made love to the maiden. Then he transformed her into a snow-white heifer to hide and protect her from Hera, his jealous wife. But the goddess Hera was well-aware of the wandering ways of Zeus and soon saw through the deception. In a fit of fury, she sent a gadfly to chase the heifer far from her native home. With the biting fly in hot pursuit, Io ran bucking and kicking along the Asian shore of Ionia, which bears her name.

From there, she sped northeastward and swam the Bosporus, or cow ford, which is also named after her. Finally, she fled far to the south, leaving the gadfly behind and finding haven in Egypt. Safe at last in the land of the River Nile, Zeus restored Io to her former youthful figure. Or so goes the Hellenic tale.

The Persians claimed that the double abduction of two eastern princesses, Europa and Medea, prompted Paris to retaliate. Paris, a prince of the Asian city of Troy, responded in anger and lust by capturing Helen, the queen of Sparta. With beautiful Helen whisked away to Troy, the kings of Hellas reacted in rage. Together they launched a thousand ships filled with their fiercest warriors. Sailing northward from Euripus Strait, then eastward across the broad Aegean Sea, they planned to retrieve the Spartan queen and plunder the prosperous city of Troy.

For ten tempestuous years they waged their bitter war. Blood from countless battles stained the earth from the Trojan walls to the Hellenic tents and ships that lay along the shore. The furious fighting *sent down to Hades many valiant souls of warriors, and made the men themselves* — the lifeless bodies on the beach — *to be the spoil for dogs and birds of every kind*.[53] In the end, proud and prosperous Troy was sacked and left in ruin, smoldering and choking in ash and dust.

Paris, the prince of Troy, had acted like the greedy dog in Aesop's fable. The dog had all the meat he could eat clutched firmly in his mouth. But he lost it all when he opened his jaws to grab for even more.[54] Paris had the royal wealth of Troy at his disposal, and all the women he wanted at his command. But by taking Helen, he lost his life and the lives of tens of thousands more.

As a legacy, he left his ancestral land in desolation. And worse, the Trojan War sparked eight centuries of conflict between the empires of Asia and Hellas. Hundreds of thousands of mortals, belligerent and blameless alike, perished on both sides.[55]

The same disregard for humans and gods that kindled the Trojan War also caused the armies of Hellas to further provoke the divine wrath. Odysseus and his Ithacan army had joined their Hellenic countrymen in the ten-year quest to conquer Troy. In the final months of fighting, Odysseus, clever and cunning as ever, devised the Greek victory by building a massive wooden horse. As the Hellenes launched their fleet and headed toward home, they left the horse to tower above the sandy shore, appearing as an offering to Poseidon.

When the Trojans discovered their hasty retreat and the huge horse looming above the beach, they shouted aloud in triumph. Quickly, they hauled the wooden hulk inside the city's impregnable walls and placed it as a gift near Poseidon's temple. After a day of drunken debauchery, the city slept soundly that night.

Unknown to them, the lifeless horse bristled inside with bloodthirsty Hellenes, pressed into every corner. Once all was dark and quiet, the waiting warriors stealthily slipped to the ground and opened the city gate for the returning Hellenic army. Ten years of bitter rage was unleashed at last as the Hellenes ruthlessly slaughtered Trojans—men and women, young and old. For this horrific massacre, and for the mock offering of the horse, Poseidon promised to punish the mastermind, Odysseus, when he sailed for home on the stormy sea.

Thus, it happened that Odysseus won the war only to be *driven far astray after he had sacked the sacred citadel of Troy*. While trying to return to his island kingdom of Ithaca, Poseidon condemned him to wander the merciless waters for ten more years. All the while, Odysseus endured countless hardships and close encounters with death. Many were *the woes he suffered in his heart upon the sea, seeking to win his own life and the return of his comrades* to Ithaca, where his long-suffering wife, Penelope, patiently waited.[56]

Odysseus and his starving men, while lost and adrift on the angry sea, made landfall one day on the gently sloping shore of a sunlit island. This paradise in the middle of the Mediterranean Sea bore the name Thrinacia, because of its three jutting headlands and strange triangular shape.[57]

From ages past, the island had offered a favorite haven for immortal gods.[58] Here, Apollo grazed his handsome herd of sacred cattle, safely secluded.[59] Like him, Demeter—the goddess of farming and harvest and protector of green and flowering plants—loved the island for its lush verdure and pastoral charm. She even called on Zeus to honor the pleasant isle in heaven, where it shines as a simple TRIANGLE bound by three stars.

But sorrow soon followed on Thrinacia. Demeter's dreamy daughter, Persephone, loved to wander with her maiden friends through the island's dewy meadows, laughing softly and gathering fragrant flowers. Her soothing voice and glowing countenance captured the heart of Pluto, the god of the underworld. Pluto rarely witnessed anything other than darkness and death. But from the depths of a shadowy chasm, he often watched the girl's delightful form as she glided on dainty feet through the glistening fields.

One sunny day, Persephone spied a colorful blossom dancing in the breeze near a deep crevice. Lured by its beauty, she left her maidens and hastened to the beckoning flower. As she approached, Pluto burst from below and carried the frightened girl to his dreadful domain to make her his wife.

Demeter, on learning of her daughter's abduction, wailed in inconsolable anguish day and night. She pleaded with Zeus to punish Pluto and return her daughter to her tender embrace. Zeus, in time, intervened. But he could only compel his brother, Pluto, to allow Persephone to spend half of each year with her mother, in the delightful world she loved.

Thus, for six months, as Demeter grieves for her daughter, the cold darkness of winter descends upon the earth. But with the return of Persephone to her mother's arms each spring, the earth abounds in flowering plants and the songs of birds.

Tragedy struck again on Thrinacia when Odysseus' famished men ignored their king's strict command and killed and ate some of Apollo's sacred cattle. For this sacrilege against the gods, and for rousing the wrath of Apollo, Odysseus and his men ran headlong into a fearsome storm as soon as they sailed from the island. As the crashing waves cracked the beams and shattered the ship into splinters, every member of the crew floundered and drowned in the dark and swirling waters.

Only Odysseus, who had abhorred the actions of his men and prayed for divine forgiveness, was spared. But he suffered the dreadful sorrow of being the sole survivor of the proud Ithacan army that had sailed for Troy so long ago. As further punishment, the deities delayed his homeward return for several more years.

Men were not the only mortals to fail in their devotion to the gods and suffer the result of divine wrath. Even a few of the animals most trusted by the Olympians fell out of favor after putting their own interests first. Such was the case of the Crow—Apollo's favored bird and close companion.

One day, Apollo called on the Crow to bring him water from a sparkling spring on Mount Olympus so he could offer a holy libation. In those days, the immortals often affirmed their allegiance to one another by pouring pure streams of water as a sign of esteem. This began long before wine was invented and used for the same purpose.

The Crow swiftly obeyed Apollo and seized a gleaming Crater—the goblet of the gods—in his talons. Searching high and low, the Crow scanned the slopes for a spring that offered a draft of water worthy of a divine libation. Soon he arrived on the shady bank of a shining pool. As he began to fill the Crater with crystal water, his gaze fell on a voluptuous fig tree bending low with the weight of its fruits.

Hungrily, greedily, the Crow hopped from limb to limb, waiting for the figs to fully form so he could fill his belly before returning to Apollo. One day turned into two, and two into three. Finally, the fruit was ready, plump and ripe, and the Crow gorged himself with delight.

With his appetite now satisfied, he began to ponder Apollo's reaction to his delay. After a moment's hesitation, he grabbed the Crater in one claw, and in the other a wondrous water snake that guarded the sacred spring. Then he flew fast and true, with all possible speed, to Apollo.

His head remained bowed, and his eyes cast down as he tried to explain his lengthy stay at the spring. With many reluctant stops and starts, he told a lie about how the huge snake had drunk the water dry, day after day, and kept him from filling the goblet. But Apollo was not so easily fooled. He punished the Crow and all of his kind by making them go without water for days at a time, with cracking throats and rasping calls. While they soar above the fields and forests, they caw aloud for a soothing draft to quench their nagging thirst.

As a further warning to those who chose to put their personal greed before the gods, Apollo placed the CROW in the nighttime sky. There, the boisterous bird, with wings held high, pecks at a serpent, much like the snake at the spring. Just out of reach of the Crow is the starry CRATER, holding a cool draft of water.

Centaur (Centaurus) and Wild Animal (Lupus), depicted on the *Farnese Atlas* Celestial Globe. See Appendix 3. National Archeological Museum, Magna Graecia, Naples, Italy. Photo by author.

Trojan Horse replica used in the movie, *Troy,* in 2004. It now watches over the Hellespont at Canakkale, Turkey, near Troy. Photo by author.

# Chapter 7.  THE PERSIAN TEMPEST

*Recalling the words of Pappos*

IN OUR OWN TIME, the same disdain for gods and mortals infected the Persian Empire and erupted into catastrophic invasions of Hellas.[60] The Persians attempted to justify their actions by arguing that eight hundred years earlier, the Hellenes had begun to extend their conquest of Troy by founding other colonies along the Ionian coast. They claimed to be simply righting a wrong by taking back what the Hellenes had stolen from western Asia.[61] As a further insult, the Persians declared that they only wished to bring the blessings of a higher civilization to the *barbaric* Hellenes.

The conflict began fifty-two years before I was born, when the Persian army of King Cyrus conquered the Ionian Hellenes and expanded the empire from India to the Aegean Sea. For the following forty-eight years, the Ionians chafed under Persian rule until Miletus and other Hellenic cities along the coast rebelled and called upon Athens and other poleis for aid and alliance.

Athens responded by sending a fleet of twenty trireme warships, and Eretria contributed another five. But the role of Athens and Eretria in the capture of Ephesus and the burning of Sardis only provoked greater hostilities. The Persians used these attacks to justify retaliatory invasions of Hellas.[62]

Darius, king of Persia, sent his son-in-law Mardonius to crush the Ionian Revolt.[63] In return for his success in the bloody deed, Mardonius received command of an army and navy with orders to launch a full campaign against Athens and Eretria. Darius also encouraged him to conquer as many other Hellenic cities as possible. Mardonius obeyed, moving his forces west from Asia across the narrow strait of the Hellespont. But his formidable army and navy rushed headlong into unforeseen trouble.

Off the coast of Mount Athos, a fierce storm caught the Persian fleet and sank three hundred ships. In one blow, twenty thousand men died by drowning and shark attack in those infested waters. At the same time, the Persian army, which was marching along the coast beside the fleet, fell under heavy attack, and Mardonius himself was wounded. The invasion ground to a halt and Mardonius' forces limped back to Asia in defeat.[64]

I was five years old when Darius sent a far greater force against Hellas. Avoiding the previous disastrous route, his entire host crowded aboard ships and crossed the Aegean Sea. They sailed from the island of Samos to Icaria, then to Naxos and Delos on the way to Eretria, and killed, captured, or drove off Hellenic families along the way. The little polis of Eretria was understandably panicked by the approach of the largest army and navy that had ever invaded Hellas. The Eretrian leadership divided over whether to defend the city and die or surrender the city and hope to live.

I remember the frightening day when the Athenian delegation meeting in Eretria fled by jumping into boats and rowing the forty-four stades across the Euripus Strait to Oropus. Thousands of refugees followed frantically in their wake in any vessel that would float. Many drowned as they lost control of their tiny crafts in the high winds and choppy waters.

Most of those who survived lived for months in makeshift shacks on the outskirts of Oropus. Others hid in thickets and caves like wild beasts and struggled to stave off starvation. We often encountered forlorn beggars—men, women, and children—destitute and in despair after losing their families and all their possessions. But they still fared better than those who remained in Eretria.

The Persian army lost no time laying siege to the city, and in six days captured and destroyed it. Then, in retaliation for their losses at Ephesus and Sardis, the invading army burned the capital along with its temples. Those who survived the rape and murder at the hands of marauding soldiers faced further horrors. They were beaten, bound, and driven into the dark and filthy holds of foreign ships, where they suffered for months while awaiting deportation and a lifetime of slavery in Asia.

An entire generation of Eretrians was swept away. To this day, seventy years later, the polis has not fully recovered from the devastation and depopulation, or from the bitter anguish that constantly haunts them. They cannot dismiss the memories or thoughts of loved ones living in brutal enslavement far away.[65]

While plumes of smoke still billowed from Eretria, the Persians launched their fleet and floated down the strait toward Athens. We peered from forested cover, in terror, as the hated ships, packed from bow to stern with savage faces, sailed past us in endless waves. With heavy packs of provisions slung on our backs, we followed the fleet while remaining concealed in the shadowy woods along the shore. All the while, we watched for a landing that would force us to flee to the mountains. I recall anxious whispers about caves and hollows where water might be found, and where we might burrow and hide until the murdering horde had satisfied its thirst for plunder.

At last, we watched in relief as the vast fleet of ships continued past us down the strait. Many of us, young and old, followed the enemy host further along the rocky coast as if to escort it far from our families and homes. We kept the hideous, painted sails and prows in constant sight until we reached low hills overlooking the coastal plain of Marathon. There the Persians moored their ships and flooded ashore. They appeared in the distance as an innumerable mass of ants filing into formation.

Soon, tiny bands of courageous Athenians came into view to our right as they rushed onto the plain. Once they amassed, they numbered ten thousand, but the Persian force numbered many times more. From our vantage point, the Hellenic army seemed like a mouse stepping forward to challenge a lion. We wept at the prospect of inevitable slaughter.

Later we heard that the warlike Spartans had planned to assist the Athenian defenders. But a religious festival demanded their attention when the moment of need finally came, and they could not be convinced to interrupt their rites for fear of losing the favor of the gods. And so, the Spartans abandoned the Athenians to their fate.

But six hundred Plataeans remained loyal to the alliance and arrived to join the fight despite the impossible odds. Most of the Athenian commanders argued for surrender as the only option in the face of a far superior enemy. But one named Miltiades convinced them to defend Hellas rather than suffer the awful consequences of conquest and enslavement.

With trembling limbs and nervous whispers, we watched in dread as the Hellenes formed ranks in the face of death and extended their battleline dangerously thin to match the breadth of the Persian formation. How does one describe the intensity of the moment, when a helpless army stands between you and death, or a lifetime of abject slavery? I thought of the thousands of poor Eretrians already shackled deep within the hated ships on the shore.

Suddenly, the tiny line of Athenians lunged forward at a run. With no cavalry or archers of their own, they hoped to reach the Persian line before it could inflict crippling damage with its missiles of arrows, javelins, and slingshot. The Persians reacted promptly and released an astonishing barrage of arrows that hung in the sky like dark clouds, then rained down like a furious storm.

Thousands missed their marks as they struck the sand behind the rapidly advancing Athenians. The sheer insanity of the all-out charge unsettled the Persian line. They were accustomed to terrorizing enemies with their vast numbers and fearsome appearance, but now they fell back in dismay.

As the fighting wore on, the Hellene center broke, and the enemy flooded into the breach. But to our amazement, the Hellenic flanks closed on the Persians like a vice, and the enemy line disintegrated. Now, with ferocity heightened by the prospect of victory, the Athenians and Plataeans rushed the retreating horde, forcing it to the beach and slaughtering thousands of Persians while capturing ships. Those Persians that survived the onslaught scrambled aboard the remaining vessels and launched into the surf. Safely at sea, they regrouped and set sail for Athens in a race to beat the Hellenic army to the unprotected city.

With no reprieve, the Hellenes marched and limped at double-time the 230 stades to Athens. When the Persians arrived, they discovered in shock that the Hellenic army stood reassembled and waiting. At Marathon, the invaders had lost 6400 men compared to only 203 Hellenes killed. Now the Persians feared a bloody repeat in the shadow of the lofty Acropolis. After sitting offshore in counsel, they grudgingly weighed anchor and sailed for Asia with their Eretrian plunder and slaves.

The demoralizing defeat that the Persians suffered at Marathon quelled their ambitions for another ten years until Darius' son, Xerxes, determined to succeed where his father had failed.[66] Fully aware of perils at sea and on the battlefield, Xerxes first attempted to coax his prey into peaceful submission. He began by declaring that Hellenes and Persians shared a familial connection as distant cousins through the ancient marriage of Perseus and Andromeda.

In the tales of the remote past, Perseus was a Hellenic hero who saved the life of the Asian maiden Andromeda. Their marriage produced a son—Perses, for whom Persia was named.[67] For this reason, argued Xerxes, Persia and Hellas should live in peace as a family, but under Persian rule, of course.

When this ploy failed to impress the proud Hellenes, Xerxes launched an unprecedented invasion, greater than any his forebears had dared, and called upon his brother-in-law, Mardonius, to lead the largest army and navy ever assembled.[68] I was fifteen years old by this time and remember well the new wave of hysteria that swept over Hellas when scouts arrived with news of Xerxes' approaching host.

Upon reaching the Hellespont, the enemy soldiers left Asia behind and advanced into Hellas by crossing the strait on a bridge of ships moored side by side. Then they marched westward along the coast through lands occupied by Persia's vassals—the Thracians and Macedonians. The Persian army arrived at Thermopylae untouched, without having faced real resistance. But that was about to change.

Thermopylae is an area of thermal hot springs on a route that narrows between inaccessible cliffs to the south and rough waters of Euripus Strait to the north. The pass is only a half-stade wide and at some places the road is no more than an ox cart trail, making the location easy to defend.[69] Here, a small force of entrenched Hellene hoplites awaited Xerxes while the Hellenic fleet protected the sea approach at Artemisium.

When the outnumbered Hellenic fleet lost three ships to the advancing Persian navy at Sciathos, it fled to Chalcis near Eretria and allowed the Persians to moor along Cape Sepias, on the mainland opposite Sciathos. Now the size of Xerxes' horde became obvious, and a shudder of despair shot through the poleis of Hellas. By all accounts, the enemy armada included 1,207 triremes and 3,000 vessels for transporting troops, supplies, and horses.[70]

Herodotus later estimated that more than two million fighting men marched in the Persian army, although some have suggested higher or lower numbers. Regardless, the invasion force on land and sea measured many times more than all the men and ships that the combined Hellenic allies could hope to muster. Even worse, the entire enemy host had reached our doorstep unscathed and in high morale. The Persian flotilla was so vast that it anchored at Cape Sepias in eight rows, ship beside ship from shore to sea. But this led to its undoing.

One morning before dawn, a furious storm struck from the northeast and raged for three days, turning much of the Persian fleet into flotsam. Some Athenians still claim that their prayerful pleas to Boreas—the north wind— did not go unheeded. They say that Boreas swept down on the Persian invaders just as he had vanquished the Persian navy off Mount Athos twelve years earlier.

As a result of the storm at Cape Sepias, four hundred Persian ships filled with sailors, supplies, and weapons sank into the depths of the wine-dark sea or washed ashore leaving wreckage along one hundred stades of coastline. Meanwhile, the Hellenic fleet remained safely harbored on the leeward shore of Euboea at Chalcis.

With news of the Persian losses, the jubilant Hellenes sailed boldly toward Artemisium to face an enemy force that still outnumbered them many times over. As the surviving Persian ships slipped to a safer anchorage at Aphetae, fifteen of them mistook the Hellenic ships as allies. Sailing forward to greet them, the Persian ships fell into Hellenic hands and raised our morale still further.

At the same time, at nearby Thermopylae, 4,200 soldiers from several Hellenic poleis assembled under the command of Leonidas, king of Sparta, with three hundred of his countrymen. The tiny army stood stalwart, serving as an advance guard to hold the pass until the remaining Spartan force could conclude religious rituals and join their comrades. Spartan rites again outweighed the pressing needs of the moment, as at the Battle of Marathon ten years earlier. Before the delayed Spartan army could arrive, the Battle of Thermopylae was over.

The fighting began when Xerxes sent a battalion to capture a few Spartan soldiers and bring them back alive. In Persia, he had heard much about their prowess and was impressed by their reputation for unflinching valor. Now, while in Hellas, he hoped to collect some Spartan specimens and keep them as caged animals for his own amusement. But soon he discovered that Spartans preferred to fight to the death rather than kneel in subjection.

When the mangled Persian troops returned with no Spartan captives, Xerxes' fascination turned to fury. To teach the Hellenes a deadly lesson, he commanded his elite fighters, which he called the *Immortals*, to force their way through the pass. As they swiftly advanced, the Spartans utilized one of their most effective battlefield tactics. They feigned a retreat to encourage the enemy to rush upon them in confident chaos. Then they suddenly turned in tight phalanx formation to mow them down.

Xerxes was aghast at the mauling of his *Immortals* and searched for another means of crushing the small band at Thermopylae. A Hellene traitor named Ephialtes now stepped forward to reveal a secret mountain path that the Persians could use to outflank the Spartans and their allies. The Persians moved swiftly into the mountains at night and reached the summit at dawn. There they defeated a force of Phocian guards assigned to defend the route. Then they slithered down a mountain trail toward the exposed Hellenic flank.

On receiving news of the approaching Persian host, Leonidas determined that his Spartans would fight to the end. To save the lives of his Hellenic allies, he sent them home to fight another day. But he commanded the Thebans to remain in the ranks, and the valiant soldiers of Thespiae stayed of their own accord. Leonidas now prepared his three hundred Spartans to make a final stand.

Some say he was acting upon a prophecy that declared either he would die in this battle or Sparta itself would be destroyed. So, he chose to sacrifice his life to save his kingdom and his country. Facing certain death, the Hellenes fought with reckless abandon, forcing back wave after wave of the enemy and trampling countless Persians into dust. Among them, two of Xerxes' brothers perished in the assault.

After the Hellenic spears had splintered and their swords and knives were swept away, they continued to fight with their hands and teeth until no one remained alive to defend the pass. Among the dead lay Leonidas and his three hundred Spartans, except for two who the king had sent as couriers before the final battle began.

Nearby lay Dianeces, who they say fought bravest of all the Spartans. Before the battle, he had heard the arrogant Persians boast that they would launch arrows in such great numbers that their shadows would block out the sun. To this, Dianeces laconically retorted that the Hellenes would, therefore, fight in the shade.

Two memorials now stand on the site where the Hellenes fell. The first honors all who fought at Thermopylae to defend their homeland. It contains the simple inscription: *Here once were three million of the foe, opposed by four thousand from the Peloponnese.*

The second monument stands in memory of the Spartan Three Hundred, and says: *Stranger, tell the people of Lacedaemon [Sparta], that we who lie here obeyed their commands.*[71] Sixty years have come and gone since the Persian army passed this way, but the memorials remain. Now the narrow glade is a peaceful place for travelers to rest and remember the terrible sacrifices of those darkest days.

During the same three days that the Battle of Thermopylae raged, the opposing fleets engaged in combat off the coast. Despite the damage sustained by the Persian navy at Cape Sepias, it still vastly outnumbered the combined Hellenic flotilla of 271 allied vessels. The Athenians had contributed almost half of these when it sent 127 fierce triremes, which they built in the aftermath of the battle of Marathon.

The Persian navy was so much larger that it safely divided into two fleets to catch the Hellenes in a vice. One, the primary Persian fleet, prepared to attack the Hellenes at Artemisium. The second squadron, with two hundred ships, sailed secretly down the north shore of Euboea. From there it entered the southeast entrance of Euripus Strait to cut off a Hellenic retreat.

The Hellenes, however, received word of the maneuver and held a hasty council. They considered fleeing the main Persian force under cover of darkness and engaging the smaller enemy squadron in the lower strait. But instead, they made the bold gamble to launch a frontal assault against the primary strength of the Persian navy.

As the intrepid Hellenic squadron approached, the Persian commanders scoffed aloud and ordered their ships to encircle and crush it. But on a predetermined signal, the Hellenic ships suddenly turned their sterns together with prows facing the enemy in every direction. With the Persian fleet bearing down upon them, a second signal sounded. The Hellenes now burst forth with lightning speed and furiously rammed entire rows of enemy oars to sheer them off.

Amid flying splinters and shrieking sailors, ship after Persian ship fell lifeless in the churning sea, unable to move forward or backward without their oars. Before they could recover from the shock, the Persians lost thirty of their finest vessels to the Hellenic attack and withdrew as twilight descended over the darkening sea.

That night, another violent storm struck with lightning that crackled across the sky and filled the sailors' hearts with dread. The storm surge washed wreckage and bodies from the day's battle to Aphetae where they became entangled in the oars and mooring lines of the Persian fleet. This, following the loss of ships earlier that day and the losses from storms off Cape Sepias several days earlier, caused the enemy to despair.

The smaller Persian squadron fared much worse. As it rounded the southeastern tip of Euboea, it fell victim to the same storm in open waters and was driven off course. In pitch darkness, it ran aground and broke up along the rocky shore of Coela—a gaping coastline close to the mouth of Euripus Strait. The entire squadron with its screaming sailors plunged to the bottom of the sea.

News of the Persian disaster reached the Hellenic fleet the following day along with the arrival of fifty-three ships sent as reinforcements. That afternoon, the main Persian flotilla sat sullenly in the harbor at Aphetae, except for a small detachment which the Hellenes promptly attacked and damaged.

On the third and final day of naval engagements, which was also the third and final day of fighting at Thermopylae, the remaining Persian ships, still much superior in numbers, attacked in a crescent formation to encircle the Hellenes. But with too many ships involved in the maneuver they became entangled and crashed into each other. The Hellenic fleet suffered damage but inflicted more. Even so, with no army left at Thermopylae to protect, the Hellenes abandoned Artemisium to the Persians and sailed down Euripus Strait to protect Athens. As they passed Oropus, we joined a throng of thousands who waved, cheered, and shed joyful tears for the valiant Hellenic fleet that had wounded a giant.

Hoplite warriors appear on this memorial plate that mourners left at the burial site of Plataeans who died in the Battle of Marathon. Marathon Museum, Attica, Greece. Photo by author.

Hoplites in phalanx. Spartan vase painting, classical era. National Museum of Magna Graecia, Reggio Calabria, Italy. Photo by author.

# Chapter 8. OUT OF THE JAWS OF DEATH

*Recalling the words of Pappos*

BY NOW THE MASSIVE PERSIAN ARMY had marched away from the carnage at Thermopylae and pursued a southward route through the provinces of Trachis, Doris, and Phocis. None but the people of Phocis dared to stand against the foreign host, as they also had at Thermopylae, but they faced severe punishment as a result. The Persians made a point of destroying their croplands and orchards and burned their houses and temples to the ground.

Xerxes' army split in two, with him leading the main force through Boeotia into Attica. The Boeotians offered no resistance and submitted to Persian rule to avoid wanton destruction. But they could not prevent the devastation left in the wake of a wolfish horde that survived on foraging and plunder.

The smaller Persian contingent marched on Delphi, with its rich store of treasures amassed over centuries by Hellenes making offerings at the temple of Apollo. As the enemy approached, storms over Mount Parnassus rushed down upon them and rockslides hurled boulders at them until fear of Apollo's divine wrath forced them to flee to Boeotia. With the army reunited, the full force of Persia now bore down on Attica and its capital city, Athens. Beyond Athens stood the wealthy poleis of the Peloponnesus, including Corinth, Argos, and Sparta. Xerxes coveted all of these as plump grapes ripe for picking.

As the Persians approached their fair city, the Athenians learned, with faces flushed in fury, that the Peloponnesians had abandoned them to the enemy and begun building a wall across the Isthmus of Corinth to protect themselves. Athens, with powerful influence over the entire naval force of Hellas, responded by commanding every Hellenic ship to sail to their city and ferry their terrified women and children to safety on the nearby island of Salamis. The naval commanders obeyed and swiftly converged from the far reaches of the Aegean Sea with 378 triremes and smaller fifty-oared penteconters.

Xerxes, having crushed Plataea and Thespiae for their roles in the battles of Marathon and Thermopylae, now ordered the savage rape of the Attic countryside. The main Persian force spared us by remaining south of Oropus, but roving bands still menaced all of Attica while searching for food and plunder.

During sleepless nights and anxious days, we watched and waited for swarms of barbaric warriors to emerge from the woods without warning. Finally, with nerves frayed, we fled to somber forests and burrowed in dark and dismal hollows and caves. From there, we kept our eyes open and ears alert to the dreaded thud of heavy footsteps.

For most of a month, hunger and thirst nagged at us and the cold air caused us to shudder beyond control. Twice, the sound of foreign shouts caused us to huddle close and subdue our whimpers and trembling limbs. But after days of silence, we risked venturing out and found that all the wandering warriors had been recalled for a focused attack on Athens.

At fifteen, I was too young to join the Athenian army and remained at home near Oropus. But I did not sit idle. All civilian males from ages seven to seventy armed themselves with spears, knives, clubs, bows and arrows, and tirelessly trained to use them. With our military called away to battle, we stood prepared to defend our homes or flee with families if all else failed.

Some of our neighbors rushed to join the refugees who gathered at the protective harbor and heights of Salamis. As they passed through the once-bustling capital city, they witnessed the eerie spectacle of Athens sitting silent and still ahead of the impending invasion. Shops and homes stood empty. Dogs and vermin wandered deserted streets.

But on the lofty Acropolis, temple officials and others who refused to retreat barricaded themselves against the coming onslaught and prepared to rain missiles down upon the enemy. From their vantage point, they watched with dread as the approaching army engulfed the surrounding hills in a solid mass and flowed in human channels through every winding street toward the Acropolis.

Too late, the defenders realized the folly of resistance. But to their credit, they fought furiously as they placed their hope in Athena's divine protection. With weapons exhausted, they hurled objects of every sort and delayed the inevitable slaughter. But the Persians spied an exposed section of wall atop a sheer cliff and managed to scale the heights.

With the wall breached, the gates fell open to the bloodthirsty enemy. The end came quickly as fierce warriors swarmed the civilian defenders. Some Hellenes jumped to their deaths while others begged for their lives and were hacked apart, even as they knelt in submission.

The outrage continued from there. The Persians plundered the temples and put them to the torch, including Erechtheus' beloved sanctuary that housed

Athena's sacred olive tree since time immemorial. This sacrilege, and the earlier attack on Delphi, worried Xerxes to no small degree. He feared the Hellenic gods and shuddered at the thought of divine retribution.

On Salamis, Athenian refugees watched in abject horror as smoke billowed from the Acropolis. That which could never happen had happened. Their ancient city, the golden child of the goddess Athena, had fallen.

Panic gripped the island. Even the naval commanders who had fought so bravely at Artemisium lost heart and prepared to flee from the harbor and sail to the Isthmus of Corinth. There they hoped to support the Peloponnesian army at the newly erected defenses.

But one among them, an Athenian named Themistocles, feared that once the fleet left the harbor it would fall apart. The panicked crews would sail to their own home ports to defend their families, leaving themselves easy prey for the Persians. Themistocles insisted that only a unified fleet could fend against the superior Persian navy. He further argued that engaging the enemy in the harbor would keep Xerxes from marching on the Peloponnesus. But every point he made met with bitter debate and grave opposition.

When arguments failed, Themistocles resorted to threats. He warned the allies that if they abandoned the bay and the Athenian refugees on Salamis, then the Athenian triremes would desert from the Hellenic fleet, leaving it crippled and doomed. The triremes would then rescue the refugees and sail for the coast of Italy to begin a new life in a distant colony. The Peloponnesians, without a powerful naval force, would be left to the fate they deserved.

His threats changed the minds of many, but other allied commanders still prepared to depart. Some say that Themistocles, in exasperation, now leaked word to the Persians warning of the imminent departure of the Hellenic fleet. Xerxes, hoping to destroy the entire navy in one blow, immediately ordered his ships to rush to Salamis and trap the Hellenes in the bay.

Until then, the Persian navy had taken its time withdrawing from Artemisium. It had stopped to make repairs and steal supplies from the countryside of Euboea. Some of the seamen had even taken the time to visit the ghastly battlefield at Thermopylae and gawk at the slain Spartans whose corpses remained scattered on the ground. But upon receiving Xerxes' order, the Persian force now sailed with speed down the Euripus Strait.

From rocky bluffs we watched the hideous sails and prows fly past again, as they had on their way to Marathon ten years earlier. The feeling of dread that had overwhelmed me as a child of five now haunted my mind again. I wondered which of the hated ships and sailors had been here before, and how many had returned from Asia to seek revenge for the embarrassing defeat at Marathon. As before, if the Hellenes failed to vanquish the horde, the survivors would have no place to hide from death or foreign enslavement.

The Persian fleet rounded the coast of Attica and rushed to blockade Salamis Bay at both ends, trapping the warships within.[72] In doing so, the Persians made the fatal mistake of forcing the Hellenic fleet to remain intact with 380 triremes and many smaller ships of war. Themistocles' plan had worked.

The naval commanders of Hellas, with their plans of escape now foiled, devised a desperate strategy against a far-superior enemy. On their command, anxious crews rushed aboard deck, launched their ships, and maneuvered into formation. The Persians reacted at once, attacking from both entrances of the bay. Xerxes and his army watched from the heights along the opposite shore as his fleets quickly converged on the outnumbered Hellenes.

The Persian naval captains knew that Xerxes held a record of each ship's sails and insignia, and that he kept a scribe by his side to record instances of bravery or cowardice, which he would later reward or punish. This prompted his captains to compete with each other and push ahead to sink as many Hellenic vessels as possible.

But this worked to the disadvantage of the Persian navy. In their scramble to impress Xerxes, the tightly packed mass of ships hurried to outmaneuver each other in the narrow harbor. Soon they became entangled, running afoul of their own oars and rigging until the whole formation fell into disarray. The Hellenic flotilla, with its powerful core of warships sent by Athens and Aegina, spied the opportunity to seize the offensive and rushed into the melee to cut the Persian navy to pieces.

Thousands of Persian sailors sank with their ships and drowned in the sea because few knew how to swim. Those who frantically scrambled to climb on flotsam met with Hellenic spears and oars that pushed them beneath the surface time and again until they rose no more. Agonized screams and widespread panic forced the remaining Persian fleet to scatter, only to be run down and destroyed.

Xerxes stared in shock as his dream of conquest became a ghastly nightmare. Confusion turned to fear as he imagined the victorious Hellenic navy sailing from Salamis to the Hellespont to cut off his retreat to Asia. If that happened, a slow war of attrition might annihilate his entire army and deliver him personally into the hands of the furious Hellenes.

In desperation, he cried for the hasty withdrawal of the main army while leaving 300,000 men under the command of Mardonius to keep the Hellenes in check. As Xerxes and his frightened host fled back across the same ravaged, corpse-ridden wastelands that they had created, they fell victim to their own brutality, dying by the thousands from starvation and disease.[73]

In Hellas, hope soared like never before and softened the bitter shock of death and destruction. The bickering poleis of Hellas now united with a common purpose in mind—to combine their forces and obliterate the loathsome foe once and for all. The ranks of the army and navy swelled in the months to come as men ventured from hideouts near their smoldering homes and seized weapons from fallen soldiers to fight for revenge.

Mardonius still commanded a formidable army that remained larger than any force that the Hellenic allies could amass. But Persian morale had plummeted as they watched Xerxes and the main army retreat, leaving them alone, far from home, to fight the ferocious Hellenes.

A year passed as Mardonius retrenched his men in Boeotia. His every movement brought counter movements from the opposing force that shadowed him and his troops. Day by day, as the Hellenic army reinforced its ranks, it crept closer to the enemy and converged near the Gargaphian Springs at the foot of Mount Cithaeron.

This abundant source of freshwater rests near the town of Plataea, and overflows into the River Asopus. From there, the Asopus meanders along the Attic-Boeotian border and spills at last into the salty sea near Oropus. Garden spots like Gargaphian sometimes attract thirsty armies that leave them muddied and bloodied by bitter combat. But as the years pass, battlefields reclaim their natural beauty, and mourners adorn them with monuments and shrines to fallen heroes.

The largest Hellenic force of the Persian Wars now stood above the Gargaphian Springs and spread along the verdant banks of the Asopus. More than 100,000 men, including 38,700 hoplites and 69,500 light infantrymen, prepared to fight the enemy host of 300,000 Persian troops and their 50,000 vassals from northern Hellas. Face to face, the armies approached the river and glared in defiance from opposite banks, daring each other to cross.

As tensions mounted, Mardonius commanded his cavalry to ford the river up and downstream of the Hellenic lines and launch crippling forays against their flanks. At the same time, he sent tens of thousands of Persian archers to spread along the north bank and slay Hellenic soldiers as they attempted to fill their rams-horn flasks with water. This forced the thirsty men to depend on the Gargaphian Springs alone. But the Hellenes still held their position.

By the twelfth day, Mardonius lost all patience as his army's supplies ran low and the Hellenic camp continued to receive daily arrivals of provisions and reinforcements. In response, he sent an elite mounted unit to block and pollute the Gargaphian Springs. With the loss of their water supply, the Hellenes abandoned their camps and slipped stealthily southward during the night toward Plataea, twenty stades away. Instead of maintaining an orderly withdrawal, the armies of the Hellenic poleis departed at different times along separate routes.

At dawn, Mardonius ordered a massive cavalry charge to crush the thirsty enemy once and for all. But to his surprise, he found their camps near the springs deserted. Hoping to rout the retreating army, he pushed southward in rapid pursuit. Upon seeing the Hellenes scattered in separate units, he sent his entire force into the chase and watched as his men broke ranks to run them down. As the Persian soldiers fell upon the Spartan army, the Spartans suddenly spun about in solid phalanxes and fought with furious tenacity, like their countrymen had at Thermopylae.

The bewildered Persians fell back, formed a wall of wicker shields, and launched a barrage of arrows. But the Spartans marched ahead with their heavy bronze shields in place and their bristling spears thrust forward until they breached the makeshift Persian wall. Then, with disciplined precision, they pulled their swords and shredded the light-armored Persian force like farmers swinging sickles at harvest. At last, they defeated Mardonius' elite bodyguard of 1,000 men and then killed the commander himself.

A short distance away, the Athenians fought with equal valor and gained the upper hand over the vassals of the Persians. The battle now became a rout as the enemy host and their allies fled in all directions. Most made their way to a wooden fortification at Thebes. But the Spartans and Athenians pursued them, firing the walls and slaughtering the men within.

Hellenic losses proved minimal with only fifty-two Athenians and ninety-one Spartans killed. Among the fallen Spartans lay Aristodamus, one of the two couriers who had survived the loss of their comrades at Thermopylae.[74]

The final defeat of the Persians at Plataea brought an end to eleven years of carnage. But to this day, reminders of those terrible times appear along the banks of the River Asopus and the coast of Euripus Strait. I have often stumbled on bronze arrowheads, spear points, pieces of armor, and ship wreckage partially buried in the sand. Sometimes I wonder if the souls of those thousands of vanquished warriors still haunt the dismal forests along the banks as they kneel to drink from the soothing waters of the Asopus.

While the Battle of Plataea raged, an allied fleet lead by Athenian triremes destroyed a Persian flotilla near Miletus. As fate would have it, the hostilities which began at Miletus twenty years earlier with the Ionian Revolt now ended in victory off the coast of the same Hellenic city. Athens emerged from the war as the primary maritime power of the Aegean Sea and assumed the offensive against remaining Persian cities in Ionia.

At home, victory brought an era of self-confidence that became evident in democratic experiments in politics. Power was placed in the hands of the Ecclesia—the full Assembly of citizens. Judicial decisions became entrusted to the populace, which formed juries of peers. Art, architecture, philosophy, and science flourished.

Panhellenic cooperation also reached new heights as hundreds of poleis joined a maritime alliance called the Delian League. Every member polis provided naval support to the alliance by building warships and training crews. But most poleis eventually chose to send money to Athens to finance the building of the fleet rather than constructing their own triremes. As a result, the Delian League became more of an Athenian Empire, and weaker poleis fell under her dominion.

Not long later, Athens took advantage of her commanding position and began asserting her authority at the expense of her neighbors. Eighteen years after the formation of the Delian League, the island of Naxos opted to leave the confederation. But Athens forced her, under threat of war, to remain and pay tribute to finance the fleet.

Despite these heavy-handed tactics, military cooperation among the Hellenes resulted in general peace in the Aegean Sea. Thirty years after the Battle of Plataea, Hellas freed the last of the Ionian cities from Persian control. Two years later, in a burst of national pride, a statesman named Pericles used Athens' newfound wealth to rebuild the Acropolis that had sat in ruins for thirty-three years. Within a decade, the Parthenon, the temple of the maiden goddess Athena, stood as the crowning glory of Athens and the entire Hellenic world.

Sadly, Athens vaunted her wealth and power, and incited resentment among her neighbors. Before long, Sparta and other poleis reacted by invading Attica and marching on Athens. As Spartans roamed the region like marauding packs of wolves, our countrymen took refuge within the walls of Athens or the port of Piraeus, or within the parallel walls that protected the road connecting the two.

Athenian commanders knew that the city would be doomed if she lost access to her seaport and fleet, so they assigned all able hands to defend the parallel walls. *In the daytime the citizens guarded the battlements by relays; during the night every man was on service except the cavalry; some at their places of arms, others on the wall, summer and winter alike, until they were quite worn out.*[75]

I was sixty-four at the time of the first Spartan invasion. Ama and I agreed that we were too old to pack and move to the capital, so we stayed on the farm and took our chances. The decision proved fortunate for us because plague soon spread through the crowded city. Many of those that seemed healthy *were seized with violent heats in the head and with redness and inflammation of the eyes. Internally the throat and the tongue were quickly suffused with blood.*

Coughing gave way to vomiting, and *the internal fever was intense; the sufferers could not bear to have on them even the finest linen garment; they insisted on being naked, and there was nothing which they longed for more eagerly than to throw themselves into cold water.* Most people struck by the disease died, and others lost eyes and extremities. Under these circumstances, with the specter of death ever present, social constraints failed. Hysteria and lawlessness prevailed.[76] Within four years, one-fourth of the population of Athens wasted away and died.

As the plague raged within the city walls, the Spartans raged without and devastated Attica. They made annual forays into the countryside, spreading fear among those who remained on the farms. Those of us who remembered the Persian Wars lead our kinsmen to the same hidden refuges in the mountains we had utilized then, whenever we spotted marauders in the region.

Once, as we returned from seclusion, we received word that our son had fallen while fighting as a hoplite in the Athenian army. He had left his wife six months pregnant. But soon she rejoined him as her soul departed while giving birth to twins.

Those are the realities of war. War destroys innocent lives, devastates crops and homes, and brings bitter despair to those who survive the losses. In the end, all war seems to accomplish is a desire for revenge and an excuse for another war. After ten years of bloodshed, an uneasy truce halted the fighting between Athens and Sparta. Athenians celebrated by beginning the construction of another Acropolis temple—the Erechtheum. We can only hope that peace will prevail and the temple will stand through the ages.

Entrance to one of the ancient Laurium Mines. The silver from these mines funded the building of a fleet of triremes that defeated the Persians at the Battle of Salamis in 480 BC. Following the victory, Laurium silver paid for construction of the Parthenon, Erechtheum, and other temples on the Athenian Acropolis. These temples symbolize the height of classical culture. Photo by author.

Athenian silver drachma extracted and minted from ore of the Laurium mines in the 5th century BC. Marshall Collection, Loma Paloma, Texas. Photo by author.

# Chapter 9. THE DARKEST DAYS

AS I SAT ALONE AND FORLORN in the dark, the memory of Pappos' tragic tales filled my eyes with tears. A feeling of homesickness swept over me as I longed for the mother and father that Bronte and I had never known. Staring sullenly into the dwindling fire, I forgot about the flock and the reason for my night long vigil. But a noise in the nearby brush grabbed my attention. As I glanced up, a dark object lunged for the enclosure.

Before I could react, the wolf seized a screaming ewe by the flank. I grabbed a burning torch and hurled it in his direction. But rather than release the sheep, he strengthened his grip while snarling viciously and glaring at me with furious eyes. Returning to the coals, I picked up two more firebrands and rushed upon the wolf, causing him to lose his grip and move grudgingly out of the enclosure.

At the first available moment, I threw more branches on the embers and stoked them into a bonfire while keeping an eye on the shadowy figure that paced back and forth on the fringe of light. After an interminable standoff, a purple streak at last appeared on the horizon. The wolf remained nearby but seemed wary now. His pack had lost interest and wandered away.

Suddenly, his glowering eyes jerked to attention as he peered beyond me. Then he bolted back into the woods as quickly as he had appeared. I turned around and followed his line of sight to the figure of Bronte approaching over the rise to take his turn with the flock.

Never had I been happier to see him. My heart welled with emotion from the trials of the night and the sudden relief that made it all right. I ran to my brother and hugged him, to his astonishment, and my tears caused him to sob as well. Rather than leave Bronte alone with the flock, we cleaned the torn flesh of the bawling ewe and headed for home.

After that night, Bronte and I grew closer than ever. The wolf attack made us realize that we would always set our occasional differences aside if one of us truly needed the help of the other. Another year passed as we assumed more of the responsibilities of the farm and flock and worked together as one to complete chores that would typically be left to a grown man.

With the coming of spring, we tossed the knucklebones again to see which one would be first to take the flock into the high country. As the little bones clattered to the ground, I shook my head at the expected result, examined the knucklebones suspiciously, and handed them back to Bronte. He simply grinned and shrugged.

I could never understand how he did it. The odds should allow me to win a toss more often than one time in four. Though I never believed in luck, I had to wonder if he had it within him. He also seemed to win most races, wrestling matches, and rock throwing contests. It was a rare day when I got to wear the victor's wreath that Pappos had woven five years before.

Hefting my knapsack and provisions, I gave tender hugs to Pappos and Ama and strode to the sheep and goat pen. The flock bleated in anticipation, knowing the time had come to nibble the fresh mountain forage. As my woolly companions and I climbed a rise on the western edge of the farmstead, I stopped and looked back at our little hut and the fragrant smoke curling upward from beneath the porch.

Farther below, I saw Bronte standing in the grainfield with a hoe in his hand and the wreath tilted back on his head. As he watched me walk away, he raised his hand in farewell. I returned a wave with a heavy heart and turned my face toward the hills.

Three nights in the mountains passed without problem, but on the fourth morning I impatiently gazed toward the east and grumbled aloud. Bronte should have arrived at my campfire by dawn to take his turn with the flock. The sun had already climbed high above the eastern horizon. As it reached noon and began its descent, I felt uneasy and sick to my stomach.

Bronte had never been late. Perhaps he, Pappos, or Ama lay hurt or sick and needed my help. I gathered the flock with haste and started for home.

Before I topped the final rise, I knew that something was dreadfully wrong. A plume of smoke billowed from the direction of our hut but was much too large to be Ama's cookfire. My face flushed then turned cold as I ran ahead of the flock.

Anxiety turned to a numb chill. I dropped my knapsack and stumbled, dazed, toward the ruins of our little home. The earthen walls were an empty shell, scorched from the inside, and filled with the debris of a collapsed roof. Timbers smoldered and crackled as coals consumed all that remained within. Clothing and utensils lay scattered and broken about the yard.

Suddenly my entire frame shook, and I fell to my knees with hot tears rushing down my cheeks. Pappos was lying nearby, face down in the earth with a staff near his hand, his white hair matted with blood. Ama sat slumped inside the door, blackened by the flames that had engulfed her. Unable to accept the reality of what I saw, I staggered slowly and aimlessly about the homestead and called feebly for Bronte. On the edge of the field, I found his wreath but no other sign of him.

As the sun descended in the west, darkness consumed my soul. Gathering two shredded blankets that lay strewn in the yard, I covered Ama's tiny figure. I had never realized how small and vulnerable she was.

Then, as the last light of day departed, I covered Pappos and collapsed by his side in utter exhaustion. During the long, cold night I never left him, but slept a while and cried a while. Lost in a half-conscious stupor, and longing to hear his voice, I lay awake looking into the heavens and recalled that priceless winter five years before, when I snuggled close and listened to Pappos' tales:

*Recalling the words of Pappos*

As mortals came to disdain their fellow beings and divine deities, selfish struggle and strife drove them to war against each other. The gods, indignant, fumed in anger. Even Astraea, who had loved humans as innocent children, walked away in sorrow. Zeus himself, who had chuckled in mirth at the child-like folly of men, now turned bitter toward them and became capricious and cruel. Innocent people suffered along with the rest, as the stories of Callisto, Arcas, and Phoenice attest.

In the distant past, the maiden Callisto dwelled among the dark forests and jagged crags of Arcadia. Hermes had been born in this wild and rugged country, in a rocky cave on Mount Kyllini. And Pan, *the goat-footed, two-horned rowdy*, and patron of savage beasts and shepherds' flocks, still haunted the deep hollows and dizzying heights.[77]

The mysterious mountains enchanted Callisto. She often wandered beneath the moon through meadows glowing in subtle light and forests shrouded in darkness. In euphoric suspense, she sometimes stopped and stood silent and still in the shadows.

She listened intently and peered through the gloom for a glimpse of the wild and wary creatures that prowled around her. Sometimes, when food ran scarce, she searched for a deer and felled it with an arrow. Then she sat beside it and shed a grateful tear for the sustenance it provided.

Callisto followed in firm devotion the divine example of Artemis — goddess of the hunt and matron of the moon. Like Callisto, the goddess delighted in spending days and nights softly stalking through somber woods in search of wildlife. Artemis, the virgin goddess, also championed female chastity, and Callisto had sworn to abide by that code.

But the dictates of fate were not for her to decide. One morning, while Zeus was seeking solace in the dusky woods, he spied Callisto from a distance as she glided silently from tree to tree, fully focused on the hunt. The maiden remained unaware of his presence as he followed her through the forest until she met him face to face. Unable to fend off his advances, she conceived a child and gave birth the following spring to a son.

Forlorn and afraid of Artemis' anger at the conception and birth, Callisto bundled her baby and held him close, concealed in her cape. But the virgin goddess heard the crying child and found that the girl had not remained chaste. In misplaced rage, she rashly blamed Callisto for the indiscretion.

As punishment, Artemis snatched Callisto's son away and transformed her from a graceful maiden into a blundering bear. Her tender voice became a grumble and growl. Her silky hair turned course and matted and covered her body from head to foot. Condemned to ramble the woods on four feet as a brutish beast, Callisto was constantly hunted by her own countrymen. The barking of dogs and shouts of the chase that had once filled her with thrills and excitement now brought fear and foreboding.

Many loathsome, lonely years passed, and Callisto's infant son, Arcas, grew to be a sturdy youth. Raised by a rustic goatherd in the rugged heights of Arcadia, Arcas earned his keep with a drove of goats and sheep and the meat he brought home from the hunt. One calm morning, while his flock lazily grazed beside a trickling spring, he spotted a she-bear on the fringe of the forest.

With a leap and a shout, he gave chase, unaware that the bruin was his own woeful mother. All that day, he pursued the frantic beast through brambles and brush, down rocky ravines and across cold mountain streams. At last, he wore her down. As she lay exhausted before him with her head on the ground and her pleading eyes turned upward, he held high his club to deliver the fatal blow.

The loud shouts of the hunter and the lamentations of the bear caught the attention of far-seeing Zeus. As he watched the tragic drama unfolding below, he felt sudden pity for Callisto and Arcas—his long-lost lover and child. In haste, he forestalled the evil fate that threatened to make one the victim of her son and the other the murderer of his mother. There, on the leafy forest floor, with a word from Zeus, the two suddenly knew their true relation and rejoiced in the reunion.

From that day forward, Callisto, who knew every shadowy haunt and hollow, led the way down hidden trails as she and Arcas roamed far and wide through the forest. Arcas always followed close behind her, faithfully protecting his mother. Finally, to offer her safety and solace forever, Zeus placed her in the highest heaven where she shines as the constellation Arctos—the BEAR. Here she circles the north celestial pole in peace, with nothing to fear.[78] But she still keeps a wary watch on the stars that mark the mighty hunter named Orion.[79]

Arcas came to rule the rugged mountain kingdom, which was later named Arcadia in his honor. He lived a long and happy life in his forest home while shepherding his people well and forever revering his lustrous mother above. When he came to the end of his days, Zeus set him in the cosmos as the Bear's protector and called him BOOTES—the Shouter.[80] His brightest star is Arcturus—the BEAR GUARD—so named because of his constant watch over his mother's constellation. With a shepherd's staff in the right hand and his left hand reaching fondly toward her, he follows close behind in the northern sky.

When Zeus intervened to reunite the mother and son, Artemis learned the truth, that Callisto had conceived the child through no fault of her own. In deep remorse for her unfair judgment and brutal reprisal, the goddess bowed her head in shame. Too late to make amends, she vowed to never take that cruel path again.

Years later, Zeus, the wanton god, lustily followed Phoenice who was another faithful admirer of Artemis. Phoenice, a daughter of the Phoenician race, was much like Callisto in manner and morals. No sooner had Artemis detected Zeus' interest in her than she took fast action to protect the innocent girl. Reacting in pity, rather than rage, the goddess changed Phoenice's feminine form into that of a bear before further harm could come.

But Phoenice was never forced to wander the woods in fear, like Callisto. Instead, Artemis set her securely in the sky as a constellation, close to her larger companion, the Bear. To distinguish the two, Phoenice is called the LITTLE BEAR.

At the apex of heaven, she stalks swiftly forward through the night in a rapid circle above the Bear. The two stand out from earthly bruins because of their long and splendid, starry tails. The Little Bear's tail curves upward, so she sometimes carries the nickname Cynosura, or *dog tail*.[81]

Zeus continued to pursue mortal women. To seduce them, he sometimes dazzled their senses and captured their affections by appearing in the form of magnificent animals. As a spectacular, snow-white swan, he gained the love of Leda of Sparta, who bore him twin sons, Castor and Polydeuces, and daughters, Helen and Clytemnestra.

The two boys later emerged as heroes of Hellas and journeyed with Jason and the Argonauts. Helen gained renown for her unrivaled beauty, and married Menelaus, the king of Sparta. Her abduction to Troy sparked the Hellenic siege of that prosperous and powerful city. Helen's sister, Clytemnestra, wed Agamemnon, the king of Mycenae, who commanded the seaborne invasion of Troy.

Zeus celebrated his liaison with Leda by placing a constellation in the sky in the shape of a swan. The swan, simply called the BIRD, shines bright among the dense assembly of stars in the glowing Milky Way. There, he appears as if *wreathed in mist* and soaring *like a bird in joyous flight*.[82]

Zeus assumed the shape of another stunning creature, a snow-white bull, to win the affections of the maiden Europa. From childhood, the cheerful Europa had always loved the coastline of her native Phoenician home, much as Callisto adored the forested mountains of her motherland. Europa often wandered along the Asian shore, laughing at the splashing surf and savoring the salty breeze. She watched for delicate shells and other treasures dropped at her dainty feet by the benevolent sea.

One warm day, as Europa strolled along the balmy Mediterranean beach, she froze in her footsteps, entranced by the sight of a beautiful bull that grazed the seagrass near the shore. Approaching slowly, she petted the white, curly locks between his horns. She picked pretty flowers and fashioned a garland to adorn his head. At last, she grasped his supple mane and slipped atop his broad back for a wade in the rolling surf.

Suddenly, the docile bull sprang to life and lunged into the waves. Swiftly he swam, rapidly plunging through the waters toward the west and sweeping Europa out to sea. As she desperately clung to his curly mane, she glanced behind and watched in dismay as her homeland dwindled and disappeared.

The copper-rich island of Cyprus soon loomed ahead. But the bull continued to batter the waves, bounding toward the setting sun. At dusk, the island of Crete came into view and seemed to swell on the horizon as they swiftly approached. Here, at last, the bull with his maiden prize waded ashore to rest on the sandy beach.

Europa collapsed near the crashing surf, sobbing in woe and foreboding, and homesick for her family. But at sunrise, the charming island enticed her to wander its pleasant and peaceful shores. Soon she discovered that graceful beaches encircled the elegant island. Her sorrow gave way to glee as the birds sang a welcoming song and the gentle sea breeze soothed her soul and softened her tears.

Crete captured her heart and became her adopted home. The following year, she brought forth a son and named the baby Minos. As a toddler, the son of Zeus traipsed hand-in-hand with his mother along every sunbaked beach of the island. And, like his mother, he treasured the gifts of the sea.

While still a youth, he hiked the hills alone and came to love the land — every cave, cliff, mountain, meadow, and forest. Soon he knew all the native beings of the island by name — the plants, animals, and people. So, no one seemed surprised when the day came that Minos, the son of Europa and Zeus, reigned as king of Crete.

Zeus was pleased to see the happiness of the mother and son. In satisfaction, the powerful god, ever proud of himself, commemorated his cunning theft of Europa by placing the BULL in the nighttime sky. The majestic beast blazes among the stars, half-submerged and splaying his forelegs in the same manner that he swam across the heaving sea.

The Bull is called a constellation *rich in maidens*, because he bears several sisters on his back, just as he once bore Europa. The seven sisters, called the PLEIADES, appear as seven stars that ride high on his hump. Their five half-sisters, the HYADES, shimmer as heavenly lights on his head.[83]

Minos ruled the people of Crete with fairness. But he fell into the common folly, far too often repeated, of showering his affection on one of his several children while neglecting the others. In fact, Minos adored his son, Androgeus, more than the rest of his family, his friends, and his entire kingdom.

Androgeus developed into a talented athlete under his father's constant attention, with lavish expenses paid for coaches and training. When the youth traveled to Athens and won the victory wreath at the Panathenaic Games, all of Crete rejoiced beside the beaming father. But many Athenians fumed at the thought of a foreigner wearing the triumphal wreath of the city.

Several ruffians banded together in the dark and inflamed each other with angry words. Riled in a fit of fury, they followed Androgeus and crowded close to kill the youth. The people of Crete reeled when they heard the hateful news. Minos locked himself in his palace, unseen for days, distraught beyond words and weary of the world's wicked ways.

At last, his sorrow succumbed to rage. In brutal retaliation, Minos imposed a terrible tribute on Athens. The wrathful king forced the fair city to send seven of its sons and seven of its daughters as annual sacrifices to the man-eating Minotaur.

The monster, half-man and half-bull, dwelled in the deep, dark labyrinth — a twisted maze of Cretan caves beneath Minos' palace. Alone in the dreary domain, the hideous, half-starved creature raged within his wretched world, bellowing day and night for another screaming victim to consume.

If the Athenians failed to pay the horrid tax of human flesh, Minos, the powerful king of Crete, promised to burn their city and level their land. For many years, Athens saw no option but to pay the dreadful debt. As yet another year approached, the Athenian Councilmen, wringing their hands in anguish, tried to decide which of their fair children to send to their gruesome deaths.

At that moment, a brave young man named Theseus stepped boldly forward. To their speechless surprise, he proposed to journey to Crete, posing as a sacrifice. There he would battle the beast in the labyrinth and win a cease to the grisly tax. The Councilmen opposed the plan in theory, but not enough to dissuade themselves of its merit. In the end, they accepted Theseus' offer.

Now the Athenian ship, with its confident hero and thirteen tearful boys and girls, found its way across the wine-dark sea to moor on the coast of Crete. Theseus, tall and fiery, was first to set foot on the sandy shore. Immediately, without his knowing, he captured the eyes and heart of Ariadne, a daughter of Minos.

Without hesitation or need for further thought, the Cretan princess determined, then and there, to save the handsome youth from the Minotaur. As the curious crowd of gawkers departed and an opportunity arose, Ariadne sidled close beside him. Softly, she whispered hurried words of advice in his ear and slipped him a simple ball of thread.

Thus armed, Theseus entered the labyrinth with confidence while the other six boys and seven girls trembled and wailed at the entrance. Leaving them there, he silently stole through the gloomy cavern. As he slipped warily forward, he unwound the skein along the path to provide a guide for escaping the twisted lair.

Far down the dismal route he roamed, passing fly-infested heaps of putrid bones. Suddenly, he stumbled upon the foul fiend in the darkness. The battle raged, with the two powerful enemies beating and butting each other until they fell to the blood-soaked floor, exhausted. Heaving and frothing, Theseus was first to catch his breath and regain his strength. With bare fists, he pummeled the Minotaur until the monster's eyes glazed over in death.

Now the hero made his ascending escape, following a simple, indispensable string—his lifeline from the mind-bending maze. As he strode out of the somber gloom, he shaded his eyes against the bright and cheerful light of the sun. From somewhere near, the other Athenian youths, still shaking with fear, heard the frightening sound of approaching footsteps. But soon they stared in disbelief and cried in overwhelming relief as their comrade came into view. Ariadne, having saved Theseus by a thread, rejoiced in silence from her hiding place in a nearby grove of trees.

Undetected by the palace guards, Theseus and his thirteen friends dashed toward the Athenian ship, hidden on the coast, where the hopeful crew awaited. Beside them ran the Cretan princess. Her mind firmly fixed, Ariadne abandoned her father and country and sailed in haste with the hero in hope of a new life and love in Athens.

At mid-voyage, while resting on the island of Naxos, the maiden, with her body, mind, and emotions fully exhausted, fell into deepest slumber. For days she lay so silent and still that Theseus feared she had passed into peaceful death. Every attempt to revive her failed. Finally, with his happy heart now broken, Theseus left her lying in sweet repose and resumed the long journey without her.

With judgment clouded by grief, he forgot the promise he had made to his father to hoist a white, billowing sail as the ship approached the Athenian shore. The sail was to serve as a signal that Theseus had found his way home alive and well. Instead, as he slept, the unknowing crew drew the ship close to the coast with the traditional black sail of mourning still hoisted high on the mast.

Theseus' father had sat day after day with his eyes fixed on the horizon. At Poseidon's temple at Sounion, on a precipice above the crashing surf, he watched and waited for his son's return. When in the distance he beheld the dreaded canvas, billowing black above the sea, he grieved at the loss of Theseus and the thirteen youths who he thought had fallen to the ferocious Minotaur.

In sorrow and despair, he cast himself off the cliff into the churning waters far below. When Theseus stepped ashore, he heard the horrific news. At once, his victory evaporated like a fresh drop of dew on a blazing summer day, whisked away by the double tragedy of losing his father and Ariadne.

Back on the island of Naxos, Ariadne finally awoke to find her loved one gone and herself alone. The poor girl could not be consoled. In so short a span, she had lost her family, her friends, her homeland, and now her beloved hero.

Her mournful sobs and deep distress attracted the attention of the god Dionysus, who frequently wandered the wooded island. In pity for the trembling maiden, he soothed her brow and stroked her hair and soon fell fast in love. At last, she set her sorrow aside and vowed to go with him to the heights of Mount Olympus to be his bride.

There, the delightful wife of Dionysus became a favorite among the immortals. Many years later, when Ariadne passed away, all of Olympus mourned. Dionysus, in deepest sorrow, set his loved one's wedding wreath among the stars. There it blazes from afar as the NORTHERN WREATH—a befitting tribute to beautiful Ariadne.[84]

In the age of bronze, the belligerence of mortals and gods brought countless sorrows upon the Earth. Still, in the end, good prevailed. Zeus' seduction of Leda was shameful. But the resulting birth of the twins, Castor and Polydeuces, provided the world with two heroes who faithfully served both gods and men.

Likewise, Zeus' abduction of Europa was a dastardly act, but it led in later years to the birth of a granddaughter—Ariadne. The sweet and gentle girl saved the lives of Theseus and thirteen other Athenian youths, while helping to rid the world of the monstrous Minotaur. As Dionysus' wife, she delighted the gods and gained their everlasting love.

Zeus, forever the philanderer, fathered other children by three of the seven sisters known as the Pleiades. But, once again, good prevailed in the end. The three children born of these trysts rose to greatness among mortals and immortals alike.

Maia, the fairest of the Pleiades, brought forth the infant Hermes, who later flew through the sky as the messenger god so dearly loved by humans. Maia's sister, Taygeta, bore a son named Lacedaemon, who founded the kingdom of Sparta. Electra's son, Dardanus, became the father of the Trojan race. These excellent children offered further proof that good may come from even the darkest beginnings.

Bear (Ursa Major) and Little Bear (Ursa Minor) depicted in the *Astronomicum Caesareum* of Petrus Apianus, 1540. Rare Books Collection, Texas Tech University, Lubbock, Texas.

Zeus abducting Europa from the Phoenician shore. Stone relief, 560-550 BC. Archeological Museum, Magna Phoenicia, Palermo, Italy. Photo by author.

# Chapter 10. SOMEHOW LIFE GOES ON

PAPPOS' WORDS DRIFTED AWAY as I woke to the sound of birds chirping in the branches above. The sheep and goats had followed me off the hill and now nibbled tufts of grass nearby. I glanced at Pappos under his blanket beside me and unbearable grief welled again. My heart was torn from my chest and cast away, leaving me lifeless and without purpose. I wondered how the birds could play and the flock could graze as if nothing had happened.

Half the day passed before extreme thirst nagged me to my feet. I brushed the dirt and leaves away, slowly picked up a jug, and staggered with a heavy heart to the spring. I would only fetch water for one this day. After washing my filthy, tear-streaked face, I returned to Pappos and Ama. At a total loss for what to do, I simply sat back down on the ground and hung my head low.

In the afternoon, I heard a young voice on the path nearby. My heart leapt as my eyes searched for Bronte returning home. Instead, the forlorn countenance belonged to a friend who lived at a neighboring farm. He was some four years older than Bronte and me, and his expression revealed the same despair that I felt in my heart. He clutched the hand of his three-year-old sister, who was unaware of anything amiss, or that her life had changed forever.

Their faces were dirty and their clothing filthy from sleeping in the woods through the night. They gladly drank from my jug. Then the boy stammered the bitter tale of the day before.

With tearful interruptions, he recalled how the two had gone to a nearby hollow to gather firewood. Upon hearing a commotion, they hurried back to their farm. From the edge of the forest, they witnessed the rape and murder of their mother and father, and the plunder and destruction of their home.

For much of the day, the three of us sat together without a word, sobbing to the point of exhaustion. The pangs of hunger finally prompted us to search for help. I filled the empty goatskin flask that still remained looped around my neck, and we set out in search of neighbors.

After passing two smoldering farms, we discovered another, sheltered deep in the woods, that had survived. An old couple, unaware of the tragedy that struck their neighbors, was tending their tiny plot. Upon hearing our plight, they dropped their tools, took us in their arms, and we all wept again.

They fed us and let us stay the night on worn blankets arranged on the porch. In the morning, the kindly elders shuffled beside us as we searched for

Bronte. One by one, we combed the ruins of the neighboring farmsteads, covered the dead, and gathered tearful survivors.

From scattered accounts we began to piece together a sickening story. Two boys had witnessed the approach of three merchant ships off the coast, southeast of Oropus. Their description of the blood red sails with the black emblem of a diving seabird remained branded in my mind. The marauding crews had moved swiftly inland, killing and pillaging along the way before fleeing at dusk to sail down Euripus Strait toward the open waters of the Aegean. The two who had watched from cover believed the men spoke an Asian tongue.

As the months passed, the story became clearer. Earlier that year, the Athenian fleet had launched a formidable, ill-fated invasion of Syracuse—a distant polis allied with Sparta. With few ships left to defend Hellenic waters, foreign merchantmen turned to piracy, launching coastal raids on small villages and homesteads—plundering, killing, and capturing slaves.

We found no sign of Bronte besides his little wreath, which I kept and cherished in his memory. We could only assume that he was either killed or forced aboard a ship and sent in shackles as a slave in foreign lands. The thought stung me deeply and left me distraught and helpless, with no recourse to right the wrong.

The description of the ships and sails led Athenian officials to believe that the crews who raided our farms came from a port in Pamphylia, on the Asian mainland north of Cyprus. I knew nothing of the region, but from that day I nursed a bitter hatred for the country and its people.

For the time being, however, I had to push those thoughts aside as we prepared our loved ones for burial. I sat silently at a distance and glanced on and off as neighbors laid out the bodies of Pappos and Ama on planks and bathed them as best they could. Pappos lay on his back while Ama, with her legs curled beneath, rested on her side.

After anointing them with perfumed olive oil, the mourners wound them in clean white cloth. They left their faces exposed and placed an obol in each of their mouths so they could pay Charon to ferry them across the River Styx to Hades. They broke up a honey cake and placed a piece in each of their right hands to placate Cerberus, the ghastly hound that guards the gate to the underworld.

For another day, the bodies rested with heads on little pillows, and chests adorned with wreaths of spring flowers. In the evening, a dozen friends came dressed in dark colors with ashes in their hair and tears freely flowing. Some beat their chests and wailed aloud. Their deep remorse and tender affection caused me to cry again.

They buried Pappos and Ama on the farm, not far from the burnt remains of the hut that Pappos had built, and where he and Ama had witnessed the birth of their only son, and later Bronte and me. Ama had called the place her home since her wedding day so long ago. She had arrived here in a procession, and she left in one as well. The simple ritual took place at twilight with four adults carrying each of the planks while others lifted torches high. A few mourners poured libations along the path to the burial site.

Most of the personal possessions of Pappos and Ama had been stolen or destroyed by flames. What little remained was placed in the grave beside them. After a neighbor covered the bodies with fresh earth, he poured a final libation that splashed and seeped into the ground. How appropriate it seemed that they had returned to the same earth that they had cultivated and cherished; the same earth that had nourished them for most of their lives.

The procession now returned up the path. Each person who handled the dead took turns washing faces and hands in a basin of water for purification. A ceremonial pot of water also sat outside the charred door of our hut, although no one would be going inside to sprinkle its purifying waters in the customary way.

Because of the shortage of food and the number of dead among the neighboring farms, we had to forego the feasts for the deceased that typically took place on the third, ninth and thirteenth days. But for several years, I annually honored the burial with memorial scraps of meat, sacrificed on behalf of my beloved Pappos and Ama.

I remained alone near the graves that night, mesmerized by the mournful hoot of an owl. In the morning, I gathered my few possessions and prepared to drive the flock toward the home of the aged couple. I needed a place to stay, and they could use a strong back to work their tiny farm. As I slowly walked away from home, I felt my childhood hesitate and stay behind. From that moment, I took up the heavy burden and somber demeanor of an adult.

I spent the following year struggling to escape terrible thoughts and bitter rage. To this end, I thrust myself into the work of restoring the couple's exhausted farm. Their hut begged for a coat of plaster, tiles on the roof to turn back the rain, and a better hearth than the charred spot on the bare ground where they had made fires to cook and keep warm. Upon completing repairs, I chopped logs for a pen for the flock, pruned the few remaining olive and fruit trees, borrowed a pair of donkeys to plow a larger field, and stacked a worthy supply of tinder and kindling for the winter.

With the farm in fair order, I returned to school as often as possible to further the learning I had come to love. The pursuit of traditional studies—reading, writing, arithmetic, memorization, and music—turned my focus toward something good and put my mind at a degree of ease. Then, at the age of twelve, physical training became a crucial part of the curriculum.

This, I believe, served the purpose of producing well-rounded citizens—men of *arete* who could participate effectively in society. But it also prepared the youth for the compulsory military service that began at age eighteen. I had no qualms about this. I longed to join the army and seek revenge against foreign pirates and other enemies of Attica.

With this in mind, I dashed onto the training field in Oropus, hoping to hone old skills and learn new ones. Soon I felt the burn of strenuous labor designed to build strength, speed, endurance, and stubborn persistence. My classmates and I trained under the constant scrutiny of a stern coach, and under the gaze of Hermes—the divine patron of gymnasiums—whose statue stood in splendor on a pedestal near the field.

Spectators sometimes peered over the walls that otherwise kept us secluded from the public. Our only other audience was a troop of younger boys who furthered their musical skills by piping lively tunes that lifted our weary spirits. Flutes stirred the hearts of competitors and spectators alike at every athletic contest in every Hellenic polis.

As we prepared for the daily workout, we stripped our clothes and covered our bodies with olive oil, scraping off the excess with a strigil. Training was tough and grew ever tougher. The one-stade, two-stade, and four-stade sprints remained our favorite races, but the twenty-four-stade run, round and round the field, brought many grumbles and groans. Our coach was not moved to compassion but made us run the distance again and again.

We also practiced the long jump with weights in our hands and learned to hurl the discus. For the javelin toss, we wrapped a thong around the shaft and secured it to our fingers. With this, we launched the javelin with surprising velocity and gave it a spin for accuracy.

The technique demanded exhaustive practice, but the student who excelled could one day depend on the weapon in warfare, hunting, or athletic competitions. One javelin contest was measured in distance. The other called for accuracy and required that we aim for a target.

As part of our training, we also wrestled, boxed, and kick-boxed until we collapsed in exhaustion. Whether we won or lost, we called upon the strength within to stand up straight and walk away with bruised bodies, bloodied faces, and grim defiance despite our throbbing wounds. The coach demanded that we bury our pain and exhaustion, grit our teeth, and push relentlessly forward. At night, while resting and nursing wounds, we found further motivation in dreams of one day winning the pentathlon at the Panathenaic games, or perhaps at the Pan-Hellenic games devoted to Zeus in Olympia.

The following morning, as we wrestled, raced, jumped, and threw the javelin, there was not one among us who failed to envision the winner's wreath being placed on his head. We imagined returning in triumph through the crowded streets of Athens, with doe-eyed girls gazing our way, and the adoring public offering free meals for life. Even if the fantasies were all we ever achieved, then the work was worth it. Once, while I wrestled a worthy opponent, my mind wandered to thoughts of grandeur until, with a thud that rattled my teeth, I found myself flat on my back.

At the age of twelve, catastrophic events disrupted my education. The proud Athenian fleet that had sailed for Syracuse and left our waters unprotected, suffered sudden, disastrous defeat. This major blow to our military power encouraged the warlike Spartans to break the truce and invade Attica again. But rather than launching scattered forays into the countryside, as before, the Spartans boldly built a fortress at Decelea, between Athens and Oropus, and dared Athenians to retaliate against the intrusion.

From Decelea, foraging parties roamed the region, plundering local crops and livestock. To make matters worse, the Spartans incited forty thousand slaves from the silver mines to cast off bondage and flood the countryside. Athens reeled at the blow and the economic distress from the shutdown of the mines, and the free citizens of Attica trembled at the presence of a large host of escaped slaves.[85]

The wandering slaves scoured the land in search of food, as might be expected. But some also terrorized families of farmers, trampling grainfields and cutting down vineyards and olive groves for no other reason than spite. The widespread damage of olive trees was so immense, it would impoverish three generations of farmers. Yet, none but a few of these hardworking families had ever owned slaves, and many even spoke out against slavery. Now they faced the wanton destruction of their livelihood and source of survival while the wealthy slaveowners cowered behind the city walls.

Backcountry folks often fled their homes out of fear and lived like animals in caves and hidden hollows. But the old couple with whom I lived refused to leave their tiny hut. So, I stood by their side and hid our meager supply of food in the forest, hefted high in the limbs of trees.

On occasion, small bands of haggard slaves or hungry Spartans emerged from the dense forest and slowly approached our hut with weapons in hand. Each time, we gave them what little we had in the hut. Without a word, they gratefully nodded and backed away. We thanked the gods that those we encountered were not as hostile as foreign foes and pirates.

From their new fortress at Decelea, the Spartans launched furious assaults against the strongholds of Attica. They also took advantage of sudden Athenian naval weakness and built a fleet of their own. Then they bullied members of the Delian League to break the alliance and join them. Athens and the Attic countryside had not faced bitter defeat like this since the razing of the Acropolis some seventy years earlier.

During these trying times, the polis welcomed me into the phratry—a brotherhood of fourteen-year-old boys. A ceremonial sacrifice and shearing of our hair announced to our countrymen that we had become young men. Some of us foolishly thought that we should now be allowed to join the army and take up arms against the Spartans. But Athenian commanders held firmly and wisely to the old tradition that allowed only men of eighteen years and above to prepare for battle.

When that day arrived, four years later, I reported for compulsory military service with less enthusiasm than I had felt as a boy. By now, I had shouted hoorays to older friends as they marched away to service and never returned. Many of those who finally found their way home bore grievous scars and amputations. With heads bowed and tears in their eyes, they told of command errors that cost the lives of many men. They told of brutal foes who chopped off Athenian heads and hands as trophies to hang at crossroads and city gates.

Many of us who marched from home into the unknown wondered where our commanders would send us. In the navy, our ship might be rammed, sunk, and left to spiral down into the black depths as we drowned or fell prey to swarms of sharks. In the army, we might be stabbed, hacked, trampled, and left alone in agony to die. It was little consolation, but I preferred to meet my demise with the firm earth beneath my feet and the hope of a proper burial.

My father had fallen while fighting in the ranks as a hoplite. In appreciation, the polis granted me a helmet, breastplate, and greaves, and trained me to be a hoplite like him, as was the custom. Hellenes believed that fighting in phalanx as an armored hoplite was preferable to serving as an archer in the light infantry. Too often, archers fell prey to the enemy's thundering cavalry. In this way, I was fortunate.

When my comrades and I first donned our gleaming armor, we stood so straight and proud that we hardly noticed the weight. We glanced down the ranks in formation with weapons bristling and faces fierce and could not imagine that any force on earth could defeat us.

Our phalanx, along with other phalanxes in front and behind, often clanked past admiring throngs of Athenians. The high-crested helmets had nose and cheek guards that partly concealed our faces. On sunny days, the armor glinted from head to foot, highlighting breastplates, back-plates, greaves, and boots.

In our left hands we held bronze shields cast with the head of Gorgo — intended to frighten the enemy and fend off evil. In our right hands we hefted eight-foot ashen spears tipped with bronze in front and back. Double-edged swords hung from our shoulders.

Our chests swelled proudly amid shouts and spirited cheers. But once we had marched away from the crowds, we cursed the stifling heat of our armor in summer and the stinging cold in winter. During marches and maneuvers, we groaned beneath the wearisome weight of seventy pounds.

As a brotherhood, we swore a solemn oath to stand steadfast and never break rank and flee. But for the next two years we faced no foe to force an advance or retreat. Instead, we trained as hoplites day after day, in heat and cold, marching in mountains through blowing dust, and slippery mud and snow. At times, we spied Spartan soldiers in the distance, but our commander held us back due to our lack of training. He knew how to pick his battles by assessing enemy strength and position.

We trained hard in fierce competition, jabbing with the spear and swinging the sword. But our foremost effort was to drill day and night as a phalanx. Our bodies and minds toughened to the task of meeting the enemy as a solid, immovable mass. We had to remain unflinching even in the face of superior forces. We learned to march as a unit in every commanded direction, without hesitation, while preventing gaps in formation.

In our left hands we carried the heavy shields that protected ourselves and the man to our left. This often caused each man to drift to the right as they sought protection behind their neighbor's shield. When many men made the same mistake, the entire phalanx also drifted right.

We trained without ceasing on every terrain to prevent the rightward drift and maintain the proper space between comrades on either side. When we stood in the front ranks of the phalanx, we hefted our spears at shoulder height in our right hands, pointed forward at the foe. In the reserve ranks to the back, we pointed spears upward at attention.

One of the surprising discomforts of army life came from keeping our feet confined in stiff boots all day and night. For a backcountry boy, bare feet meant freedom. In my youth, I had climbed, run, jumped, and swam without constraint, and resorted to sandals only when my feet screamed for relief from the sharpest rocks and thorns.

Now, in the army, my feet yearned to break free from their leather wardens. But I had to admit that they served their purpose on rugged routes and frozen marches, and they guarded against trampling boots in the crowded ranks of the phalanx. After my service, however, I never again wore anything more than sandals, except in ice and snow.

Foot soldiers served as the backbone of our 32,000-man army. Most of us trained to fight on the battlefield, but the infirm and older soldiers remained stationed at fortifications.

One in twenty men rode with the cavalry, and another one in twenty supported the infantry as lightly clad archers, slingers, and javelin throwers. Although we jeered at the light infantry, they often tipped the battle in our favor with constant barrages of missiles that pummeled and scattered the enemy ranks. In truth, we would not have survived without them.

When we trained in maneuvers, the cavalry defended our flanks. They galloped together in stately procession, sitting tall on spirited horses festooned with fine harness and saddles. They wore long hair that flowed behind them like Spartans. But they also wore a superior sneer that made these sons of wealthy Athenians the butt of many jokes among the hoplites.

When we completed our training in phalanx, the commanders bestowed great honors on us with spears and shields of our own. But these remained unstained for another year as we patrolled the wilds of Attica away from Spartan strongholds. Most commanders preferred to reserve combat for those with two or more years of training, while keeping the remainder in watchful waiting, ready for immediate action.

Meanwhile, we maintained a sharp routine of drilling and marching through frozen passes in snowcapped mountains; through dense forests in humid valleys; and through stagnate marshes and swollen streams. The wilderness was our home. But at times, we marched past rustic farms and home-steads where wary faces peered out at us, first in fear, then relief as they smiled and waved at the passing phalanxes. We were their primary protection from marauding foes.

Wrestlers. Marble relief, c. 510 BC. National Archeological Museum, Athens. Photo by author.

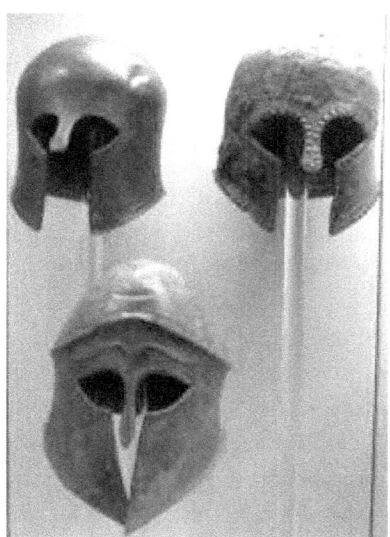

Bronze helmets, 7th to 5th centuries BC. Archeological Museum, Olympia, Greece. Photo by author.

# Chapter 11. A RAID ON THE ASIAN SHORE

AT AGE TWENTY I COMPLETED TRAINING and entered full military service. Morale was low. The Spartans still occupied much of Attica and their fleet had recently inflicted an embarrassing defeat on the Athenian navy at Aegospotami on the Hellespont. Most of the army remained on high alert at defensive locations around Attica. But commanders pulled three phalanxes aside for an incursion along the Asian coast.

Ships from Phoenicia, Cyprus, Lycia, and Pamphylia continued to take advantage of Athenian weakness by raiding coastal settlements. Ten years had passed since that bitter day when wolfish pirates murdered Pappos and Ama and killed or enslaved Bronte. Since then, many more families had suffered the same fate until our combined cries finally prodded Athenian politicians to action.

Despite my reservations about naval service, I found myself clambering aboard a transport ship at the port of Piraeus in full battle gear. As we launched into the open waters of the Aegean Sea, the choppy waves shook and rattled our bones. We lined up at the railing, vomiting into the churning seafoam below. Several older veterans leaned back with arms folded and chuckled at our misfortune from across the deck. But one among them at last took pity and ambled over to offer encouragement.

The man's long experience at sea soon became evident. In a kind and steady voice, he assured us that favorable signs had promised a safe voyage despite the high waves and heavy waters. He explained that this was a good time of year to cross the sea.

After all, it was summer. Hesiod had said that *sailing is in good season for mortals for fifty days after the solstice, when the summer goes to its end…. You will not wreck your boat then nor will the sea drown your men.*[86]

Athenian fleet commanders usually heeded Hesiod's warning against sailing later in the year. The Boeotian philosopher had advised that in the autumn months, *when the Pleiades, fleeing Orion's mighty strength, fall into the murky sea, at that time blasts of all sorts of winds rage; do not keep your boat any longer in the wine-dark sea.*[87]

Orion's constellation always follows close behind the Pleiades' starry cluster, and his disappearance over the western horizon serves as a second warning to avoid autumn storms. During the cold months that follow, one must remain increasingly wary, because *a swift blast of wind from on high unexpectedly strikes a ship's mast and rips it from its stays, wedges and all,* leaving a crew hopelessly adrift at the whims of the merciless sea.[88]

The veteran continued his sage advice, warning us that at all times of the year, before lying down at night, a wise sailor *shortens sail for fear of the morning sea.*[89] None can know for sure what might transpire in the night and bring devastation by morning. Homer quoted Odysseus' recollection of one terrifying night far from home: *When it was the third watch of the night, and the stars had turned their course, Zeus, the cloud-gatherer, roused against us a fierce wind with a wondrous tempest, and hid with clouds the land and sea alike, and night rushed down from heaven.*[90] Every man except Odysseus perished in that storm.

The constellation of Goat Horn and the two stars called the Donkeys that ride on the back of the Crab offer further warnings against off-season sailing. Experienced seamen know that when the sun appears in Goat Horn following the winter solstice, *then is the frost from heaven hard on the benumbed sailor.... The sea ever grows dark beneath the keels, and like to diving seagulls, we often sit, spying out the deep from our ship, with faces turned to the shore* as we anxiously search for a safe harbor.[91]

The old soldier further assured us that, in addition to the seasonal markers, the weather signs favored our voyage. If the two Donkeys or their manger had darkened or disappeared behind clouds in the night sky, then rain or storm would be on its way. If clouds had hidden one of the Donkeys, then we could expect the wind to blow from the direction of the clear star toward the obscured.[92] But this was not the case, as we could see for ourselves by simply gazing into the night sky. The stars promised fair weather ahead.

A soft, rosy dawn also signaled seasons of calm. Had the morning sky shone fiery red; had the cranes and seabirds circled above the sea and fled; then we would have secured the deck for fear of a raging tempest. From childhood, I had learned to follow different signs on land: the excited chatter of sparrows at first light; the swarms of bees and wasps during the day; the wandering toads and salamanders; the singing frogs; the sputter and spark of an oil lamp that is difficult to light. These warned of approaching rain or storm.[93]

The old soldier told us more. When sailing southern waters near the Egyptian shore, we should always watch the constellation called the Incense Altar. *Ships in trouble pain her heart,* so she sends warnings of imminent storms at sea. If she appears bright but banked with clouds, beware of the coming tempest.

The veteran spoke of skeptical sailors who disregarded the Incense Altar's warnings. For those who *heed her favoring signs and quickly lighten their craft and set all in order, on a sudden lo, their task is easier, but if from on high a dread gust of wind smite their ship, all unforeseen, and throw in turmoil all the sails, sometimes they make their voyage all beneath the waves.*[94] One can also watch the crescent moon, the full moon, and the sun as they portend wind, rain, or storm with increasingly dark hues or halos.

Those of us who had never ventured upon the trackless sea out of sight of land came to appreciate the man's sociable nature and knowledge of seafaring lore. During the voyage, one of the young men panicked at the sight of a shooting star off the starboard bow. Our old friend stood back, leaning against the railing while thoughtfully waiting until the commotion had settled. Then he stepped among us and whispered assurance that all was well.

He explained that the gods often send shooting stars with trails of sparks as signs for seamen and soldiers. These bring good as well as evil tidings.[95] After all, Hera had guided the Argonauts through a safe passage at sea by the path of a shooting star.[96] He counseled us not to worry about fleeting celestial events, as the superstitious Persians do. Instead, we should follow the fixed signs that the gods placed in the sky and interpret them according to well-established lore.

With shining stars above, we approached the hostile Asian shore under cover of darkness. Word passed through the ranks that our target was a seaport harbor on the coast of Pamphylia where a fleet of raiders often traded plunder and slaves. My heart began to beat rapidly as questions crowded my mind.

What if we fought the same pirates who had brutally murdered my family? What if this proved to be the very port where Bronte, if living, had been dragged in chains and sold into slavery? What if he labored through life in this harbor town, or perhaps on the docks, or toiled in a neighboring field? How I longed to take my revenge on those evil men and rescue my brother! Though the chances seemed small, my hope rose to new heights and my spirit soared like never before since that spring day ten years ago.

The commander's booming voice suddenly disrupted my thoughts. As he announced our imminent arrival, we buckled on armor and grabbed our weapons with hands that shook with nervous excitement. A bundle of thyme was thrown on the coals in a large metal brazier on the deck.

Its soothing smoke spread through the ranks and toward the stern with a pungent smell. Most of the men now laid shields and spears at their feet. Using both hands, they bathed in the smoke and inhaled the incense that is known to impart courage.

Our commander now began to prepare our minds for battle by repeating Jason's words to the Argonauts: *And now in our hands we hold our children, our dear homeland, and our aged parents; and on our venture depends whether Hellas wins dejection or else great fame.*[97] In response to our enthusiastic shouts, the commander roared a reminder of the many Hellene warriors of the past, like Achilles, Ajax, Diomedes and Odysseus, who had also stormed the Asian shore.

These heroes shone bright like the star Sirius — *keenest of all blazes with a searing flame* — as they ran across the moonlit plain toward their Trojan foes.[98] Likewise, Polydeuces, the Argonaut, became animated by the approach of battle, appearing *bright-eyed* and much *like a heavenly star, whose twinkling is most beautiful when it shines through the evening darkness.*[99]

Before dawn, we made landfall on a beach twenty stades from the seaport and formed ranks for the march. Our rapid advance followed a hilly and winding road, and we scattered flocks of sheep and goats as they ran for pasture in the morning mist. Some of our men captured shepherds to keep them from shouting alarms, then bound them with ropes and rejoined us.

The first light of morning broke over the harbor town as we clattered into view. Lazy smoke rose from rooftops, and several merchant vessels sat silently moored along the shore. I had planned to scan for the hated red sails described to me long ago, but the ships rested unrigged near the docks. As we paused for an instant, I pondered the peaceful scene and imagined how quickly it would turn to mayhem.

We now lurched forward at a quickening pace until the steady thud of our feet matched the deafening heartbeat pulsing inside our helmets. Dogs began to bark, doors flew open, and frantic folks of every age raced for the woods. As a small line of light-armed soldiers quickly formed to oppose us, we broke the silence with a deafening roar and invoked the aid of Apollo with a reverential yell of *ie ie!*[100] Their defenses immediately melted, and we redirected our march toward the ships.

Gathering embers from hearths in surrounding houses, we made a bonfire on the beach and began to fire the vessels. To our surprise, Pamphylian sailors had remained at their posts overnight, sleeping aboard. Now the ships burst to life and the enemy rained missiles down upon us from their decks. As we rushed aboard, they engaged in close combat. But they were no match for our superior weapons, armor, and disciplined use of sword and spear, and those who survived were forced to flee. We burned every ship to the waterline.

Our commander now ordered several public buildings torched before we made our hasty retreat. He was experienced enough to know that victory can quickly turn to defeat when an army tarries and allows the enemy to form ranks and launch a counterattack. We marched swiftly back the way we had come, boarded our ship, weighed anchor, and set sail toward the west.

My heart was broken. I had desperately longed to search the town, interrogate the people, and make every effort to discover whether Bronte had passed this way. Later, upon quiet reflection, I saw my folly. Ten years of feeble hope had fanned a spark into a flame, but it suddenly sputtered out forever. At last I had to accept the cruel fact that I would never see Bronte again.

After three more forays along the coast of Lycia, our ship sailed westward under a steady breeze. The journey home was long and lonely. I fell into melancholy while my comrades wondered why I kept to myself. Disembarking at Piraeus, we marched to Athens amid half-hearted cheers. Through many years of sporadic warfare, the people had watched countless hoplites come and go, and became numb to victories and defeats that failed to bring a final peace.

Upon receiving furlough, I returned once more to my dear old home near Oropus. Portions of the scorched earthen walls still stood, as did the stone markers on the overgrown graves. I stayed the afternoon, sitting on the ground near Pappos and Ama, then wandered up the rocky path to the moss-covered altar overlooking the sea.

After running my hands over the weathered stone, I pulled from my knapsack a child-sized wreath—the one that Pappos had fashioned for Bronte and me in this very place. I gently laid it on the altar, ran my fingers over the braided twigs once more, and set a slender rock on top to hold it safe.

At last, I looked toward the white-capped sea, turned my back on the sacred site, and walked away with tears in my eyes. I could no longer bear the bitter thoughts and had lost all hope of avenging my family. My only recourse was to start a new life and hope that time might soften some of the burning rage and helpless feelings inside.

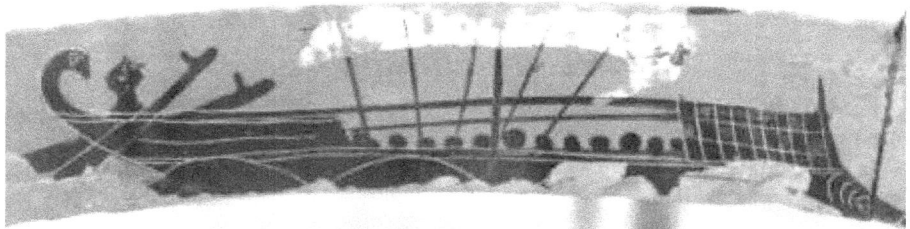

Hellenic ship with helmsman observing the sky. Vase painting from Attica, 5th century BC. Archeological Museum, Magna Phoenicia, Palermo, Italy. Photo by author.

Hoplite warriors in mortal combat, armed with bronze helmets, breastplates, greaves, shields, swords, and spears. Vase painting from Athens, 520-510 BC. Getty Museum, Malibu, California. Photo by author.

# Chapter 12.  A NEW BEGINNING

AFTER FIVE MORE YEARS AND MANY FORAYS in the military, I mustered out, moved to Athens, and married a childhood friend. Tempe had grown up on a farmstead near ours. It was her and her older brother who had wandered upon me that dreadful day so long ago when I sat beside Pappos' body near our smoldering home. She had lost her parents in the same brutal raid and was sent to Athens to live with an uncle and aunt. Now she was eighteen and I was seven years older.

This was a late marriage for most girls of Attica, who typically wed at sixteen, and sometimes as young as twelve or thirteen. Hesiod had suggested that a man wait until the age of thirty to marry. Then he should marry a girl of sixteen, preferably one that he hardly knew.

But I had waited long enough. Before I marched off to join the army, Tempe and her family had often returned to visit their kin near the old homeplace. Despite the difference in age, I had come to know her well.

Her uncle, who was born in Athens, thought it strange that I talked directly to Tempe about marriage instead of simply negotiating a dowry with him. But country people in Attica enjoy looser social norms between male and female. We spend more time with each other and are comfortable discussing matters together, even before marriage. Her uncle apologized because Tempe brought little dowry, but her dreamy eyes and gentle soul provided treasure enough for me.

With a formal agreement between guardian and groom, Tempe and I became betrothed. The wedding followed a few days later and simply served to move the bride from her uncle's home to mine. In traditional manner, we married during the first full moon after the winter solstice. This is the time of year that is sacred to Hera, the goddess of marriage.

Evening festivities began with a feast at Tempe's uncle's house, which was festooned with branches of olive and laurel. Tempe captured my gaze in a full-length chiton that she had made for the occasion, and a veil and wreath with *lovely garlands around* her locks.[101] She appeared as pretty to me in homemade cloth as she would have in the finest Corinthian linen. Her plaited and flowered tresses reached her waist.

After we tasted the sesame seed and honey cake that was meant to promote fertility, Tempe's grandfather spoke a few words and quoted Homer: *For nothing is greater or better than this, than when a man and a woman keep house together sharing one heart and mind—a great grief to their foes and a joy to their friends.*[102]

He now offered a solemn sacrifice as Tempe gave up her childhood treasures—her doll, ball, and little drum. With silent tears, she parted with these tokens of her youth and devoted her toys to Artemis—the protector of maidens. To Hera she offered a lock of hair.

Tempe's younger friends tended to her as they pressed close in support and shed soft tears together. But soon they dried their eyes and giggled and whispered among themselves. After receiving some simple gifts, Tempe and I withdrew from the house and traveled by donkey cart, accompanied by a small crowd of well-wishers carrying torches. Along the way, they lifted their voices in wedding songs and piped their flutes. Older people spoke of the days when a mock abduction marked the departure of bride and groom, a custom still practiced in Sparta.

Upon arriving at our own little home, the guests showered us with nuts and figs. Then they motioned us in, closed the door, and stood outside singing loud and boisterous songs until neighbors demanded they leave. Fifty years have come and gone, but I remember that evening like last night's dream. I had become a captive of love—*that bittersweet, irresistible creature.*[103]

Tempe remained my closest friend and companion. Her cheerful light chased darkness from my heart and brought us together as one. My home was wherever she happened to be, in country or city, indoors or out. Without her I felt alone and far from home. Some feel otherwise about their wives or husbands. Like Hesiod said: *A man acquires nothing better than a good wife, but nothing more chilling than a bad one... who singes her husband without a torch.*[104]

After a bustling year in Athens, we returned to the peaceful countryside of Attica. Neither of us could bear the emotional burden of returning to our old homeplaces, so we searched and found an abandoned hut fifty-one stades southeast along the coast. Together, we repaired our rustic home and plowed the neglected grainfield. We settled with ease into the lives of farmers—the livelihood we had always known. Tempe understood the demands of a self-sufficient farm and gladly accepted her lot in life along with the satisfaction and freedom it offered.

The virtue of hard work had been embedded within us from birth. We remembered the words of Hesiod, who charged his fellow farmers and shepherds to be diligent at labor and charitable toward others, rather than being an idle person with no purpose in life, forever seeking handouts. While an honest worker's reward is a full larder, a fine reputation, and a strong sense of purpose; the idle person, who only works hard at avoiding work, *is always wrestling with calamities.*[105]

In the fall, I plowed a field measuring one-half stade by one. We sowed half the field with wheat and barley, leaving the other half to rest in fallow. We planted a small vineyard and pruned a few tangled olive trees standing forlornly apart. This, we hoped, would provide enough for a family, leaving a bit for barter. Our flock began as a billy and three nannies, to which we added a ram and ewes as soon as we could afford them.

Like other farmers, I carefully followed the celestial signs. *As the seasons rolled on, and the months waned, and the many days were brought in their course,* we counted on the stars to faithfully measure the passage of time.[106] Wise men of old told that the gods gave us the sun by which to awaken and work, and the stars and constellations to tell us when to plant and harvest.[107] The *twelve signs of the Zodiac mark the great year—the season to plough and sow the fallow field and the season to plant the tree.*[108] They also announce the rainy season when the sun passes through the constellations of Goat Horn, Water Bearer, and the Fishes.[109]

Each morning before light, when I walked to the spring for water, I watched the eastern horizon for a star or constellation that might make its heliacal rising that day. Again, at dusk, I scanned the eastern and western horizons for stars that marked the seasons. The rhythm of our lives and the success of the farm depended upon these signposts.

The bright star named Bear Guard in the constellation Bootes serves as one of these markers. Three hundred years ago, Hesiod proclaimed the star's role as a harbinger of early spring. He taught us that *sixty wintry days after the [winter] solstice, the star Arcturus [Bear Guard] is first seen rising, shining brightly just at dusk, leaving behind the holy stream of Oceanus. After this... the swallow rises into the light for human beings.*[110] This is the season to pull oneself away from the warmth of the hearth and march to the fields with freshly sharpened pruning hooks to trim the grapevines.[111]

A month later, at the time of the vernal equinox, spring bursts free from winter with unfettered vitality. In this season, poor Persephone escapes from her dreadful home in Hades for a six month stay with her mother—the earth goddess Demeter. With Demeter's grief for her missing daughter assuaged, winter turns to joyful spring and the earth abounds in flowering plants and the songs of birds. Now is the time for farmers to hoe the fields, chop the weeds, thin the crowded stalks of grain, and cover roots exposed by wind and rain.[112]

Two months later, the heliacal rising of the Pleiades announces the time to sharpen sickles and hasten to harvest the grain.[113] Threshing and winnowing follow close on the heels of the harvest at the rising of the constellation Orion. For this, we borrowed a yoked pair of oxen or donkeys and tethered them to a post in the center of our hard-packed threshing floor. Once we unbundled heaps of harvested stalks on the ground before them, we goaded the pair forward in circles to trample the stalks and separate chaff from grain.

As they lumbered along, we searched for untouched stalks and threw them under the animals' heavy hooves.[114] The threshing site stood on a knoll exposed to the wind, which helped us winnow the grain. Again and again, we tossed the pulverized husks high overhead and watched the breeze blow the chaff away from the heavier grain. Then we gathered the grain into baskets and bundled the stalks for fodder.[115]

Each year, we rushed from dawn to dusk to complete these heavy chores before Sirius, the Dog Star, rose in the east to announce the sweltering Dog Days of summer. If we failed to finish our tasks by then, the sun's brutal heat would beat down upon us, and itchy chaff would stick to our sweaty skin while we worked. [116]

The Dog Star is the brightest star in the sky. Some even say its intense rays make the earth hotter for the fifty days following its first appearance each year. People of the past prayed to Zeus for relief from the oppressive heat, until at last he sent the annual Etesian winds rushing down from the north as a respite for forty days.

Despite the cooling breezes, the Dog Days often blaze too hot for hard labor.[117] Every farmer agrees with Hesiod, who said: When the cicada *pours forth its voice in the most dread heat*, it is best to set tools aside and rest in the shade, drinking wine mixed with water from a cold spring, and nibbling bread, cheese, and meat.[118]

As the Dog Days drift away, the stars called Bear Guard and Herald of the Vintage shine at dawn on the eastern horizon to announce the time to glean the vine.[119] Following Hesiod's directions, we gathered at the vineyard to *pluck off all the grapes and take them home, set them out in the sun for ten days and ten nights, then cover them up in the shade for five, and on the sixth draw out the gift of much-cheering Dionysus [wine] into storage-vessels.*[120]

Wealthy owners of large vineyards pay wage workers to stomp their grapes in a vat, urged on by the lively rhythm of flutes. But we simply sang and laughed together while pressing our smaller yield by hand. With the wine fermented and safely stored, we ceremoniously sampled the vintage. I have never partaken of the famous wines from Lesbos or Rhodes but cannot imagine them pleasing the palate more than our own humble vintage.

By this time, the olive trees beckoned to us as autumn breezes shook their leaves and showered their fruit upon the ground. The time for harvest varied across Hellas depending on elevation and preferred degree of ripeness.

With baskets in hand, we picked up the fruit, plucked it from lower branches, knocked down the upper olives with sticks, and climbed the trunk or a wooden ladder to reach the remainder. We laughed aloud as we tried to catch them tumbling down. Some we stored for eating. The rest we pressed into golden oil and poured it into jars for cooking and lighting lamps.

The time for plowing now drew near. Each year, as I roamed the woods, I searched for a holm oak trunk or bough with suitable size and strength to serve as a plow. It needed to have a hand-width trunk for a running board and an angled branch for a handle. On finding one, I noted the location and returned in winter to chop it down. I seasoned the wood for at least a year, then shaped it with an axe. At last, I attached the sharpened plowshare of iron.

At the end of the olive harvest, I watched the western horizon each morning to catch sight of the setting of the Pleiades, followed fast by the Hyades and Orion.[121] When the time came, I attached the plow to one end of a laurel pole. To the other end, I tied the yoke.[122]

I borrowed a pair of oxen, though if none were available, I resorted to donkeys. Oxen are most highly prized for pulling plows, threshing grain, and leaving a rich layer of manure behind.[123] Hesiod observed that a pair of nine-year-old oxen and a forty-year-old man make the best team for plowing, because they are mature enough to keep to their chores and not too old for hard labor.[124]

At first light, Tempe and I fed and yoked the beasts, then pulled them into position. Tempe prodded them forward as I pushed the stubborn plow and struggled through the day to finish the field. At last, we sat and smiled at the smell of fresh-turned earth and held each other close as darkness descended.

At dawn, I returned to the field and walked the furrows, reshaping them and breaking clods with a mattock or hoe. If autumn showers had blessed the soil with moisture enough for planting, Tempe followed close behind me and sowed the seeds while rhythmically covering them with her dainty feet.[125] But if the soil felt dry, we waited for rain before planting, and prayed it arrived before winter.

102

Hesiod stressed the need to plow and sow as early in the season as possible to beat the wintry blasts. If you wait too long and *plow the divine earth first at the winter solstice, you will harvest sitting down, covered in dust, grasping only a little with your hand*.[126] He also urged an early start to every day, saying: You are better off *getting up at sunrise, so that your means of life will be sufficient. For… dawn gives you a head start on the road, gives you a head start on your work too*. An early start also allows a person to avoid the wind and rain of evening, and the scorching heat in summer.[127]

Every year, I pushed hard to complete the plowing and planting, the firewood stacking, and other outdoor chores before bitter cold descended. Winter blasts of snow bend low the pine and fir trees of the forest. And man and beast bend equally low, as though turning old while trudging through the snow.

Even woolly sheep seem to fear the frigid winds. To defend against the worst weather, I donned a wool himation that reached my feet and pulled on boots of oxen leather padded with wool. A hooded coat of goat or sheepskin stitched with heavy sinew helped me repel the ice and snow.[128]

Tempe fashioned these and all our clothing with nimble and talented fingers. She sheared the sheep, washed the wool, fluffed it full, and rolled it on her leg into serpentine strips. She spun the strips on a handheld spindle and wove the thread on a wooden loom that rested on the porch.

She spent many fair-weather days there, sitting on a reed mat on the ground and singing to pass the time as she spun and wove. The himations she made compared quite well with the high-priced cloaks that Athenians buy in Megara. I considered her homespun wool a symbol of freedom from debt and dependence.

Tempe fashioned her own chiton from a square woolen cloth with one-fourth folded down from the top. She wrapped it around her left side and pinned it at the shoulders, then cinched her waist with a sash, and drew some cloth over the sash to form a pocket. In winter, she added a wool himation of her own making and slipped her feet into little sandals. She wore no hat, but only a shady hood shaped from the folds of her chiton.

Tempe showed no interest in fancy clothing and held that her hood provided more protection than the parasols coveted by wealthy women. We had both grown up with rustic values that advised: *Do not let your mind at all put to shame your outward appearance*.[129] Like most backcountry women, she never painted her face. But she boiled petals to make perfume and plaited her hair in lovely braids, often festooned with flowers.

While spinning and weaving, she remained alert to our infant son and followed him wherever he wandered. She milked the goats and made the cheese. She ground the grain with a pestle and mortar of stone, then shaped the flour into flatbread and fried it on a griddle.

To supplement the flatbread, she gathered sweet peas, chickpeas, lentils, cabbages, onions, and garlic from her garden. For flavoring food, she picked sesame, mint, and thyme from a smaller plot. She also sprinkled thyme in her bath and burned it as soothing incense. Our only other seasoning was salt, which *harmonizes so well in combinations pleasing to the palate.*[130]

For the main evening meal, Tempe usually served sweet peas, chickpeas, or lentils cooked with olive oil, salt, and herbs. These, she poured into bowls alongside pieces of flatbread for scooping. As an added treat, we often ate olives, onions, garlic, fruits, or berries according to season.

When my arrows flew straight and true, she roasted venison, hare, duck, thrush, or partridge from the hunt. Or we might eat fish or cheese. For special events, she dazzled us with desserts of figs, nuts, or cakes of grain and honey. On frozen nights, we drank a steaming draft of barley porridge and thyme before burrowing deep in bed.

Some folks called us poor, but we knew true contentment. After the sorrows and deprivations of our youth, we now found comfort, joy, and loving devotion. We delighted in self-sufficiency and freedom. We beamed within our humble means and refused to suffer debt. Nor did we want for more than the earth provided in fields and forests.

During the year, we traveled to local festivals at the temple of Rhamnous and the sacred spring of Amphiaraus.[131] While there, we sometimes bartered our surplus perishable goods—grain, oil, vegetables, fruits, olives, or figs—in return for salt or iron. Rhamnous, a bustling, fortified port, was only twenty-nine stades southeast, and gave us access to all the goods of Athens and the entire Aegean world. But we felt little need for them.

Olive harvest. Vase painting, c. 520 BC. British
Museum, London.

Olive press, 2nd century BC. Capernaum,
Israel. Photo by author.

# Chapter 13.  WARRING WITH WOLVES AND SPARTANS

OUR LIFE OF CONTENTMENT WAS WHISKED AWAY when the army called me back to war. Athenian soldiers serve in active duty for only two years, or longer if they choose, but remain in reserve to the age of fifty. As a young man, I had marched in raids on Asian shores and repulsed Spartan incursions into Attica, but I had never been part of the main action. At Aegospotami on the Hellespont, the Spartan navy had defeated the Athenian flotilla and swept southward to blockade Athens, forcing her to surrender her fleet and fortifications.

Sparta then compelled Athens to humbly submit to the rule of the Thirty Tyrants, who promptly murdered hundreds of Athenians regarded as political threats. The following year, Athens reacted in rage by deposing the Thirty Tyrants and restoring democratic rule. Then an alliance of furious Athenians, Corinthians, Thebans, and Argives fought back against the heavy-handed Spartan foe.

Spartans clung to an archaic culture far removed from most Hellenic poleis. They descended from barbaric Dorians who had conquered and enslaved the native helots of the Peloponnesus. But the helots vastly outnumbered them, so Sparta responded by maintaining a militant kingdom and bullying the helots of the region into submission.

Even Spartan maidens participated in the harsh regime. As girls, they raced, wrestled, threw the discus and javelin, and competed like boys in little or no clothing. As women, they remained athletic and conditioned to bear strong and valiant children.

Spartan boys faced a far more rigorous life. From infancy, harsh discipline demanded that they obey every order without question, accept their meager rations, brave loneliness and darkness, and shed no tears. At age seven, they left their mothers to become the property of the polis and struggled through relentless military training until the age of twenty.

They developed endurance and martial skills and embarked alone on bitter ordeals that taught them the harshest lessons of survival. Even in youth, they learned to spill human blood without flinching. The commanders forced many into an initiation rite that required them to search by night and capture and kill their first helot. Beyond this brutal military life, they gained little education. They sang and played the flute, but only in martial tunes.

As young men, they marched barefoot across rugged terrain, with shorn heads and beaten bodies. Their commanders denied them baths and provided each man just one cloak to wear each year. Food remained meager, bland, and coarse. But upon completing their training, they formed the ranks of invading armies and gorged themselves on the spoils of war in Attica and other poleis.

At last, Athens marched against them to exact revenge, and I was in the hoplite ranks. We passed through regions fully despoiled by eighty-five years of fighting. Living off the land proved almost impossible and left us at the mercy of faulty supply lines that stretched a great distance from Athens.

At night, we drifted to sleep among rocks and brambles and awoke with empty stomachs. When fortune chose to favor us, we came upon ripening crops or hidden stashes of food and marched away with all we could carry. Our hunger made us almost as shameless as Spartans.

To restore morale, the commander proclaimed that the Delphic Oracle had uttered a prophecy favorable to our campaign. My cynical mind often wondered whether Pythia's pronouncements would save or destroy us. For further divine protection, the commander ordered several soldiers to carry a portable altar bearing a fire sparked from the eternal flame on the Acropolis. During pouring rain and high winds, we sometimes peeked to see if the flame still burned. I doubted that the fire helped our cause, but feared the loss of morale that would spread through the ranks like a fever if it ever flickered out.

As we tramped toward a hostile camp, our allies joined us one by one. In the Athenian army, each tribe maintained its own ranks and set its own pace to the shrill sound of flutes. At last, we topped a rise and spotted the enemy line waiting in tight formation on a neighboring hill.

With haste, our commanders formed a line of battle and ordered the phalanxes into position. Though outwardly composed and steady, we shook in our boots with nervous anticipation. For the first time, I felt grateful for the endless training that now allowed us to march in formation without having to pause and think. We remained fully focused on rushing the Spartan foe and mowing them down like barley.

In close alignment with comrades, shoulder to shoulder, I could hear every courageous shout and muffled fear. But the thought of fleeing refused to enter our minds. To flinch or veer from formation would open a gap that invited certain death. To run would bring slaughter from behind while the enemy cavalry slashed or trampled us into the ground. We had sworn an oath to never retreat. But that meant little now. Stark reality kept us standing our ground.

After a brief pause, the commander barked an order to forward march. A moment later, he shouted double-time and we rushed toward the enemy. The Spartans reacted in kind and quickly closed the distance. From the third rank, I stared beyond my comrades' bobbing heads at the advancing Spartans with their menacing crests and fearsome faces.

The command now came to lower spears, and mine fell forward in unison with the phalanx. Then, with a tremendous shock, we crashed headlong into a wall of spears and shields. Without delay, we recoiled, reformed, and thrust forward again.

Our training helped us remain unshaken as we fought mechanically, filling the gaps left by fallen friends and comrades, and marching over their wounded or lifeless bodies. We did not even stop to consider our own fate now that the battle raged. The anticipation had proved more unnerving than the action itself.

Without a thought, we hefted our swords, slashed and stabbed, withdrew in unison, then advanced and butchered again until the signal came to stand at attention. Only then did we notice our gaping wounds, our utter exhaustion, our missing comrades, and the outcome of the skirmish. We cheered aloud as the enemy slowly withdrew with heavy losses. But the commander, aware of Spartan tricks, forced us to maintain ranks and allow them to retreat.

For five more years, I served on active duty, fighting Spartan phalanxes, raiding their supply lines, and participating in minor victories and defeats. Finally, we marched under the command of Iphicrates, a native of Rhamnous, and crushed an entire battalion. The lull in fighting that followed allowed me to return home to Tempe.

But, as she attests, I emerged from the war as a different man. I now walked with a cocky swagger that came partly from long association with rugged companions, partly from pride in battlefield victory, and partly to hide the wretched reflections of war that plagued my mind.

One autumn day, I finished the plowing and planting, stored the tools for winter, gathered my weapons, and gave Tempe a tender farewell. With a bow, arrows, pelt, and knapsack slung on my back, I hefted a javelin and club in my hands and headed into the mountains to hunt for half a month. Tempe pleaded with me to take an able companion for safety. But I only scoffed. I had survived in the wild for much of my life, had vanquished Spartans face to face, and felt no fear of woodland beasts.

After several days on Mount Parnitha, I noticed common wolf tracks mingled with larger ones scattered along a muddy bank. I paid little heed, but thought it strange that, day after day, wherever I camped, the tracks appeared near a neighboring stream. The pack was probably following me in hopes of stealing game felled by my arrow. But the presence of a persistent pack put me on alert. I kept a wary watch and always had my weapons handy.

Early one morning, as I slipped silently through the forest, I spied a buck in a misty glade. With his head hung low, he grazed with abandon and remained unaware of my presence. Slowly, I lowered my javelin to the ground, wrapped a pelt around my left forearm, notched an arrow, and drew back the stoutly strung bow.

The arrow flew true, and soon I was dressing the deer. On completing the bloody work, I walked to the stream to wash my hands and face. As I returned toward the carcass, the pack appeared for the first time. Among them stood a strikingly large wolf with a dark coat, defiant eyes, and a light gray mane. A brief shudder spread through me as though I was nine years old again, fighting for my flock and my life.

But I was more angry than worried. I had hunted in foul weather for days, had dispatched the deer and dressed it. Now, I stood at my post with a piercing stare and loudly dared the marauders to snatch it away. After a brief standoff, I grabbed my javelin and advanced to force a retreat.

The pack snarled and slowly skulked away. But the large wolf stood his ground and glowered at me with the most unnerving eyes I had ever seen. Then he rushed for me with his teeth bared.

The javelin sliced his flank but failed to slow him down. Leaping through the air, the cunning beast threw his weight at my shoulder and knocked me to the ground. In an instant, he lunged for my throat, but my arm served as a shield. I shouted as his savage teeth ripped the flesh and scraped down to the bone, then held me in a deadly grip.

Face to face, I stared into his evil eyes, heard his guttural growl, and smelled his loathsome, carrion breath. Searing pain seized me, but I kept my presence of mind. Grabbing a rock with my other hand, I brought it crashing down on his head.

He backed away, dazed, then lunged at my leg and tore another gaping wound. A second swing of the rock cracked his jaw, and he jerked back with a startled yelp. As I gathered my wits and awaited his next charge, he paced nearby, snarling and searching for an opening. Then he sniffed and licked his wounds and backed toward the carcass while warily watching me.

He now began to tear into the deer, growling viciously and snapping at the pack as it ran to join him. I dragged myself slowly away, aware that if the wolves rushed down on me now, all would be lost. My javelin lay close to the carcass and my club, bow, and arrows sat useless at the stream.

At last I reached the muddy bank and lowered my torn limbs into a shallow pool. After gulping handfuls of water tainted with my own blood, I gritted my teeth and washed the bleeding wounds. I tore off pieces of clothing, wound them around the shredded flesh, and tied the cloth as tight as my ebbing strength allowed.

The pain advanced quickly now and the loss of blood caused me to swoon. I crawled to the coals of last night's fire, dug deep in the ashes, and gratefully cradled a glowing ember. With tinder and kindling still scattered nearby, I built a blaze and pulled myself close to dry my body and clothing.

My appetite was gone, but I nibbled some figs from the knapsack to keep my strength. I remained too weak to swing a club and lacked strength enough to pull a bow. But I propped upright on a log, pulled out my knife, and sharpened the tip of a straight and sturdy branch. Then I shoved it into the glowing coals to temper.

If the pack attacked, I could only thrust the makeshift spear with one good arm. I also kept my knife and arrows by my side, although I knew they offered little protection. Even so, I felt compelled to prepare for the worst as best I could. At last, I slumped in exhaustion and rested where I sat while awaiting the coming darkness.

At twilight, the pack appeared on the fringe of camp, but the large wolf was not with them. I stoked the fire to a roaring blaze and held my sharpened stick in hand. The wolves, with stomachs stuffed with venison, slowly withdrew and wandered away. As they vanished into the darkness, my head began to swim, and pain and nausea tightened their grip.

I rested my head on the log and gazed at the shimmering stars. The eternal sources of light peered down upon me, unimpressed by my frail and fleeting presence on earth and my utterly worthless pride. Thoughts of Pappos crept into my mind. For the first time in thirty years, since that bitter night when I lay beside his broken body, I heard his clear and consoling voice, calling me to listen to the lessons of the stars:

*Recalling the words of Pappos*

The gods had come to disdain mortals because of their failure to offer proper respect and devotion. Arrogance, above all, provoked the deities because it created strife among humans and made men believe that they ruled all beings, mortal and divine. One man, Orion, loomed large and mighty among men, but stumbled and fell into the same folly of conceit.

In stature he stood like a giant, and his prowess as a hunter impressed all who saw him. Odysseus himself called Orion *the tallest, and far the most handsome* of men. *In his hands he held a club all of bronze* and the pelt of an animal, the trademark of a hunter.[132]

Orion came of age in the way of the warriors and hunters of Hellas. From childhood, they carry a simple array of weapons into the chase — a club, a pelt, and a knife. Although very young, they sharpen their senses by wandering alone, far and wide, through fields and forests. They learn to detect the slightest movements among the blades of grass and leaves of trees. They listen for subtle sounds that betray the presence of prey.

As they grow strong and hardy, these hunters of Hellas become brave and bold. Some swagger as if they are brandishing weapons in battle. Their glowing confidence and sharpened skills of observation, combined with their self-discipline and tireless stamina, pave the way for success in every endeavor.[133]

Hunters, young and old, often wander the winding woodland trails with one or more canine companions. The respect between dog and man is mutual, and their firm friendship is often portrayed in hunting scenes painted on pottery. Both play an important part in the chase and share in the feast that follows. Hunters highly value their dogs, especially those of fine form and solid training. They depend on them, not just for stalking hares, the favored game, but for protection from large and lethal predators, like wolves, boars, bears, and lions.

Like many Hellenes, Orion enjoyed hunting the hares that appear in abundance across the mainland and islands. He exulted in the quick and lively chase that caused his heart to pound. He savored the succulent meat and valued the plush pelts that are sewn together for warm cloaks and bedding.

In the way of the woodsmen, Orion used an animal pelt to ensnare the hare while his club came hurtling down. In his belt dangled a dagger for skinning and dressing the game. After he roasted the meat on a spit, he used the knife to slice a portion to place on the burning coals as an offering to the gods. Only then did he stuff his ravenous mouth and toss a piece of meat to the hungry hound.

Rarely did Orion miss a chance to follow his dog in pursuit of prey. The canine would wander warily ahead, quick of eye and keen of scent, with paws toughened by years of roaming rugged terrain. He was not solid in color but spotted—a sure sign of good breeding. His hind legs stood long and strong with plenty of spring for leaping and perfectly formed for the sprint.[134]

On the trail, the hound trusted his sharpened sense of smell and followed his nose while sniffing the earth for any sign of prey. For this, Orion favored a crisp morning in spring or fall. In winter, the frozen ground conceals the scent of prey. In summer, heat disperses the smell from the sunbaked clay. Orion also never waited until after dawn to release his dog, because the scent of the previous night grows faint and the rising wind of day whisks it away.

As they wandered the woods together with the dog silently searching for a scent, Orion whispered a prayer for success and pledged the first portions of meat for Apollo and Artemis, the twin gods of the hunt. Suddenly the dog trembled and shook in his tracks upon detecting a tempting smell.

The hare, somewhere nearby, remained silent and still as a statue. To hide himself in a half-dug hollow or clump of grass, his head and body lay prostrate with legs tucked underneath. His long ears lay flat on his back.

With a frenzied yelp, the dog shot along the line of scent, swerving left and right like an unfletched arrow. He followed close on the course while *barking freely* and running *fast and brilliant in the chase*. At the last possible moment, the hare bolted and fled with ears held high. Twisting and turning, teasing his tracker, he darted down secret shortcuts. He ran the unsuspecting dog through brambles and briars, then up, always up, the steep and slippery slopes.

The cunning hare knew from instinct and experience to *cross brooks and double back, and slip into gullies or holes*. He usually outsmarted the hound. But the dog and Orion never seemed to mind. Tomorrow's dawn would bring another delightful chase.[135]

Nothing in heaven or earth could distract Orion from his love of the hunt until the day he laid eyes on the Pleiades. The darling girls, the seven daughters of Atlas and Pleione, had attracted many men, but none had been more deeply smitten than he. Like a woodsman after a wary deer, he pursued them with an obsession. But it was all in vain.

Before now, no maiden had escaped his affections. Some say even Artemis, the champion of chastity, almost fell for his manly charms. But the apprehensive Pleiades resisted his every impassioned ploy.

At last, the beleaguered sisters begged Zeus for protection. The god of sky and storm obliged and changed them into a peaceful covey of softly cooing doves. Later, he granted them immortality among the stars, where they rest forever, nestled together in each other's lovely company.[136]

Orion reeled at the rebuff. Deeply wounded, he wandered back to the woods to return to his first love—the hunt. Now his pursuit of game became excessive as he tried to bury his feelings for the Pleiades behind a show of bravado.

Orion boasted loudly that he could vanquish any beast, large or small. Gaea, who is Mother Earth, had finally heard enough. She abhorred his blasphemous bellows against nature and shuddered in fear that he might come near to destroying all the fauna she dearly loved.

So, Gaea, who once sent the monstrous Typhon against the gods, summoned a Scorpion, colossal and cruel, to slay Orion. Like Aesop's cocky rooster, Orion had crowed too loudly and lured a predator down upon himself.[137] The mighty hunter now became the prey.

While Orion walked in the woods one day, the Scorpion, born of the earth, burst to the surface. On spying Orion, he bore down hard and fast, scurrying swiftly forward on eight arachnid legs with pinchers snapping. Orion raised his thunderous club and fended off the claws with lightning strokes. But soon the Scorpion brought his stinger into play.

The stinger stretched longer than Orion's club and dripped with poison more potent than the venom from a hundred vipers. Dodging the deadly dart, the embattled man struggled to reach the monster's head and crush it with a savage blow. As Orion pushed desperately forward, with eyes wide and watching in every direction but down, he tripped on a boulder and stumbled to the ground. In an instant, the Scorpion shuffled forth and pierced him through the heart. Thus, the mighty hunter fell to the *fiery sting* of a scorpion *proving mightier*.[138]

When ORION died, Artemis fell to her knees and grieved. She pleaded that the hunter might receive a home in heaven. Zeus complied. But because he despised immoderate pride in mortals, he placed the SCORPION in the cosmos as well. There, the beast forever follows Orion and offers a lesson for all who see to avoid conceit for fear of a fall.

The massive Scorpion stretches so far across the celestial sphere that he occupies more than his fair share of the starry sky. To remedy this, his powerful pinchers became defined as a separate constellation called the CLAWS.[139] As the Scorpion appears on the eastern horizon, Orion seeks shelter far to the west. But when the Scorpion is hidden from sight, Orion seems happy in his heavenly home, and no one shall ever *see other stars more fair*.[140] With his enormous stature and radiant glow, as well as his prominent position among the stars, he shines down upon all the people and places of the Earth.

From on high, Orion still pursues the Pleaides across the sky. And yet, he prefers to hunt the celestial prey with a pelt in his left hand, a club held high in his right, and a glittering knife tucked into his belt. Even the mighty Bear *circles ever in its place and watches Orion* with suspicion.[141]

But the Hunter's attention is fixed on the HARE, who races ever underfoot with ears erect. Here Hermes, the messenger god, placed the Hare to honor his awesome agility and speed. Like his earthbound counterparts, the heavenly Hare sits silent and still among the stars, and manages to stay just beyond Orion's reach as though he enjoys the chase as much as does the hunter.

Orion's spotted comrade, the DOG, also joins him in the sky. Bounding through the astral lights, he bursts forward on long legs toward his prey and stays close on the heels of the cunning Hare. Like Orion, the Dog's constellation burns brilliantly in the night. On his muzzle he bears the brightest star in the sky, the DOG STAR that some call Sirius.[142]

Alongside the Dog frolics a playful pup — the smaller dog of Orion. The puppy's constellation is named HERALD OF THE DOG because he rises above the horizon before the larger canine comes to view. The little dog likes to join the hunt with his tiny tail happily wagging. But lacking the steady self-control of the older hound, he sometimes jumps ahead and spoils the stalk. Or he straggles behind and pauses to nip at flowers, as playful puppies will do.

On his muzzle he carries a single star. On his flank glimmers a far more luminous light called HERALD OF THE DOG STAR, or Procyon. This star shines only slightly less bright than Sirius.[143]

High in heaven, Orion and his dogs hunt at the mouth of the *deep eddying* River Eridanus. The sad River, now a stream of stars, recalls the tragic fall of Phaethon who, like Orion, was punished for his pride. Phaethon's father reigned on high as Phoebus Apollo — the shining god of the sun.[144] But the boy was born a mortal child, raised by a caring mother named Clymene and his older sisters, the lighthearted Heliades.

The sunny sisters loved to play among the trees on the riverbank, spreading their arms and fingers wide like the branches above and adorning their hair with colorful autumn leaves. Sometimes they mimicked the cheerful songs of birds that flitted from twig to twig.

Phaethon joined their happy outings and often paused with the girls to watch the wondrous sun as it rose and fell in the sky. First, it dispersed the darkness of early morning. Then, it followed a golden arch over land and sea, across the broad, blue expanse above. The children knew they should be back home by the time it arrived on the western horizon.

From the beginning, Clymene told her children the truth—that the shining sun was indeed their father, Phoebus Apollo. She assured them that he smiled down on them daily and tanned their faces and gave their cheeks a rosy glow. Phaethon longed to be like his glorious father, but alas, he found himself forever bound to earth.

As the years passed and the restless boy grew bolder, he assumed the visage of invincible youth. With childhood fears left far behind, he decided to face his father at last. He packed a bundle, slung it over his shoulder, and marched for many weary days to the base of Mount Olympus. Undeterred by the lofty peaks that towered above, he began to climb slowly and steadily toward the top.

Upon surmounting the shining summit, he promptly found Apollo's resplendent palace. Without delay, the brash boy pushed open the gates and entered. Soon he stood in the sun god's beaming presence.

Apollo welcomed Phaethon warmly, as a father to a son, and promised to hand him his heart's desire. The boy had no need to consider his response. At once, he declared his undying wish, his lifelong desire, to drive the chariot of the sun for a day. From there he hoped to behold all the world on high, from earth to sea to sky.

Aghast at the reckless request, Apollo tried to dissuade him. None but himself, he said, could manage the fierce and fiery team of horses that draws the chariot across the cosmos. Not even Zeus would dare to take up the task.

The climb up to heaven was far too steep, Apollo warned, and the descent was even more dizzying and dreadful. In addition, dangers dwelt among the stars. The Scorpion, the Crab, the Lion, and the Bull glowered at the deity's daily intrusion. How quickly they would maim a mortal youth—stinging, pinching, clawing, and goring!

Phaethon only smiled at Apollo's words of warning, and the sun god saw for himself the folly of trying to take back his promise. Bowing his head and shaking it slowly, he whisked his son away to the sunlit stable in the east. There he prepared the blazing chariot and team of spirited steeds. Then he returned to his throne, sullen and troubled, to watch with deep foreboding the fateful day unfold.

Dauntless as ever, Phaethon leapt into the chariot and grabbed the reigns as if he were right at home. In an instant, the chariot jolted forward and shot into the air like an arrow, climbing at an alarming rate. Soon the team parted the puffy clouds and hurtled high into the blue sky. Fear gripped Phaethon now, and he ventured an anxious glance below. He watched in great distress as homes, towns, islands, and mountains dimmed and finally disappeared in the distance.

As Phaethon began to shake with fear, the stormy horses detected the driver's lack of control. Flushed in frenzy, they seized command and fought and jostled among themselves for a new path to follow. Without warning, they began wheeling in every direction.

Into the highest heaven they flew, disrupting the peaceful abode of the stars. From there, they streaked toward earth in fiery descent and slammed across mountaintops, leaving them leaping in flames. The lofty peaks—the sacred pinnacles of the gods—now burned and billowed in ruin.

Even Olympus began to blaze. Forests followed, engulfed in violent infernos, and the waters of many rivers boiled away into suffocating steam. Flora withered and died. Fauna scattered and fled. And humans wailed aloud as their homelands blackened into ash.

Gaea screamed for action from the immortal gods, demanding they save her lovely earth and all its living beings. Zeus finally stepped forward, furious at the widespread destruction and the chaotic disruption of his peaceful skies. He seethed, too, at the conceit of a brazen youth who dared to assume the role of a god.

With a single stroke of his lightning bolt, he felled the tempestuous team of horses and struck the rider and chariot from the sky. Phaethon, with *fire ravaging his ruddy hair*, tumbled through the air with the burning wreckage, *as sometimes a star from the clear heavens… seems to fall*. Into the River Eridanus he shot like a flash. With a deafening splash, he caused the waters to hiss and steam.

The naiads of the river sullenly retrieved his burned and broken body. Then they reverently buried the boy, *still smoking with the flames of that forked bolt*. At last, in great solemnity the river nymphs engraved his epitaph: *Here Phaethon lies. In Phoebus' car he fared, and though he greatly failed, more greatly dared*.[145]

Phaethon's inconsolable sisters, the Heliades, gathered close around his grave. There they mourned for their brother so steadfastly, without stirring from the spot, that they took root on the riverbank and assumed the form of poplar trees. With quaking leaves, they shed sweet tears of amber that showered down upon the rippling waters and verdant grass below. Zeus tried to assuage the sorrow of Phoebus Apollo by assigning the RIVER a home in the sky in memory of his children. Now a stream of stars pays tribute to the once proud flow of water known as *Eridanus, river of many tears*.[146]

Another young and haughty hero, Bellerophon, suffered a similar fate. None could deny that he had performed amazing deeds. First, he found and approached the wild and unruly winged horse named Pegasus. In time, he softened the stallion's rampaging heart with his gentle hands and soothing voice. Then he cautiously climbed on his back and rode the steed until they became like one in flight.

Now the horse and hero flew far and wide to find adventure. In the east, they engaged in battle with the she-warrior Amazons, who despised all men so much that they even discarded their own infant sons. In the furious fight that followed, Bellerophon vanquished many of the warlike women. Flushed with victory, he now pursued an even deadlier foe. Leaping proudly on Pegasus' back, he flew aloft toward the menacing mountains to face the dreaded Chimaera.

The Chimaera, the odious daughter of Typhon, concealed her lair among desolate heights and rocky crags. Only through the air could the horse and rider find her. Huge and hideous, her body was that of an agile mountain goat that allowed her to leap from peak to peak.

She had the flesh-eating head of a lion and a tail that coiled and writhed like a snake, with striking, venomous fangs. At night, the cruel beast incessantly stalked the valleys, *breathing out, terribly, the force of blazing fire*.[147] She hated every living being, but most of all, abhorred the sight of humans.

As soon as she spied the horse and rider hovering above, she roared forth a wrathful flame that singed their hair and baked their skin. The two bellowed in pain but maintained the pursuit. Circling at a distance, Pegasus dodged the fire and fangs while the young man pierced the creature's body with a steady rain of arrows. At last, the Chimaera grew faint and plummeted to her death in the valley below.

Now that Bellerophon had laid low the fierce foe, he assumed himself invincible, claiming victory even over death. He began to imagine that he, who seemed immortal, must surely deserve a divine home. Climbing once more on Pegasus' back, he goaded the horse to soar through the sky toward the summit of Mount Olympus. Here, he expected to join an applauding pantheon of gods.[148]

As Bellerophon spurred his winged horse higher and higher above the clouds, Zeus delivered a woeful welcome—a gadfly to render a painful bite on Pegasus' back. The horse began to buck wildly, dislodging Bellerophon and causing him to fall through the pale blue sky and down to the dusty earth. A giant thorn bush saved the tarnished hero from sudden death but left him battered and bruised in body and mind. Despised by the gods, and lacking his former strength and self-esteem, he wandered alone until the end of his days, *eating his heart out, and shunning the paths of men*.[149]

Despite his heroic achievements, his fatal flaw—his arrogance—doomed him in the end. Once again, the deities delivered the stern warning, in no uncertain terms, that pride precedes a fall.

Red Deer stag. Vase painting, 525-500 BC. Archeological Museum. Island of Rhodes, Greece. Photo by author.

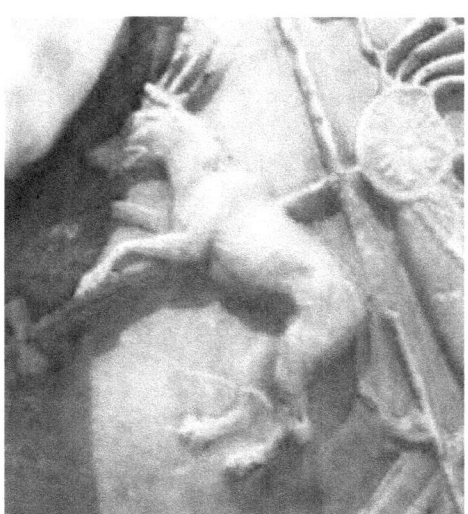

Dog (Canis Major) with the brilliant light of the Dog Star (Sirius) radiating from his head. Depicted on the *Farnese Atlas* Celestial Globe. See Appendix 3. National Archeological Museum, Magna Graecia, Naples, Italy. Photo by author.

# Chapter 14.  A COUNTRYMAN LOST IN THE CITY

AT THAT MOMENT, PAPPOS' VOICE FADED in my mind. The stars blurred and the fire became a hazy glow as I drifted into unconsciousness. I regained my senses a few days later at home in my own bed.

Tempe had never shaken the ominous feeling that welled within her as I left for the hunt. A few days later she begged two neighbors to search for me. For a few days more, they doggedly tracked my steps until they found me crumpled beside the ashes of a fire, caked with blood and unconscious.

Fortune had smiled on me in the end. The wolves had not returned. With a hastily assembled stretcher made from branches, the men laboriously toted me out of the mountains. Tempe took one look at my ashen face and urged the foot-weary men to find a doctor in Rhamnous.

Before this, I had avoided physicians and their fees. Instead, Tempe usually stitched my cuts and set my broken bones. But the wolf's nasty fangs left deep gashes that she knew invited infection.

I changed my opinion of doctors when I finally came to and peeked at my lacerated limbs, purple, swollen, and stitched, it seemed, with a spindle-full of thread. Fate smiled on me again; I had remained unconscious while he cleaned and sewed the ragged flesh.

The doctor had departed before I woke. He told Tempe that I might have bled to death if not for the freezing mountain weather. He left salves for her to apply, then hurried back to his other patients in Rhamnous.

Tempe assured me that he had studied medicine in Athens and did not resort to magic spells and incantations like other healers. Instead, he invoked the aid of Asclepius, the great physician. Then he closely diagnosed my condition, probing for broken bones and smelling for infection.

He proved most expert at stitching wounds and setting bones. And he applied medicinal roots and herbs to fight infection. He told Tempe that most cases were not so involved, and many patients simply required bleeding or purging to correct their bodily balance.

Tempe constantly tended my wounds in the months to come and gently soothed my body and mind. She sang soft melodies to me and played her childhood flute in mellow tones that filled my soul. She helped me return to the humble person I was before the war, and our love grew stronger than ever before.

By early spring, I had healed enough to hobble around and help her prune the grapevines. Three months later, after the harvest, our young son and a neighbor assumed most of the labor on my behalf. At the request of the deme, I began spending half my time in Athens.

There I engaged in the affairs of the polis, as was expected of citizens no longer active in military service. Most farmers of Attica participate only marginally because the distance to the city is prohibitive and they prefer to remain with their crops and flocks. As a result, Athens, with its majority population and number of active citizens, tends to control the polis.

The Athenian polis, encompassed by Attica, is divided into ten tribes which are subdivided into ten local demes per tribe. I had engaged in the business of the deme in Rhamnous and had attended tribal meetings to manage land holdings. But at the Assembly, which is open to all male citizens, we focused on the affairs of the polis.

The Council of Five Hundred presided over the general Assembly. Demes and tribes that desired more representation nominated trusted men to join the Council. But some men, those with political ambitions, nominated themselves. Any citizen over age thirty could gain nomination, but the final decision fell to the beans. The drawing of black and white beans determined who was elected, or as some believed, determined which candidates the gods had chosen.

The whole idea seemed unsavory to me. I disapproved of self-nomination for political power and social prestige. I disliked how some citizens gained greater authority by the luck of the draw. I disdained the common thought that the drawing of beans represented the will of the gods. The beans, I thought, were ascribed too much divine power, and actually had less value than those I ate for my evening meal.

As a new member of the Assembly, I made many friends with men I greatly admired. From them, I learned much about politics and the pressing foreign and domestic issues Athenians faced every day. By evening, our conversations shifted to science, philosophy, and spirituality.

On occasion, a friend would invite us to a symposium to share a meal at his home while continuing our conversation. Other men hosted symposia centered on wine, feasting, and frivolity in the company of youthful maidens and men. But the ones I frequented focused on the search for knowledge and spiritual truth. I listened, amazed at the wisdom amassed from the far-flung ends of the Earth that resided in the minds of these enlightened men. I came to understand why Athens represents the cultural center of Hellas. But I also discovered that political power attracts an unruly lot, and the worst of them often jostle their way to the top.

Many foreigners admire our Assembly as the most august body of the most enlightened country in the world. But our eyes often deceive us when we peer from a distance. Only up close can we see the truth.

While the Assembly usually functioned efficiently and contributed to the important decisions of the polis, sometimes it appeared as a gaggle of geese — rude, loud, pompous, and backward in traditions. To convene the Assembly, attendants sacrificed a pig and sprinkled its blood in a circle around the gathering. A speaker then bellowed an invocation to the gods, often calling for divine favors for himself and divine curses against his opponents who, he claimed, deceived the people.

In the meetings that followed, most members calmly discussed the matters at hand. But a few displayed the worst behavior and frequently hurled insults and vulgarities. They scuffled and shoved until the Scythian Archers, who maintained order, rushed to intervene. Meetings often lasted from dawn to dusk, but some paid little attention to the duties at hand. Instead, they spent the day spreading gossip or stuffing food in their gaping mouths. On the farm, Ama would have chased them with a willow switch for bad behavior.

One day, I watched in dismay as two rather corpulent men argued with ugly shouts and swears, then pummeled each other in anger. Their flying fists, arms, and legs sent the surrounding audience of citizens sprawling. Food scattered here and drinks splattered there until finally they fell and rolled down the hill of the Pnyx.

The guards, following close behind, finally pulled them up, shook them well, and dismissed them for the day. Later, I heard that the argument did not stem from differences of opinion on matters of the polis. Instead, it began when one stole a gulp of the other's wine.

Dealing with Athenians can be difficult at times, but the city itself is spectacular. The Acropolis glows with delightful temples and devoted throngs of worshippers. The massive Doric features of the Parthenon and the elegant Ionic style of the Erechtheum stand in beautiful contrast, and gleam like precious gems against a clear blue sky.[150] Sometimes it seems impossible that Persians once reduced the Acropolis to a smoldering pile of rubble. To gaze on it now brings deep satisfaction and reassurance that radiant beauty can emerge from the darkest defeat.

Attica abounds in marble, much of which is mined from Mount Pentelicus near Athens. Most of the quarried stone is sent to sacred sites because the general public prefers fabulous temples over fine houses. In fact, many consider personal displays of wealth as a badge of dishonor. They point to the inscription on Apollo's temple in Delphi that says: *Nothing in excess!*

Most embrace this timeless creed and work for the public good rather than private greed. But many now perceive an increase of costly homes in Athens. Some interpret this as a sign of society in decline—a society that has failed in its focus and fallen from the heights of altruism into the pitfall of materialism. Altruism promotes benevolence and peace, while materialism breeds greed and strife.

They say that societal decline prompts greedy people to grab what they can and flaunt their wealth to convince themselves and others that all is well. Some even enslave themselves in debt by borrowing money to purchase lavish homes, and all for the purpose of impressing like-minded people who they despise.

The typical homes of the wealthy and those pretending to be wealthy consist of rooms surrounding a colonnaded interior courtyard. The floors and walls are bedecked with brilliant mosaics, frescoes, tapestries, and statuary. The effect is aesthetically pleasing and stunning to the eyes, but inherently worthless and even disruptive to the pursuit of knowledge, wisdom, and truth.

Many wealthy families also boast large estates outside of Athens, with vineyards, olive groves, horses, and slaves to support their opulent lifestyle and public image. Pappos once said that the growth of a large estate suggests that poorer people are being forced from their lands, and with no recourse, move to the slums on the outskirts of Athens.

There, they search for honest work to pay for scraps of food and tattered clothing. Failing that, they trudge in desperation to silver mines to spend their lives in perpetual gloom, laboring underground throughout the day with backs bent low while dust and torch-smoke destroy their eyes and lungs. This fate often befalls the poor because the greedy, who grab their possessions, are also too selfish to share.

Many who flaunt their wealth in life do the same in death. As they face their impending demise, they commission massive monuments, ornately engraved to commemorate themselves forever. The eerie stones loom as silent sentinels of the dead in cemeteries outside the northwest city gate.

On the main road into Athens, travelers often stop to gawk at the huge slabs of marble. Then they direct their gaze toward adjoining rows of family members and slaves—the patriarch's minions in life and death. Kinfolk often pay homage at these sites and adorn them with wreaths and colorful sashes. They offer cakes and cups of wine and olive oil as refreshments for the deceased.

Other roads into Athens are warm and welcoming, but a few are cold and cruel. One might see criminals bound to stakes, wasting away from slow starvation and exposure. One might smell the foul pits where felons are hurled and left to die. Or one might witness the clay pots that hold the remains of rejected newborn babies.

Within the city walls, Athens is a pleasant and prosperous town with well-laid roads and rows of houses the size of ours in the country. There are shady parks where children play and old folks sit to reminisce. Sculptures carved in marble capture the gaze, and flowing fountains, public baths, schools, gymnasiums, and lavish stadiums adorn affluent parts of the city.

But in other sections of town the narrow and winding roads turn into mudholes when it rains. Garbage, dung, and human waste litter the streets and ooze through open gutters down the center. On some of the busier roads, gutters are covered with slabs of stone, but in them, rats, flies, mosquitoes, lice, and fleas breed and spread disease.

At night, gloomy paths become hangouts for thieves. During the day, a person must walk with care past rows of huts that hug the streets on either side. Doors open outward toward the road and sometimes knock unwary wanderers into the gutters. But many residents warn from within by pounding their door before pushing it open.

In the streets of Athens, a person often encounters signs of birth and death. Doors display an olive branch to indicate a newborn boy inside, or a bundle of sheared wool for a baby girl. Other doors exhibit a cypress branch with a purification bowl below to warn of a corpse within.

Funerals are daily events in a large city like Athens. Processions capture attention with hysterical mourners who wail, groan, pull at their hair, beat their faces and chests, rip their clothing, throw ash and dust in the air, and wallow on the ground. For most, these are acts of genuine sorrow. For others, nothing more than elaborate drama.

One day, as I scurried swiftly down the street, lost in thought, I turned a corner and ran headlong into mourners carrying a festooned casket on their shoulders. Startled, they stumbled but managed to save their load and heft it back in place. They wailed aloud, but not in sorrow. Instead, they gave an angry shout. One woman struck me with her cane while another threw ashes in my face. With profuse apologies, I beat a retreat while they disappeared down the street. In Athens, one cannot avoid the living or dead at every turn.

Like homes in the country, most city houses include a main room with a smaller adjoining space for sleeping or storage, and are built of sunbaked brick plastered with mud. But there the similarities stop. City dwellings provide little privacy. The tightly packed houses often share exterior walls or stand against cliffs and have a wall of natural rock.

Most roofs are thatched with straw, but some are covered with tiles of clay and are accessible by outside ladders or staircases. These allow families to relax and sleep in cool breezes on summer nights. One unusual type of home rests in a cluster of homes on upper and lower levels with adjoining walls on three sides.

Poseidon takes a terrible toll on these types of dwellings when he sends earthquakes ashore. Many are killed and injured as the massive structures collapse. Fire is another scourge that occasionally sweeps from house to house, turning thatched roofs into torches.

Most dwellings are cheaply built, yet many people still cannot afford them. Instead, they rent and face the threat of eviction. In hard times, they have no choice but to join the homeless masses.

These impoverished people, often through no fault of their own, sleep beneath their himations in public places or beyond the city walls. In winter, many crowd into public baths to take refuge from the cold. Some turn to crime, robbing bystanders on the streets or crashing through doors to plunder dwellings. If the door is stoutly locked, they tunnel through mudbrick or remove roof tiles to force their way inside.

Athens' overpopulation makes the problem worse. It increases the homeless crowd, adds to sewage and filth, and causes long lines to form at public fountains. There, people might wait for much of the day to fill their jugs with water. Most city dwellers keep their families small, not so much for the sake of the city, but to insure there is enough food for all. Abortion is common, and infanticide of newborn babies also occurs, especially with little girls.

All believe that to murder a child is a terrible crime, especially those more than five days old. Yet some place newborns in clay pots, set them outside the city walls, and allow them to starve or die of exposure. This heinous act is legal as long as the child is newly born and has not been welcomed by ritual into the family and given a name. Infanticide is more common in Sparta, where all

125

babies are closely examined and those with weaknesses are promptly discarded.

The practice is extremely rare in the Attic countryside, where population is not a problem, and parents feed their children from the produce of the land while teaching them to help with the labor. Some barren women even rescue newborn babies from clay pots outside the city walls. They take them to their rustic homes and raise and cherish them as their own.

While woeful conditions prevail on the fringes of the city, the center flourishes beneath the beaming Acropolis. The commercial heart of Athens is the Agora. Here, Hephaestus' temple stands in sacred grandeur and frowns solemnly on the madness of the marketplace below.

In times past, the Assembly convened here. But choking crowds forced it to the Pnyx on a nearby hill west of the Acropolis. Religious dramas also relocated to the amphitheater of Dionysus on the Acropolis' southern slope.

Today, the Agora is clogged with vendors, buyers, and barterers from the polis and beyond, all jostling to secure a favorable trade. Throngs of people engage in business negotiations and civic debates. Curious visitors, cursing sailors, and resident foreigners shout in a jumble of tongues. Stump-speakers, idle bystanders, and packs of dogs consider the place their own. I have watched a steady stream of people step over one sleeping dog who found the market a fine place for a nap.

The Agora is congested and noisy, but also mesmerizing. Here, a person can find exotic wares from foreign countries. There, a shop sells scrolls of written texts from all of Hellas and far beyond. Vendor booths are grouped by type, with one section selling pots and utensils, another vegetables and fruits, and others wine, meat, fish, cosmetics, and funeral wreaths. Even sandal makers have a section in which to sell their products, as if a person cannot make his own.

Vendors stand side by side with their competitors and try to outshout each other to attract passing shoppers. Some even grab their arms and drag them toward their booths. The hustle and bustle spills from the Agora into the nearby Ceramicus, where several hundred potters fashion clay products and stack them in piles. The place is especially popular in winter, as heat from a hundred kilns attracts the crowds.

Nearby stand booths for artisans: carpenters, coopers, cobblers, tanners, blacksmiths, butchers, and barbers, all buzzing around like bees. Any product a person could want or need lies within reach of the Agora. But the marketplace also has a dark and sinister side.

Bronze arrowheads of Scythian archers, c. 5th century BC.
Marshall Collection, Loma Paloma, Texas. Photo by author.

# Chapter 15. THE SQUALOR AND SPLENDOR OF ATHENS

THE AGORA IS ALIVE AND EXCITING, but it is also burdened with bitter sorrow. One section holds a row of auction blocks for trading slaves. Slavery is common in Athens and is widely accepted, but strongly opposed by merciful men and women who despise the inhumanity.

When I walk past the auction blocks and see the pleading eyes of forlorn children, I grieve for them, and for Bronte who might have suffered the same fate. Nausea wells within and my teeth clench in anger aimed at the cold and cruel slaveowners who add to their wealth at the expense of innocent lives. My face flushes in rage when I think of the Athenian capture of foreign slaves and how it prompts retaliatory raids against our own poorly defended shores.

Many slaves are torn away from conquered countries and families. They are beaten, raped, and shackled by the same brutal men that butchered their fathers, brothers, and sons who died defending them. They are stolen from foreign lands, but also from other Hellenic poleis that frequently fight each other.

Bronte and I were nine years old when Athens attempted to force the neutral island of Milos to help them fight the Spartans. When the peaceful people of Milos refused, Athens sent an army and slaughtered every able-bodied man. Then they enslaved the surviving population of wailing women and children and sold them right here, in the Agora. The conquered Milesians, the innocent victims, now became objects of cruelty and scorn for the rest of their miserable lives.

But not all slaves come from conquered countries. The people of Thrace, Phrygia, and other impoverished regions sometimes sell their children when they cannot afford to feed them. Debtors in Attica have even sold themselves to stave off starvation. As slaves, they receive a pittance of food and clothing from masters who want to safeguard their investments in human property.

At auction, a slave trained in a trade or craft might cost 500 drachmas. But most males lack special skills and sell for about 200. They labor in fields or mines, or work in Athenian homes. Females are in higher demand as domestic workers and fetch 250. They are used and abused for more than simple labor.

Slavery rarely appears in the backcountry, where most families value self-sufficiency and freedom, and the remaining few cannot afford the cost. Only an occasional farmer scrounges enough money to buy a single slave to work beside him in the field.

Wealthy Athenian families often own at least a dozen slaves who cook, clean, fetch water, chop wood, grind grain, spin thread, weave cloth, nurse babies, and walk the children to school. Many owners grow plump and indolent as they call upon slaves to help with every little chore. In some cases, slaves even raise a family's children on their own and frequently fill their heads with foreign ideas and customs.

Some owners adopt favorite slaves into their family by means of a simple ritual in which they sprinkle figs and nuts upon their heads. With their past erased, the slaves receive new names and join in family prayers. Those who remain loyal until death might even be buried in the family plot.

But more typically, from one day to the next, slaves never know what fate awaits them. One moment, the mistress might pleasantly laugh with her servant, and the next she might beat her for the smallest infraction, depending on her mood. The law officially protects slaves from mistreatment but also prohibits slaves from initiating a legal action. If they show resentment or resistance, they are often sent to the silver mines to join thousands of other slaves and work in the worst conditions. It is safer not to fight back.

Even so, some escape from cruel masters and hide in the countryside. They subsist by stealing from grainfields and orchards at night, and burrow into dense thickets to sleep by day. Before long the masters use dogs to hunt them down, then brand them with red-hot irons and haul them away screaming. After an attempted escape, the captives are heavily guarded, and shackled and forced into wretched labor in grinding mills or mines. Or they are sent to work on the docks of Piraeus under strict supervision, loading and unloading backbreaking cargo from dawn to dusk.

The life of a free wageworker is not much better. They too are beaten, abused, and given a pittance on which to live. Unlike slaves, they are left to fend for themselves without provisions of food, clothing, or shelter. Most wageworkers are metics—free foreigners living in Athens who earn one obol a day. Many serve in the military for the same low wage, as light infantrymen or rowers on warships.

Other metics are skilled craftsmen, working as weavers, tailors, tanners, potters, or smiths for two obols a day. Most remain poor, but some thrive in business and banking, and acquire substantial wealth. A few metics are men of great reputation who journeyed to Athens, often from Ionia, to partake of the vibrant commercial and cultural environment.

Some metics arrive in family groups, escaping poverty or famine in their native lands. To live in Attica, they must pay an annual fee of twelve drachmas per year for males, and six for females. They face restrictions in many ways and can never aspire to citizenship or ownership of houses or land. But they can possess moveable property including slaves.

They often form religious cults and freely worship their foreign gods. Some cults become so popular that Athenians convert to their beliefs. Even in these instances, metics, like women in general, remain subordinate.

Almost all women in Hellas face rigid restrictions. Tempe, at times, tells of her childhood years, which she split between Athens and the Attic countryside. In the city, she found the restraints overbearing.

From childhood, her uncle demanded that she remain out of sight, especially when strangers arrived. Upon reaching maturity, she became even more sequestered. She was banned from school, though her mind naturally longed for knowledge of the outside world. Instead, she learned at home to write her name, read simple inscriptions, recite Homer and Hesiod, and play the flute and lyre.

At our wedding, when she sacrificed her childhood toys to Artemis, she hid her most cherished possession, a simple reed flute that her father had fashioned for her when she was three years old. To this day, she holds it close, and though it is rather worn, she plays the sweetest and softest melodies.

After her parents died, Tempe's aunt taught her to cook, clean, spin, weave, care for nephews and nieces, and maintain an immaculate household. Without these skills, a woman might never marry. Most men, it seems, take a wife to keep the house and raise the children. They hope she bears a male heir to continue the paternal line. They further expect a wife to take care of them in old age and offer the proper funeral rites that assure them a better afterlife. Society generally expects men and women to marry and bear children, and ostracizes those who cannot.

Before we wed, Tempe rarely went to the market except when visiting her family in Oropus. In Athens, men did most of the shopping and kept their wives and daughters hidden from public eyes. But restrictions lightened in later years as thousands of men were called away to war. The loss of men in battle and the poverty spawned by warfare forced many women, especially widows, to work in shops as spinners and weavers, or sell their wares in the Agora. But some people still disdain all women who work in public.

As a youth, Tempe enjoyed the religious processions that granted fleeting escapes from the cloistered confines of home. On these days, she could shout, laugh, sing, dance, and play the flute in public. At other times, she and her friends arranged secret social calls under the guise of borrowing a spindle or salt.

A few women laugh in the face of taboos and public opinion. They often appear outdoors, working in the market or attending tragic dramas at the theater of Dionysus. Those most daring even frequent the risqué comedies that cause grown men to blush.

Life is far different for men. They come and go as they please and partake of the pleasures of the city. They build their own businesses and participate freely in politics. But they also devote many years to military service and put their lives at extreme risk in doing so. At all times, they remain responsible for the survival and success of their families, whom they defend to the death.

Some married men have extramarital affairs and keep mistresses, which society allows for men but not women. A woman has the right to divorce, but may have difficulty procuring one. A man, on the other hand, can easily gain a divorce but is often discouraged by having to return the dowry.

Many husbands, along with sailors and other single men, prefer to wander the streets of Piraeus, which are famous for boisterous brothels. The Ceramicus offers the same entertainment with painted women who roam the streets by day and night. They shout like vendors in the Agora while offering their wares for two or three obols.

A few women work more discreetly and charge exorbitant rates. They consider themselves high class prostitutes, and flaunt their skills as conversationalists, dancers, or musicians. They are adept at gaining control over the minds of their clients and wheedling money through seduction or theft.

Their victims—wealthy buffoons who have more money than sense—have apparently forgotten Hesiod's warning: *Do not let an arse-fancy woman deceive your mind by guilefully cajoling you while she pokes into your granary.*[151] Prostitution is the extreme exception to society's demand that women should remain aloof and secluded.

In the backcountry, social constraints are not so strongly felt. Women are mostly secluded by the distance between neighboring farmsteads and are rarely subject to prying eyes. They maintain greater control of the household while husbands are busy with farming, herding, hunting, and fishing. Some women are also more vocal at home and in public.

Outsiders often frown on this rustic female behavior. But backcountry women accept their criticisms as compliments. They know that strength of character is important when helping to maintain a self-sufficient family. Many husbands agree and enjoy equitable relationships.

The farming families of Attica are certainly different from folks in the city. Outsiders call us peace-mongers. They are correct. We see little value in foreign wars and only hope to keep our crops and homes from being destroyed. If we lose them, we lose our livelihood and perhaps our lives. For this reason, we clamor for peace but are also the first to take up arms and defend against foreign invasion.

Outsiders call us stubbornly independent. Again, they are correct. We love our self-sufficient freedom and avoid dependence on material items that bind us in debt. We ignore the squawking vendors who prey on unwary shoppers.

We try our best to grow and gather our own food, and fashion our shelter, clothing, and household goods by hand. We believe *it is fine to take from what you have. But it is woe for the spirit to have need of what you do not have.*[152] We remain contented with the bounty provided by nature.

Athens exhibits greater disparity between rich and poor. We fall somewhere in between. Or if we are poor, we rarely become aware of it. In fact, we consider ourselves quite rich, so long as we have enough to survive.

After all, we have room to move and breathe. Our water is pure and abundant. Our surroundings are fresh and clean. Our economy is usually stable, depending on the vagaries of weather and war. And we are rarely affected by foreign affairs or market fluctuations.

Unless dire circumstances arise, self-sufficient farmers see no need to *go onto ships; for the grain-giving field bears them crops.*[153] We see no need to enslave ourselves to usurious lenders. We clearly perceive that a borrower is a slave to his debt. And if he fails to repay his debt, he could even become a slave to his lender.

Commerce at any level can open the door to debt, dependence, and entangling economic ties. Our own polis faces this problem. Athens has the advantage of producing surplus wine and olive oil that other countries covet. The huge demand for these products requires vast numbers of amphorae for transport, and five hundred potters in the Ceramicus work all day and night to supply the need.

Athens exports these and many other products to foreign countries in exchange for grain. But Athens has become more dependent on grain than those countries are on oil and wine. She has placed her head in a foreign stranglehold, and gasps for breath whenever those countries decide to squeeze. Our mighty merchant fleet offers the impression of commercial control, but it makes us slaves to imported goods.

While serving in the Assembly, constant problems of economy, society, and politics plagued me. I felt that the woes of the world were breaking my back. For a rural farmer, life in the city can be a heavy burden to bear. Having loved being the former, I admit a bias against the latter.

And yet, I cannot help but love the squalor and splendor that is Athens. To walk in the footsteps of a hundred generations of ancestors; to climb the Acropolis where Athena and Erechtheus promised to protect the polis; to gaze upon the dazzling marble temples that shine as jewels on top of the world; these wonders tug at my heart and fill my mind with a surge of Athenian pride.

From the rocky height, I often peered northward toward the home and family I dearly missed. I gazed southward toward the sparkling waves of the Aegean Sea. I looked westward and eastward to the green patches that mark the gymnasiums, the verdant fields of the Academy and Lyceum.

In the evening, I strolled beneath the leafy sycamores and fragrant willows of the Lyceum—the sanctuary of Apollo, with its cool springs surrounded by soft grass and marble statues. Or I wandered through the ancient grove that is now called the Academy. The shady walkways, flowing waters, and altars to the gods put my mind at ease. I marveled at the twelve sacred olive trees, transplanted from slips of Athena's tree at the Erechtheum.

A man named Plato, a student of Socrates, founded a school at this gymnasium for the purpose of *arete*—exercising the mind and soul as well as the body. Here he gathered a group of students and was often seen at the Academy alone or surrounded by attentive ears.

I heard him speak on a few occasions and listened, amazed, at the similar thread of thought between this cosmopolitan philosopher and my own rustic Pappos. One evening at twilight as I wandered the grounds, a distant voice captured my attention. I turned to see a bonfire glowing in the gathering darkness. A small crowd had ventured close to escape the evening cold and shifted their eyes toward a speaker I recognized as Plato. As I joined the curious crowd, he spoke these timeless words:

Ancient method of storing amphorae in a ship's hold. Greco-Roman Museum, Alexandria, Egypt. Photo by author.

# Chapter 16. THE WISDOM OF PLATO

*Recalling the words of Plato*

HERE WE STAND in one of the loveliest locations in Hellas, enjoying the lush gardens, listening to the babbling brook, warming ourselves by the fire, and admiring the temples of the Acropolis as they glow in the soft moonlight. If we slow our pace and stop to ponder, we find great joy in the world around us. But we tend to observe our universe only in the most limited way, through our physical senses alone. Our minds rarely venture far beyond our body. Instead, our thoughts remain restricted as if imprisoned underground.

*Picture men dwelling in a sort of subterranean cavern.... Conceive them as having their legs and necks fettered from childhood, so that they remain in the same spot, able to look forward only, and prevented by the fetters from turning their heads. Picture further the light from a fire burning higher up and at a distance behind them.*

Between their backs and the fire runs a road traveled by people carrying their loads and conversing along the way. The prisoners cannot see the people walking behind them but can only perceive their shadows cast on the cavern wall before them, and can only hear the echoed mumbles of their voices. Nor can they see themselves, or their fellow prisoners on either side. But they can talk to each other and often pass the time speculating on the shadows and echoes. *In every way such prisoners would deem reality to be nothing else than the shadows* and echoes, since they had experienced nothing more.

But what if *one was freed from his fetters and compelled to stand up suddenly and turn his head around and walk, and to lift up his eyes to the light.... What do you suppose would be his answer if someone told him that what he had seen before was all a cheat and an illusion, but that now, being nearer to reality and turned toward more real things, he saw more truly?... Do you not think that he would be at a loss and that he would regard what he formerly saw as more real than the things now pointed out to him?*

Since humans are creatures of habit, I believe he would still consider his old shadowy world to be reality. And he would consider the light and the people he now saw face-to-face to be an illusion. Now what if *someone should drag him thence by force up the ascent which is rough and steep, and not let him go before he had drawn him out into the light of the sun?*[154]

And what if they goaded him to climb atop the Acropolis and gaze across the fair city until day turned into night? And what if he perceived soft lamplight in all the windows, and blazing hearths inside the homes, then observed the dazzling temples themselves and the sparkling Aegean Sea? Surely his mind and senses would overflow in awe.

Upon peering upward, he would smile at the shimmering stars and see how *the lovely moon... in all her fullness... shines over all the earth.*[155] He would stand like a statue, transfixed by the mystical moment, and remain marveling through the night. Then he would witness the coming of dawn and the clarity that daylight brings with every contrast of light and shadow.

At last, he would witness the brilliant sun rising. He would fall to his knees overwhelmed with wonder and realize that this glorious source of light is that which *presides over all things in the visible region.... Well then, if he recalled to mind his first habitation and what passed for wisdom there... do you not think that he would count himself happy in the change and pity* his fellow-bondsmen?

He would wish to share these wonders with them, and most of all with the wisemen among them that he had always respected. But he would find them reluctant to believe his stories. Instead, they would remain quite content to maintain their esteemed positions in their own wretched world.

The foolish *wisemen* would frown and scorn him if he stirred up new ideas. His old friends would shun him while stubbornly clinging to the world they had always known. They would taunt him and call him a fool when he tried to help them imagine an ideal existence that they had never experienced.

*And if there had been honors and commendations among them which they bestowed on one another, and prizes for the man who is quickest to make out the shadows as they pass... do you think he would be very keen about such rewards, and that he would envy and emulate those who were honored?*

*If such a one should go down again and take his old place, would he not get his eyes full of darkness, thus suddenly coming out of the sunlight?... Would he not provoke laughter, and would it not be said of him that he had returned from his journey aloft with his eyes ruined and that it was not worthwhile even to attempt the ascent? And if it were possible to lay hands on and to kill the man who tried to release them and lead them up, would they not kill him?*

In the same manner as this man, a wise person transcends the limitations of sensory perceptions and searches for true reality—Truth. And when he has found it, he knows it in his mind and feels it in his soul.

My own search for Truth reveals that there is one Good spirit that *is indeed the cause for all things—of all that is right and beautiful; giving birth in the visible world to light and the author of light [the sun]; and itself in the intelligible [mental and spiritual] world being the authentic source of truth and reason; and that anyone who is to act wisely in private or public must have caught sight of this…. That those who have attained to this height are not willing to occupy themselves with the affairs of men, but their souls ever feel the upward urge and the yearning for that sojourn above.*[156]

This Good is central to our ethos and is commonly called *spirit* or *divine spirit* because it fills, envelopes, and overwhelms all things. In fact, spirit and soul are one and the same, and manifest truth far beyond the mundane.

Some people accuse me of denying the existence of nature spirits and the Olympian gods in favor of this all-encompassing spirit. That is not exactly true. I agree with those who believe that spirits inhabit and animate all things, including rocks, rivers, wind, and rain.

In our own time, most people believe that these same objects and forces of nature are gods that possess human traits. I do not refute it, although I do sometimes wonder at their ungodly behavior. I only contend that one spirit — the Good of which I speak — is the ultimate source and sum of all, including rocks, rivers, mortals, and gods.

Awareness of this one Good spirit is nothing new. It is inherent within us and has been revealed in the words of our brightest minds of old, including Thales, Anaximander, Pythagoras, Pherecydes, Xenophanes, Heraclitus, Parmenides, and many others.[157]

Within this all-encompassing Good spirit, a person may choose to honor any or all of its manifestations, including any nature deities or gods they might believe in.[158] But they would be wise to realize that these are only aspects of the one Good.

In Hellas, we are free to commune directly and personally with the Good spirit through meditation, prayers, and dreams. But in Asia, the people's minds are often enslaved by despots and priests who insist that they alone provide a path to the divine. They force the masses into submission through fear of retribution on earth and damnation in eternal life.

The mystery cults they spawn, which now appear in Hellas, are much the same. I disdain cults and religions that claim to be the chosen people while scorning others into shame. They proudly proclaim that only they are bound for eternal bliss, and gloat that others will suffer forever. They maintain exclusive memberships with secret initiations, mysterious incantations, elaborate rituals, and religious displays that range from drunken orgies to ascetic denial of meat and sex.

But people need not depend on human institutions. Instead, they may transcend the physical world and the mundane rituals of religion. They may commune directly with the Good spirit at any time, in any place. After all, the Good spirit created *the soul in origin and excellence prior to and older than the body, to be the ruler and mistress, of whom the body was to be the subject.*[159]

*When the creator had framed the soul according to his will, he formed within her the corporeal universe... The soul, interfused everywhere from the center to the circumference of heaven, of which also she is the external envelopment... The body of heaven is visible, but the soul is invisible, and partakes of reason and harmony, and being made by the best of intellectual and everlasting natures, is the best of things created.*[160]

Physical manifestations of the Good are mere images of its spiritual nature, which is the *greatest, best, fairest, most perfect — the one.*[161] The Good spirit envelopes *all things in relation to each other* as one harmonious whole. This is portrayed by the shining stars — *the brightest of all things and fairest to behold —* which are distributed *over the whole circumference of heaven* and *follow the intelligent motion of the supreme.*[162]

The one Good is the harmonious source and sum of all things physical, mental, and spiritual. To ignore this truth in favor of selfish pursuits brings turmoil to humans because they have wandered away from their true being and flounder like fish out of water. But to cherish and embrace the Good brings happiness.[163]

*When a man is always occupied with the cravings of desire and ambition, and is eagerly striving to satisfy them, all his thoughts must be mortal... But he who has been earnest in the love of knowledge and of true wisdom... since he is ever cherishing the divine power, and has the divinity within him in perfect order, he will be perfectly happy.*[164]

Most people are intelligent enough to make their way in the world, grabbing the immediate gratification it offers. But few are wise enough to transcend the world and rejoice in spiritual truth. The sophists, for example, despite their intelligence, rarely achieve the wisdom, peace, and joy of a simple spiritual person.

Intelligence must not be confused with wisdom. Intelligence can lead a person toward or away from wisdom. Learning is a commendable pursuit, to be sure, but it can be employed for the purpose of good or bad, to either embrace or exploit one's fellow beings.

Intelligence, *according to the direction of its conversion, becomes useful and beneficent, or again, useless and harmful.*[165] The sophists are intelligent, but often reveal a lack of wisdom. They excel in using persuasion to gain power, prestige, and possessions, rather than seeking the truth. They wheedle their students for money and thus teach them, by example, to be as greedy as their teachers, thereby propagating this predatory behavior.

The golden tongues of these pretentious rogues utter little of value. As Homer said, *glib is the tongue of mortals*, whose quick words often disguise a superficial mind.[166] They are too busy talking to listen and learn, so they spout uninformed opinions from the time they wake to the time they finally fall asleep. *And if anyone challenges the least particular of their speech, they go ringing on in a long harangue, like brazen pots, which when they are struck continue to sound unless someone puts his hand upon them.*[167]

When they win elections to political positions, their only qualification is knowing how to exploit the masses by flattering them for votes. And does this single skill help them further the best interests of the polis? No. It only helps them destroy it.

Their lack of qualification soon appears in their misplaced efforts to solve problems with quick fixes or a barrage of ineffectual laws, each of which spawns the need for a dozen more. Thus, that which should be simple and straightforward becomes complex and confusing.

If sophists were truly wise, they would know that exploiting other people never brings contentment. It only increases avarice. And the wealth they acquire attracts other predators, who attack them like sharks in a feeding frenzy. *A man contrives evil for himself when he contrives evil for someone else, and an evil plan is most evil for the planner.*[168]

There are two opposing human traits—*to give* and *to grab*. As Hesiod said: *Give is good, Grab is bad.... For whatever a man gives willingly... he rejoices in the gift and takes pleasure in his spirit; but whoever snatches, relying upon shamelessness, this congeals his own heart.*[169] Grabbing hurts everyone, especially the grabber, who focuses only on himself and becomes obsessed with every problem that mounts against him. Giving helps everyone, especially the person who gives, whose mind is focused on the problems of others rather than on his own.

In the same manner, a person succeeds in life when he promotes harmony rather than strife. Life is too short for dissension—too short for a squabble that no one wins. Sappho, the wise woman of Lesbos, urged us *to guard against the idly barking tongue when anger is spreading in the breast.*[170]

Men of old agreed, saying: *What need have we… to exchange strifes and wranglings?* It is best to keep tempers down and voices low. *The tongue that is the best treasure is a sparing one.* We should *avoid the wretched talk of mortals. For talk is evil: it is light to raise up quite easily, but it is difficult to bear, and hard to put down. No talk is ever entirely gotten rid of, once many people talk it up.*[171]

It is true that the sophists have made great contributions to knowledge in the areas of astronomy, physics, geometry, medicine, and the arts. But their emphasis on rhetoric and its use for persuasion and exploitation often brings them shame. The problem is a lack of perspective. Rather than humbly seeing themselves as part of an infinite physical, mental, and spiritual whole, they imagine themselves as the center of the universe, around which all else revolves. As such, they only seek to serve themselves.

Plato (c. 427-348 BC) was a student of Socrates and the teacher of Aristotle. Aristotle was the teacher of Alexander the Great.

Plato (left) and his student Aristotle (right) at Plato's Academy. *The School of Athens*, painting by Raphael, 1509-1511 AD.

## Chapter 17.  A LONG SEA VOYAGE

WHEN PLATO ENDED THE LESSON, his audience applauded. In response, he only raised his hand, smiled, and quoted Homer saying: *Praise me not too much, nor blame me.*[172] The crowd laughed with delight.

As I strolled home that night with my himation wrapped tight to turn away the cold, I recalled his words, and would ponder them often in the months to come. Plato had merged ideas that I had heard in scattered phrases from Homer, Hesiod, and other wise men and women I admired. Plato's words also aligned with the moral code that Pappos unveiled in the stories of the stars. These tales of old taught us that love and devotion result in peace and harmony, while arrogance and greed bring hatred and strife.

Slowly, I embraced a philosophy based upon these reflections. I came to believe that there is one Good that animates all—one spirit that is the source and sum of all things physical and metaphysical. We can perceive its manifestations in nature. We can know it in our mind. We can feel it in our soul. Our deepest yearning, our truest purpose, and our worthiest endeavor is to love the one Good spirit and all that is of the one. And when our physical existence ends, our spirit *flies away with joy* into perfect oneness, as Plato said.[173]

Athens certainly has its problems, but the flurry of ideas that freely flow within this cosmopolitan city are exhilarating to the mind and soul. Ideas arrive from all corners of the world to be openly discussed and debated; to be accepted or rejected. When my time came to leave the city, I believe I departed as a wiser man.

For several years, I had trudged back and forth from our homestead to Athens, farming one month and attending meetings of the Assembly the next. But at last, with a happy heart, I hurried home for good. Or that was my intention.

Calamities sometimes come our way that change the best of plans. For four autumns in a row, we watched with dismay as large flocks of cranes streamed southward, heralding severe winters. Sure enough, the months that followed brought bitter blasts from the north that howled across Euripus Strait and shook our tiny hut.

For long nights we huddled close, struggling to stay warm near the hearth. Every summer that followed brought scorching heat and severe droughts that shriveled crops and meadows.[174] Our streams turned to scattered puddles and patches of mud. The harvest failed, the livestock languished, the wildlife starved, and our stomachs grumbled.

The young olive trees that we had planted to replace those decimated by marauders proved less productive than their ancient forebears. The older trees had thrived for two thousand years, providing abundant harvests for a hundred generations of families. But suddenly, we faced a scarcity of olives for eating, and oil for cooking and lighting lamps. Besieged by hard times, I was forced to make a difficult decision.

In Athens, I had come to know merchant shippers who made regular runs to the Ionian coast, the Black Sea, Italy, Phoenicia, and Egypt. Although I enjoyed their strange tales of exotic lands, I had no desire to board a ship or make a living from seaborne trade. Nor had I forgotten the military forays that had confined me to a heaving ship on open waters and made me long for landfall. Nevertheless, in desperation, I bundled a pack, slung it on my back, and prepared to walk to Piraeus to search for a berth.

After bidding my family a tearful farewell, I turned with a heavy heart down the dusty trail. Soon, I arrived at the road that led toward Oropus, and hesitated as nostalgia welled within. My heart longed to turn toward the dear old home that had been lost to my eyes for thirty years. There, the lonely graves of Pappos and Ama, and the family altar in the ancient grove lay forlorn.

But melancholy overwhelmed me, and I sullenly cast my eyes toward Athens. From there, I walked to Piraeus where I found a ship being fitted for a six-month voyage to Joppa and other ports of call. I was not the only unfortunate farmer to show up on the docks. I joined a mismatched crew of old salts and landlubbers ranging from ages fifteen to sixty. Together, we set aside our troubles and took up the task of outfitting the ship, storing supplies, and finding our way around the floating hulk that would be our home.

Seven days later, we launched to the sound of the boatswain's whistle and the cursing crew who struggled to retrieve and coil the heavy mooring lines. When we entered open waters, the seasoned sailors stood out from the stumbling and retching landsmen. Thirty years had come and gone since I had sailed on the open sea, and I soon found myself leaning over the rail.

Our big-bellied merchant ship lumbered along, rolling and pitching as the sail tugged at the rigging and slowly pulled us forward. This was no trireme with a sleek hull, trim sail, and 170 oars that allowed it to cut through the water with ease. The sun was setting as we finally lost sight of land, but I did not sleep that night, or the next.

This was a world to which I had to adapt all over again. The sudden lurches, the slap of waves on the hull, and the wind whistling through the rigging kept me on high alert until I collapsed from exhaustion. But soon enough, I learned to slumber like a baby, even in rough weather with amphorae of olive oil and wine rattling in the hold.

We quickly discovered, to our relief, that the captain was a navigator rich in experience who had sailed the Mediterranean for many years. His cool bravery during heavy winds and sudden squalls made us confident in his abilities despite our fears. He did not hesitate to venture out of sight of land across broad stretches of open sea, even in the darkness of night.

Many captains never let land slip from their sight. Instead, they prefer to hug the coast and seek a sheltered harbor by twilight. Our captain's self-assurance flowed from a vast knowledge of navigational lore accumulated over a lifetime from other seafarers at every Hellenic, Ionian, and Phoenician port. In his head, he carried maps of coastlines. He noted geographic features, dangerous shoals, and prevailing winds and currents.

I observed with fascination as he searched from the heaving bow for coastal landmarks that revealed our location. I gazed in amazement as he stood at the stern and aligned two objects on the shoreline behind us in order to help him maintain a straight course ahead.

His keen eyes closely followed migrating flocks of birds to determine cardinal directions. In shallow waters, he commanded a sailor to lower the bell-shaped sounding weight until it struck bottom and gave him a measure of depth. Then he ordered the sounding weight hauled to the deck and examined the tallow-filled hollow of the bell. From this he surmised the coastal location according to the type of sand and shell that stuck to the tallow.

The captain observed every change of current and wind direction, and watched ripples on the water for telltale signs of these. He carefully noted the movement of the sun during the day and the stars at night as they followed their fixed courses from east to west across the sky. Most of all, he kept his eyes on the two celestial Bears—the polar constellations that mark the northern sky.

From her vantage point on high, near the northern apex of heaven, the Bear's starry light shines as a beacon for those who venture into open waters at night. Odysseus himself, when hopelessly lost at sea and attempting to return to Ithaca after twenty years of warfare and wandering, used the Bear as a guide as he sailed toward the east.

Homer recalled how *noble Odysseus spread his sail to the breeze; and he sat and guided his raft skillfully with the steering oar, nor did sleep fall upon his eyelids, as he watched the Pleiades, and late-setting Bootes, and the Bear... which ever circles where it is and watches Orion, and alone has no part in the baths of Ocean. For this star Calypso, the beautiful goddess, had bidden him to keep on the left hand as he sailed over the sea.*[175]

For greater accuracy, our captain also noted the position of the Little Bear, around which *the entire universe appears to revolve.*[176] Thales, the famed Ionian astronomer and philosopher, was the first to reveal to the Hellenes that the sailors of Phoenicia followed the Little Bear's unwavering guidance in the sky.

Thales' successors spread the word, saying *it is by [the big Bear] that the Achaeans [Hellenes] on the sea divine which way to steer their ships, but in [the Little Bear] the Phoenicians put their trust when they cross the sea. But [the big Bear], appearing large at earliest night is bright and easy to mark; but the other is small, yet better for sailors: for in a smaller orbit wheel all her stars. By her guidance, then, the men of Sidon steer the straightest course.*[177]

In addition to finding directions, our captain determined the ship's latitude—the position north to south—by using a gnomon to mark the angle of the sun's noontime shadow on certain days of the year.[178] Many coastal cities marked their latitudes in the same manner, and gave the measures to mariners so they could more easily find their port and ply their trade.

Whenever we made landfall, the captain found a patch of level ground and sank a gnomon—a simple vertical stick—into the sand. When the sun reached its highest point in the sky, at noon, he marked the tip of the gnomon's shadow and measured the angle to determine our latitude.[179] Then he glanced at a scroll that told him if a port city appeared on or near the same latitude. If so, he surmised whether the port lay east or west, and considered sailing in that direction to intercept it.

Some seamen claim to mark latitude while sailing, by measuring the height of the northernmost star that rests on the tip of the Little Bear's tail.[180] Our captain said he had tried this at times, using finger-widths to mark angles in the sky, but with little success while standing on a rolling deck.

He also attempted to measure the distance traveled by estimating the ship's speed and then approximating the amount of time that the ship had sailed at that speed. To determine speed, the captain stood at the stern and commanded a man at the bow to drop a chip of wood in the water. The captain then counted the moments until the ship sailed past the chip. From this he determined approximate speed and estimated duration and distance.

He estimated longer passages of time by watching the sun climb in the east and descend in the west. At night, he followed the fixed stars of the zodiac—those constellations, mostly in the form of animals, that pursue the path of the moon and planets. Like the sun, they climb and descend from east to west and provide a measure of time. He also showed us how readily *can the sailor on the open sea mark the first bend of the River [Eridanus] rising from the deep, as he watches for Orion himself to see if he might give him any hint of the measure of the night or of his voyage.*[181]

In similar manner, the captain observed the Little Bear as it slowly circled the north celestial pole. From these observations, the captain determined *when it was the third watch of the night, and the stars had turned their course* around the sky.[182] With a fair degree of accuracy, he knew how much of the night remained before rosy-fingered Dawn would rise to disperse the darkness.

By the time we arrived at the port of Joppa, even those of us who were new to seafaring life had learned basic navigation and become attuned to the motions of the ship. We knew how to shift our weight to accommodate the constantly surging sea. Without conscious thought, we felt and responded to changing directions of wind and current. We learned to anticipate the captain's command to trim or furl the sail.

His willingness as a teacher encouraged me to learn more about navigation by sun and stars, and how to read the weather at sea. As a farmer, I thought I knew all one could know about predicting the weather. But a sailor develops sharper skills for the sake of his immediate survival. At sea, he remains alert and attuned to the slightest atmospheric fluctuations.

Often, on a quiet night, I lay awake on the swaying deck and pondered the celestial stars and seafaring lore. Then my mind would drift into melancholy as I dreamed of Tempe waiting for me so far away, as patient as Penelope. An old verse would come to me in the whispering wind and lull me to sleep: *The moon has set and the Pleiades; it is midnight, and time goes by, and I lie alone.*[183]

On the last stage of our outbound voyage, Zephyros—the west wind—struck us from behind with an unexpected blast and rushed our ship, straining and creaking, toward its destination. I gave a sigh of relief as the Phoenician coastline came into view.

But my relief was short-lived. I held my breath again as the ship careened and bolted forth with alarming speed toward an offshore barrier of jagged rocks. At last, the captain calmly shouted for us to shorten sail, and the ship slowed almost to a stop. He ordered the oars mounted and we rowed the remainder of the way until safely in the harbor and moored at the dock.

Joppa is a bustling port on the crossroads of trade, connecting Asia and Africa with Hellas and other lands to the north and west. There, we spent a month making repairs, gathering supplies, and selling our merchandise to people of strange appearance and language. One evening, we stood near the ship, mesmerized by the exotic beauty of several Phoenician women who had come to shop.

An older sailor among us softly whispered that Joppa was the home of Andromeda herself—the lovely Phoenician maiden renowned from ancient times. There, just beyond the harbor, stood the jagged rocks hammered by the crashing surf of the relentless sea, where her heartless father had left her to die as a sacrifice to Poseidon.

That night, as I wearily lay on the swaying deck with eyes turned toward the heavens, the words of Pappos came to me and I listened again to the age-old tales:

Hellenic merchant ship, 1200-800 BC. Wooden model at the Museum of the Sea, Island of Ithaca. Photo by author.

# Chapter 18. HEROES OF AGES PAST

ORION STOOD TALL with the stature and strength of a hero. Phaethon ventured forth with the confident glow of youth. Bellerophon vanquished dark forces in desperate battle. But the three fell victim to the same invisible foe—their arrogance. They plummeted to their doom as punishment for their pride, as a mighty oak crashes to the forest floor.

They were not the only ones. Mortal women succumbed to the same vices as men. You have heard of Medusa, a monster so ghastly that those who looked upon her froze into cold and lifeless stone. But the wretched creature was once a young lady of radiant beauty. Her lovely form, flowing hair, and enchanting eyes shone like a goddess's and captured the gaze of men and women, of birds and beasts, of flowers and trees, and immortal beings.

Even Poseidon, god of the sea, could not resist her charms. From the salty surf he daily splashed ashore and, at a distance, followed her footsteps. Her allure captured his heart and conquered his mind until he yearned for nothing more. Desperately, madly, he became entranced by the maiden Medusa.

But the admiration of deities and men destroyed her. Her sweet smile slowly sank and became a haughty sneer. Before long, her pride proved so loathsome to the gods that Athena, who was also quite jealous, transformed Medusa into a gruesome ghoul.

Her fair form now slithered on the ground like a serpent. Her flowing hair writhed as a tangle of poisonous snakes. Her enchanting eyes withered all who beheld her, so that she never again looked upon joyful life without watching it decay into dreadful death.

In her new form, hatred consumed Medusa, poisoning her heart and blackening her blood. Day and night, she shouted bitter blasphemies at the gods but remained helpless to harm them. Instead, in hateful agony, she determined to murder any mortal who wandered within her dreary domain.

At last, in the seaport city of Argos, a trembling handful of heartbroken survivors came forward, forlorn, with heads held low in fear and sorrow. They had lost their loved ones, frozen forever in stone and condemned to stand as silent ornaments of anguish in Medusa's miserable lair. In despair, the survivors pleaded for the help of Perseus, a hero among them who shone with the unbound boldness of youth.

Together, they begged him to stalk and destroy the fiend. Perseus, the demigod son of Zeus and Danae, stepped forth without further thought, as heroes will do. In haste, he set off on the dangerous quest and tracked Medusa to her haunt. Drawing near, he cautiously stalked past pillar after pillar of stone-cold mortals who had all shared the same misfortune.

To avoid a similar fate, Perseus wielded an assortment of weapons given to him by the gods. A polished shield let him see Medusa's horrid reflection rather than confront her face-to-face. Small wings attached to his feet launched him fast in flight, and a magic helmet rendered him invisible to her sight. Upon reaching her lair, he took to the air and searched with keen eyes until he spied her reflection in his shield.

Then, like a storm, he burst down upon Medusa with a lightning sword. The monster swiftly spun toward the sound of the rushing wind. But she was unable to fix her eyes on him, and Perseus, with a single slash, severed her scaly neck.

The head thudded heavily on the ground, with glowering eyes wide open and serpent hair still writhing and snapping. Ever so carefully, he covered the lethal eyes and retrieved the head. In disgust, he dropped the loathsome trophy into a leather bag and made his winged departure through the air, far over the sparkling sea.

As the lifeblood flowed from Medusa's head, droplets from the blood-soaked bag fell and mingled with the seafoam far below. Poseidon mourned aloud and lamented the maiden's brutal punishment and cruel destruction. Unable to undo the dictates of fate, he decreed instead that Medusa's blood should join with his own seafoam to beget a beautiful being. For now that Perseus had released Medusa from her wretched existence, the god of the sea wished something good to come from the once-radiant woman he had loved. According to Poseidon's will, Pegasus, the winged horse, white as snow from muzzle to tail, was born of the blood and foam, and sprang from the salty sea.[184]

Meanwhile, Perseus rose in triumph on winged feet and soared for days and nights throughout the heavens, with the white-capped sea below and the approving gaze of the starry Pleiades above.[185] From his vantage point he beheld many strange and exotic kingdoms. In the far west he alighted in the land of the giant Atlas, whose wife, Hesperis, and daughters, the Hesperides, graced that tropical clime.

Perseus and the family fell into pleasant conversation. But alas, poor Atlas, more brawn than brain, spied the forbidden, blood-soaked bag. In one unguarded moment, with a curious peek at the hideous head and lethal eyes of Medusa, he froze into the North African mountain range that forever bears his name. With profuse apologies to Hesperis and her daughters, Perseus resumed his flight through the stars for three more days and nights. *Thrice did he see the cold Bears* in the northern sky, *and thrice the Crab's spreading claws* among the constellations.[186]

On the fourth day, while following his course above the shoreline of Joppa, a tiny object, far below, captured his attention. Circling downward for closer inspection, he discovered a maiden all alone and chained to the jagged rocks that jut out from the surging sea. Her delicate form stood fully exposed to the salty air and rising tide. In rapid descent, Perseus rushed to her side.

The silent girl, cold and apparently lifeless, was beautiful beyond perfection—the masterpiece, perhaps, of a sculptor inspired by the gods. But then *a light breeze stirred her locks and warm tears welled in her eyes.*[187] The maiden Andromeda, refreshed by the ocean air, shortly regained her senses. Startled at first by the stranger beside her, she soon set fear and shyness aside and told the young man her woeful tale.

Her mother Cassiopeia, much like Medusa, had boasted of her own flawless beauty. Cassiopeia, too foolish to realize how foolish she was, even claimed to outshine the Nereids, the lovely sea nymphs cherished by Poseidon.[188] The god of the sea seethed at the insult, but Cassiopeia remained self-absorbed and ignored his vengeful wrath. She failed to consider that it was Poseidon who punished wayward sailors on the storm-tossed seas. It was Poseidon who sent rumbling earthquakes and raging tsunamis to topple coastal towns and sink entire fleets of ships.

The indiscretion of Cassiopeia now prompted Poseidon to unleash Cetus, an amphibious Sea Monster, prodigious and deadly. The voracious creature ravaged the shore of Joppa, daily devouring unwary fishermen along with their boats and nets. He crunched the bodies and bones of shepherds and flocks who roamed the rocky coastal paths. In gluttony and greed, he even snatched screaming guards from atop the city walls.

At last, the husband of Cassiopeia—the weak-hearted Cepheus, king of Joppa—saw no choice but to appease Poseidon with a sacrifice of royal blood to the monster Cetus. Soon Cepheus settled on a suitable victim. Not himself,

that would never do, nor his overbearing wife who had caused the whole misfortune. Instead, he gave up their gentle, obedient daughter.

When the sobbing girl had finished her tale of impending doom, Perseus
looked up, startled to see the barnacle-encrusted beast already hurrying *toward its maiden-feast*.[189] The hero, smitten with love for Andromeda, promptly
prepared for battle. In a flash, he leapt into the sky with winged feet and a
gleaming sword in hand.

As soon as Cetus burst from the surface of the sea, Perseus attacked. Time
and again, from high to low, from front to back, from side to side, the hero
hacked and stabbed, gouging deep wounds while darting away before the
gaping jaws and gnashing teeth could snatch him from the air. At last, the
loathsome behemoth began to sway, sluggish from fatigue and loss of blood,
and collapsed with a deafening splash that almost engulfed the anxious
watchers crowded atop the city wall. With the grisly deed completed, Perseus
freed the fainting girl.

For many days and nights, the kingdom of Joppa reveled in Perseus' victory with joyful shouts and jubilation, and festive processions and songs. Andromeda, shy and silent, received a warm welcome amid petals of flowers
showered from the city wall. All the while, Cassiopeia, jealous of her daughter, pouted in the background, bewailing her own mistreatment that left her
ignored and unattended.

Although adored by her countrymen, Andromeda cared little for that, or
for anything other than Perseus. The two vowed to leave Joppa behind, and
side-by-side, begin a new life in the seaside city of Argos. Cepheus and Cassiopeia, red in the face, railed against the thought of their daughter marrying
the foreign youth. But Andromeda distrusted the judgment of those who had
sacrificed her to save themselves. With her mind made up, she took Perseus'
hand in hers.

Zeus, the proud father, saw much in PERSEUS that he admired, and honored his heroic son in the heavens. Among the stars, Perseus is clad in a sturdy
helmet and winged sandals, with a polished shield slung on his back. In his
right hand he raises a flaming sword. In the left he carries the ghastly head of
Medusa marked by a beam of light called GORGON. Behind the head trail
two stars of writhing serpent hair.[190]

To complete the scene, lovely ANDROMEDA swoons in her chains near
the hero's upraised sword. The SEA MONSTER, with gaping jaws, rises men-

acingly from the stars beneath her feet, rushing upward, propelled by its massive fins. CEPHEUS and CASSIOPEIA are there as well, forever watching the dreadful event from a cowardly safe distance.

Cepheus wears a felt cap that points forward in the Asian fashion of his country.[191] He recoils in horror at the sight of the approaching fiend. Cassiopeia, saucy and scantily clad, sits on the edge of her throne with arms upraised in suspense.

As punishment for the haughty queen, Zeus ordained that her constellation should turn head downward as she travels across the sky. In this awkward position, Cassiopeia can be neither proud nor modest. For *she headlong plunges like a diver* into the sea, as her stars set in the west.[192]

As for Pegasus, the winged horse that sprang from the sea became famous far and wide for his beauty and bravery. He often hurried to the aid of heroes involved in desperate quests. He carried Bellerophon aloft to vanquish the vicious Chimaera.

After Zeus dislodged the presuming youth from his back, Pegasus continued his ascent *and came to the immortals* on Mount Olympus.[193] On the shining summit that overlooks the world, he joined the livery of Zeus. Soon he served as the god's most trusted steed, bearing his flashing thunderbolts throughout the starry heavens.

Years later, when the mortal horse died, Zeus provided Pegasus with stars of his own. His constellation, simply called the HORSE, gallops swiftly with tremendous spirit through the sky. By his side, within easy reach of his muzzle, runs his favorite foal, Celeris.

During his earthly life, the sleek colt Celeris stood second only to Pegasus in splendor and speed. Celeris also displayed the wondrous traits of his distinguished maternal grandfather, Chiron the centaur. Among the stars, only the head of Celeris is visible as he joins his sire in their celestial race. For this reason, his constellation is called the HORSE HEAD.

In Argos, the love between Perseus and Andromeda grew profoundly with the passing years, and they brought many children into the world. Their oldest son, named Perses, became the eponymous ancestor of the Persians. Their other sons received renown as forebears of the Mycenaean kings of Hellas. One of these, Electryon, reigned justly over Argos. Electryon's daughter, Princess Alcmene, became Zeus' lover and bore him a son.

After the birth of the baby, Alcmene soon saw that her little boy, Heracles, was no ordinary child.[194] He quickly gained the strength of a grown man and showed stunning signs of his divine lineage by strangling poisonous serpents and performing other powerful deeds. Upon coming of age, Heracles followed in the heroic footsteps of his great-grandparents, Perseus and Andromeda.

Of all his amazing exploits, Heracles attained greatest fame for accomplishing the Twelve Labors, a series of seemingly impossible feats. The first labor required him to slay the Nemean Lion, a man-killer with a hide no weapon could pierce. The frightened villagers of Nemea, including nearby Kleones, had suffered dreadfully, with hundreds of lives lost to the bloodthirsty beast. The brutal Lion relished the taste of human flesh and found equal pleasure in the chase and the kill.

Many valiant warriors had tracked him down only to fall prey to his ripping claws and rending teeth. But Heracles remained undaunted. He had defeated a dozen lions with the help of his heavy club and arrows of bronze. With little trouble and less fear, he found the beast's lair, littered with bones and emitting a foul and suffocating stench. The Lion had no reason to hide his presence. He always welcomed another victim foolish enough to track him down.

As soon as Heracles entered the dreary den, he discerned the huge, shaggy hulk in the darkness and launched a volley of arrows in rapid succession. In dismay, he watched as each bounced off the impenetrable hide and clattered to the cold cavern floor. Furious at the brazen assault, the Lion lunged at Heracles with claws forward and fangs bared. As the two locked in a deadly embrace, the Lion slashed and snapped at his assailant time and again. But the powerful man held tight to the mane and slipped his muscular arms around the enormous neck, slowly choking the Lion's life away.

With the victory finally won, Heracles sat on the ground with a heavy thud and tended to his open wounds. After catching his breath, he skinned the Lion with its own sharp claws, the only tools that could sever the heavy hide. From that day on, the lionskin cloak became the hero's most treasured possession and trademark.[195]

Scarcely had the people of Nemea received the joyful news when Heracles was summoned to an equally trying task. The murky marsh of Lerna that lay near Argos had long been haunted by Hydra—the vile and vicious nine-headed swamp serpent. The monster was one of the ferocious offspring of the *terrible, outrageous, lawless* Typhon, who had once attempted to devour the gods.[196] From deep within her lair, the Lernaean Hydra slithered in ceaseless search of unwary wanderers.

For most of the day, Heracles struggled through the swamp in stagnant and slimy water up to his neck. He held a pine-torch high above his head to light a path through the forbidding fog and gloom. Suddenly he detected a slight ripple on the water. As he inched slowly forward, Hydra burst to the surface behind him. Heracles turned at once and swung his sword, severing one of her snapping heads. In horror, he watched as two more heads grew promptly in its place. Quickly he lopped off another, but again, two more emerged.

In desperation, he dispatched a third and thrust his torch onto the bleeding wound. The burning neck sizzled and boiled with a terrible stench, then fell with a splash, cauterized and lifeless. Hydra all the while struck with venomous fangs from every direction. But one at a time, Heracles managed to dismember and singe each neck.

When only three heads remained, Hydra's companion, the Crab, sidled through the mire, unseen. With piercing pincers, he tore a nasty gash in the hero's foot. Heracles shouted in pain as he brought the wounded limb crashing down to shatter the shell of the Crab. He then turned his full fury on Hydra and soon reduced the foe to one immortal head which could not be killed. This he cut off and concealed under a massive boulder, where it remains hidden to this day.[197]

As news of Heracles' prowess spread through the land, he received frantic calls to more dangerous missions. Among these was his fight with the foul, flesh-eating Stymphalian birds. The menacing, man-eating flock had descended on the people of the Peloponnesus like a dark and ominous cloud.

Day after day, the grim, ravenous birds gorged on men, women, and children, until none dared to venture outside their homes. Whole families began to die of starvation as they hid in terror under beds or blankets. Heracles rushed to the rescue. To aid him in the quest, he chose his strongest, straightest Arrow, dipped in the poisonous blood of Hydra.

Draping his lionskin over a shoulder to serve as a shield, he drew his bow and slayed first one bird and then another, retrieving his Arrow each time. By the end of the day, he had defeated most of the horrid fowl and chased the remainder far away. Now the starving people of Stymphalia emerged from cover, gaunt but grateful. With hoarse and feeble voices, they cheered their deliverer.

Heracles had little time to tarry, and pushed ahead to his final labors. In the land of the Hesperides there dwelt a Dragon named Draco, a gargantuan servant of the goddess Hera. Hera, the wife of Zeus, heartily despised Heracles because Zeus had sired him with another woman. She incessantly searched for ways to harm him, and Heracles responded in kind.

If Heracles could subdue her serpent, Draco, then he could help himself to the golden apples of the Hesperides—Hera's prized possessions. Hera had received the apple tree as a wedding gift when she married Zeus and proudly planted it in her garden on the African shore. Here it flourished under the constant care of Atlas' charming daughters—the Hesperides.[198] But the young maidens longed for the forbidden fruit, so Hera employed Draco as a more reliable watchman.

Draco, with his overpowering size and blazing eyes, proved to be one of Heracles' greatest opponents because he remained ever vigilant—never sleeping.[199] Still, the fearless hero bolted into the fray and wrestled the scaly serpent to the ground. With immense power, Draco writhed and attempted to wrap his attacker in coils and crush his life away.

All that day, the two struggled to gain a commanding grip until, at last, Heracles managed to pin the Dragon's slippery head to the ground. In an instant, he brought his heavy club down to shatter Draco's spine. As the serpent's lifeless body continued to wriggle and squirm, Heracles seized a branch from the apple tree, loaded with golden fruit, and made his departure.

Zeus applauded the astounding success of his stormy son. And when Heracles came to the end of his earthly days, the god placed him high in heaven with his other son—Perseus. In memory of one of Heracles' many battles, he appears clad in his lionskin cloak, kneeling in desperate struggle with Draco the DRAGON. His left foot pins the serpent's head while his right knee rests on the scaly back. His club hovers high, clutched in the right hand, ready to deliver the lethal blow.

Because of the position in which he is poised, the constellation of Heracles is called the KNEELER. Lurking far beneath him is HYDRA, who slithers through the stars with her one immortal head still intact. Heracles' other enemies—the crouching LION and the stealthy CRAB—also appear nearby in the nighttime sky, as does his trusty ARROW that he used to slay the Stymphalian Birds.

The honor that Zeus bestowed on Heracles, Perseus, and Andromeda showed that the gods are as quick to favor those who serve them and their fellow man as they are to punish the proud. These heroes' lives reflected courageous service without conceit. For this, they remain the most famous of mortals.

Heracles (Hercules) with Nemean Lionskin. Marble copy of a Greek original from the 4th century BC. National Archeological Museum, Magna Graecia, Naples, Italy. Photo by author.

The Nemean Lion's cave winds deep into the rugged rock. Kleones, Nemea, Greece. Photo by author.

# Chapter 19. A THIRST FOR ADVENTURE

PAPPOS WORDS REMAINED WITH ME as we completed our business at Joppa, emptying the products of Hellas from our ship's hold, and filling it with grain, dates, linens, spices, and other exotic and wonderful items from as far away as India. On the return voyage, stormy seas forced us to veer northward and hug the coast through pirate-infested waters off Tyre, Sidon, Cyprus, and Pamphylia. Once again, my aching heart longed to look for Bronte, though I realized the futility of holding onto a lost hope from long ago.

The crew pressed frantically forward to escape the dangerous waters, but often spied sails on the horizon and shifted course to avoid them. When, despite our efforts, we passed close to a foreign vessel, we armed ourselves with rusted javelins, swords, and shields stored in the hold, and stood alert on the deck to make a show of strength until safely away.

Anxious months passed as we slowly made headway through rolling waves. Every evening, we looked with longing at the sun as it set in the direction of home. Finally, we entered waters familiar to some of the men and sailed with lifted spirits across the Aegean Sea. The sight of Salamis and the coast of Attica brought hoarse cheers from the crew. Then, the Acropolis gleaming in the distance caused even the toughest sailors' eyes to glisten.

At Piraeus, we rested for a day before spending another half-month unloading the hold and refitting the ship. As we worked on the dock and walked in the port, our legs had to adapt to the steadiness of the earth. Happy was the day when I collected my pay, bought provisions in Athens, and began the walk toward home.

But a feeling of foreboding had nagged at me for the past six months. I had left my family in dire straits with withered crops, a meager store of grain, and a scrawny flock. And I could not remove the image of Pappos, Ama, and Bronte from my mind. As anxiety mounted, I pulled the load higher on my back and ran the final stades to the farm. With overwhelming relief, I found my family faring well. My son had taken good care of his mother and adapted to the drought by spending more time with fishing poles and traps along the coast.

I laughed to think that I returned from the sea to a continued diet of fish, but I had no complaints. Like me, my family had turned to the salty waters to seek a living. They fared so well that they often produced a surplus which they sold at the fish market in Rhamnous. I was proud and happily taken aback to find that my family could survive so well without me.

In another month, the rains came, and the drought finally began to break. We promptly prepared for a busy farming season. The money I had made at sea went to purchase iron for tools, and sheep and goats to bring the flock back to size. Our fortunes became less precarious and quickly improved. Three years after my return, our neighboring Thebans defeated the Spartans at Leuctra and ushered in a long-awaited period of peace that furthered our prospects of improving our means.

At home, at last, in my family's embrace and secure in my land of birth, the next twenty-five years flew faster than I could have imagined. With ample time together, we grew ever closer and valued our evenings around the hearth. I loved to tell stories of the rolling seas and strange lands in the east as my wife and son leaned forward to listen. During the day, my eyes followed migrating birds, drifting clouds, rolling waves, and the morning sun rising over the sea. At night, I watched the steady movement of stars and constellations and estimated the passage of time that led to the approaching day.

Frequent reflections on seafaring lore led my mind to Pappos, who loved to recall the ancient voyages of Odysseus and other intrepid wanderers of the wine-dark sea. One of his favorite tales was that of the Argonauts, the renowned crew that sailed the fifty-oared penteconter, the *Argo*, through unknown waters to distant and dangerous lands. Bronte and I had listened and watched with eyes opened wide as Pappos recounted the tale:

*Recalling the words of Pappos*

Heracles gained wide acclaim for completing the Twelve Labors, but he also searched for other far-flung adventures. On one such quest, he joined Jason's crew of Argonauts to sail the Aegean and Black Seas, and capture the Golden Fleece.[200]

Other heroes also committed themselves to the quest. The crew included Asclepius, the ship's physician; Orpheus, the famed musician; Peleus, the father of Achilles; Laertes, the father of Odysseus; the twin brothers, Castor and Polydeuces; Argus, the builder of the ship *Argo*; and Tiphys, the talented helmsman.

This excellent assembly of men embodied *arete*. Wherever they wandered, admiring throngs *marveled as they beheld the beauty and stature of the preeminent heroes*.[201] Beyond their physical form and noble bearing, they loomed large as men of learning. Some had even gained the gift of knowledge from the wise centaur, Chiron.

Like many enlightened mortals, they excelled in music as well. On more than one occasion, they *sang a hymn to the accompaniment of Orpheus' lyre in beautiful harmony, and round about them the windless shore was charmed by their singing.*[202] Above all, they stood tall as spiritual men who remained ever reverent and devoted to the deities.

The journey of the Argonauts arose from events that unfolded many years earlier in the kingdom of Thebes. The Theban queen had given birth to twins—a son and daughter named Phrixus and Helle. But the king abruptly sent his wife away at the insistence of his mistress, who soon wore the queen's crown.

The new queen despised her stepchildren and conspired to see them put to death so her own son would one day inherit the throne. To this end, she demanded that her husband sacrifice his own children. This, she claimed, would appease the deities that had sent a famine to plague the land. Day and night, the wicked queen screamed at the king to slay Phrixus and Helle and save the kingdom's starving subjects.[203]

At last, the king gave in to his wife's constant carping and commanded his royal servants to place the trembling children upon the pyre. All the while, the evil queen, sight unseen, sneered in the shadows. As the servants lit the loathsome fire, a splendid Ram with a Golden Fleece, sent by Hermes, suddenly darted through the chamber door.

Lowering his head, the Ram lifted the children onto his back and fled toward a safe haven in the east. Fast and far they flew. But as the Ram swam the swirling waters that divide Hellas from Asia, poor little Helle, frail and fainting, slipped into the gloomy depths and drowned. On her behalf, the inhabitants along the coast later named the channel Hellespont.

Phrixus grieved deeply for his twin sister and cried a shower of tears while clinging tightly to the Ram's woolly back. After a weary and woeful journey, the two arrived on the eastern shore of the Black Sea, at the port of Aea in the kingdom of Colchis. The exhausted Ram, his mission fulfilled, now performed his last selfless act by offering his body to Phrixus for a sacrifice to the gods.[204]

In obedience, the boy, with sorrow heaped on sorrow, made the somber offering. Then he placed the Ram's Golden Fleece in a sacred grove to serve as a shrine. There it hung in a *huge oak tree... like a cloud that glows red from the fiery beams of the rising sun.*[205]

Phrixus lived his remaining years in far-off Colchis, while Thebes and all of Hellas withered in drought, by divine decree, because of the horrid dead of the Theban king and queen that resulted in the death of Helle. Meanwhile, Phrixus' younger kinsman, Jason, was born to the king and queen of Iolcus, in Thessaly. When Jason was only an infant, his uncle usurped his father's throne and plotted to murder the child to secure his own spurious claim. But Jason was rushed to a cave for safekeeping and raised by the kindly centaur, Chiron.

Upon reaching adulthood, Jason returned to confront his uncle, the king. But the cunning uncle averted the young man's wrath and lured him into a dangerous quest that was sure to seal his doom. Jason brimmed with youthful boldness and could not say no to the venture.

The king and most of his subjects believed that the deadly drought would end and the land would flourish again if a champion could retrieve the Ram's Golden Fleece from Colchis. Thus, the cruel and crafty uncle silently schemed: If Jason somehow succeeded in returning the Fleece, then the kingdom would thrive. And if he died in the attempt, the king would be rid of a threat to his throne.

Jason surmised the king's motive but remained steadfast. In fact, he delighted at the chance for adventure and gladly accepted the task. Like him, his friends, the heroes of his generation, eagerly jumped at the opportunity and joined him in Iolcus.

Argus began to build a seaworthy ship for the distant journey. First, he crafted a keel of heavy oak and laid it on the sandy beach. To this he fastened beams and braces of hardwood and added heavy planking to hold back the furious slap of thundering waves.

He carved a stern that arched above from behind, and a stout bow that thrusted forward. He built a solid deck, then chose a mast that was sturdy and straight, and planed it to perfection. He stepped the mast into the hull and wedged it with a heavy hammer, then straightened it with stays, side to side, and fore and aft.

Now he fitted a yardarm to the mast, with blocks and halyards. He shaped a sail and sewed it, triple-stitched, so it would billow well and hold in a heavy gale. He furled the sail on the yardarm to await the launch while he fashioned a sturdy pair of steering oars and fifty more for rowing. He chose two stones for anchors and trailed them from the stern with tightly braided ropes. With these, the ship *Argo* could rest stern-to-beach and not drift off with the ebb and flow of the tide.[206]

As Argus assembled the ship, Jason trained the crew and assigned them specific tasks. At sea, Tiphys would steer from the stern while Lynceus watched from the bow. The others would work the sail when days were fine and the wind blew from behind. At other times, all hands would man the oars and row ahead toward distant shores.

Tiphys would take up the critical task of steering the ship because he was *expert in predicting rising waves on the broad sea; expert too in predicting storm winds, and in determining a course by sun or star.* His lookout, Lynceus, whose name means *lynx-like,* would aid in navigation. He had the eyes of a lynx, the keenest vision of the crew.[207] Day and night he would search the sea and sky for telltale signs, with eyes squinted against gusts of wind and glare upon the water.

On making landfall late in the day on a foreign shore, the men would secure the ship and scout for danger. Once assured of safety, some would scoop up leaves for bedding while others picked up piles of wood. Two would take up the task of sparking a fire by *twirling sticks* between their palms.[208] These men also served as cooks—a most important post. Their success or failure meant the difference between a healthy, happy crew, or one that grumbled with stomachs growling.

With the ship and restless men ready to go, and the sea rising to high tide, the time came at last to launch the *Argo.* Under blue skies and fair winds, the crew winched and shoved the heavy wooden hulk from the sandy beach into the swelling surf. Then they steadied the ship and *drew the sail to the top of the mast and let it down from there. A whistling breeze fell upon it, and on the deck, they wound the lines separately around the polished cleats and calmly sped past the long Tisaean headland. A steady wind bore it ever onward.*[209]

When the wind slackened that afternoon, the men bent to the oars. *Rowing proceeded tirelessly* as they plied the frothy waters of the Aegean Sea. At last, they left Hellas behind in their wake as a hazy sliver on the western horizon.[210]

The trip began well, but trouble soon followed. One day, while seeking supplies on the island of Lemnos, Heracles' faithful companion failed to return to camp. Heracles searched frantically for him along the shore and deep into the forest. Through the night and well past dawn he persisted, but all in vain.

*Soon the morning star rose above the highest peaks, and the breezes swept down. And at once Tiphys urged them to board and take advantage of the wind. In their eagerness they boarded right away, drew the ship's anchors up on deck, and pulled back on the halyards. The sail bulged in the middle from the wind, and far out from the shore they joyfully were being borne.*[211]

Only after the island was far behind them did the men discern the absence of Heracles. Above and below the deck, they searched but found no trace. Downtrodden, they saw no option but to keep the course determined by the wind and continue without him.

As the crew probed into foreign waters and ran ashore on strange islands, they encountered many dangers. Often, they battled with hostile bands that resented their bold intrusion. And when they entered the tempestuous strait of the Hellespont and the turbulent waters of the Sea of Marmara, the weather turned against them. The men grew weak and weary at the oars as they fought their way for days through lashing waves and heavy swells.

At last, they beached the ship, staggered ashore, and collapsed in the sand. For twelve days and nights they rested and recovered their strength while waiting for the storm to subside. On the last evening, a halcyon shore bird hovered above the drenched and dejected men as they sat in the soggy sand near the *Argo*. The halcyon arrived as a favorable sign, sent by Rhea, to herald fair weather for sailing. For this, the men offered grateful praise.[212]

Rhea is the daughter of Gaea — Mother Earth. As such, Rhea holds a degree of control over earth, wind, and sea. She is also the mother of Zeus, Poseidon, Pluto, and other powerful gods. To be in her good graces is no small matter, and so she must be appeased. Most people believe she dwells among the Phrygians when she walks upon the Earth. As fate would have it, the Argonauts had found safe haven from the storm on the Phrygian coast near Cyzicus, in the shadow of Mount Dindymum.

Before resuming the journey, the men carved a wooden likeness of Rhea and carried it up the mountain slope on their shoulders. They stood it in a sacred grove of ancient oaks and stacked flat stones for an altar. Upon placing wreaths of oak leaves on their heads, the men offered Rhea a savory sacrifice.

Jason prayed and poured libations while Orpheus taught the men to perform the leaping dance in armor while beating their swords against their shields, in the manner of Phrygians who worship the matron goddess. Rhea's closest companions, the Corybantes, praise her in similar ways as they shout and twirl the whirring rhombus and beat the resounding tympanum.[213]

When the Argonauts received further signs that Rhea had blessed their voyage, the men's spirits soared. They gladly returned to the oars and worked their way through the Sea of Marmara and the narrow passage of the Bosporus.[214] After many days, the arduous outbound journey ended at the distant port of Aea in Colchis, on the farthest reach of the Black Sea.

But there they faced fierce opposition. Aeetes, the king of Colchis, raged within when he heard that Jason intended to take the Golden Fleece to Hellas. The Fleece epitomized the glory and pride of his kingdom. It hung high in the holiest place, and its value surpassed that of his total treasury.

Still, Aeetes quickly assessed the tough and determined Hellenic crew that had come so far to tower before him. He feared the result of an outright rejection. Instead, he freely offered the Fleece to Jason if the youth would only succeed at a simple test of strength and skill.

All Jason had to do was lash a heavy oak-tree yoke atop the bulging necks of two enormous, fire-breathing bulls, then force the team to plow a furrow. Next, he needed to plant the teeth of a dragon and slay the angry army of men that would sprout forth from the dreadful seeds.

Rather than wagging his head and slinking away as most men would do, Jason shrugged his shoulders, accepted the challenge, and pondered the best way to bring it about. From a nearby balcony, the king's sorceress daughter, Medea, witnessed the wager while her longing eyes followed Jason's every move. To her, Jason looked like Sirius, the shining star, the most luminous of all, *which rises beautiful and bright to behold*.[215] Medea, the enchantress, had become the enchanted.

Throughout the night, the anxious crew remained awake and watched the constellations of the Bear and mighty Orion. As these stars crossed the sky, the men marked the passage of time until the dreaded contest at dawn. Meanwhile, Medea came to Jason in darkest night to reveal her love and to offer help with the deadly tasks.[216] First, she handed him an ointment that would repel the fiery breath of the bulls. Then she described how he should defeat the dragon-tooth warriors by simply throwing a stone among them.

Enthralled by the love of the softhearted sorceress and encouraged by the knowledge he now possessed, Jason prepared for the contest with glowing confidence. At dawn, when the laughing king unleashed the bulls, Jason stepped forward, impervious to the flames that roared from their mouths.

Promptly, he yoked them and forced them to plow a furrow while he sowed the seeds of dragon teeth. While he waited and watched for the fearsome army to rise from the field like so many stalks of grain, he swelled with courage in the way of the warrior. *He flexed his knees to make them nimble, and filled his great heart with prowess, raging like a boar*.[217] Firmly he planted his feet and faced the *earthborn men* as they sprang forth to battle. As Medea had in-structed, Jason hefted a heavy rock and hurled it among them. At once, they fell into confusion and turned on each other in furious slaughter. Jason now bolted forward, *as when a fiery star springs forth from heaven bearing a trail of light*. In a flash, he vanquished the remaining foes.[218]

Aeetes shuddered, aghast at Jason's baffling success. But he was far from ready to concede defeat. Instead, the deceitful king delayed and offered to hand him the Fleece the following day. Then he secretly rallied his royal army and prepared to overpower the band of Hellenes.

Again, Medea intervened. That night, she used a spoken charm and a po-tion of her own concoction to drug the great snake that guarded the Fleece in the sacred grove.[219] As the serpent fell into peaceful sleep, she showed the en-dangered crew the way to escape unseen with the Golden Fleece.

With Aeetes' army hot on their heels, the Argonauts flew to the ship and fled by sea. They brought Medea aboard as well, to protect her from her wrath-ful father. Heading swiftly westward, they crossed the stormy seas and straits for many days and came at last to Hellas with their hard-earned prize.

Not long later, Jason deposed his uncle with the help of Medea and came to reign as the rightful ruler of Iolcus. The Argonaut crewmen, the heroes and friends, now parted to pursue further valiant adventures in their own native lands.

For his selfless service and sacrifice, the RAM received a place in heaven. Among the stars, he is seen swimming the Hellespont with his Golden Fleece just visible above the surface of the sea. His bright muzzle turns back over his shoulder as he watches a guiding astral light, and his horns dip downward.[220] Now his Fleece shines for the enjoyment of every earthly being, rather than for one greedy king.

The ship ARGO also attained an eternal course in the stars, where it navi-gates the celestial mists of the Milky Way. Its steering oars propel it forward, and its stern arches stately overhead. The *Argo's* prow is concealed in the fog as it ventures into uncharted skies to the south.[221]

Some of the Argonauts gained the same acclaim for their service to gods and fellow sailors while on the voyage. Orpheus, *the father of songs, and widely praised minstrel*, carried his seven-stringed Lyre aboard to offer inspiration and entertainment during the distant journey.[222] The immortals themselves had entrusted this most excellent musical instrument to him.

When Hermes, the messenger god, was but a baby, the precocious child, in search of a toy, crafted the Lyre from a tortoise shell and a pair of sacred cattle horns. Apollo was not pleased when he heard that the horns had come from one of his own beloved bulls. But Hermes quickly averted his anger by handing him the sweet-sounding Lyre—the first of all stringed instruments.

Apollo, the god of the sun and the arts, beamed with delight. He cherished the Lyre and carried it constantly with him. Then, one day, he gave the instrument to his true love, Calliope, as an expression of his affection.

Calliope, the Muse of epic poetry, soon discovered that the Lyre provided a perfect rhythmic companion to recitations of the stories of old. It proved to be of further worth as an accompaniment to singing, in happy harmony. Later, when Calliope's son, Orpheus, showed an amazing aptitude for music, she passed the instrument down to him.

In his talented hands, the Lyre offered a delightful addition to sacred songs and epic stories. Thus, in all the ages to follow, every bard of ability has plucked the vibrant strings of a lyre while reciting the tales of Homer and other notable poets.

With the divine instrument carefully cradled in his hands, Orpheus performed stories and songs so enchanting that he wooed the wild beasts that wandered the woods. He even *charmed the hard boulders on the mountains and the course of rivers with the sound of his songs. And the wild oak trees, signs still to this day of his singing, flourish on the Thracian shore... where they stand in dense, orderly rows... charmed by his Lyre*.[223]

At the bidding of Chiron, Jason had invited Orpheus to join the Argonauts. The musician immediately proved his worth. On the very first day, he revealed how the Lyre offered a steady rhythm for rowers. The instrument also served to calm frayed nerves, ruffled by the rigors of the voyage.

Once, when conflict broke out between two members of the crew, Orpheus grabbed the Lyre in his gifted hands and began to sing a soothing song. *He sang of how the earth, sky, and sea, at one time combined together in a single form... and of how the stars and moon and paths of the sun always keep their fixed place in the sky; and how the mountains arose; and how the echoing rivers with their nymphs and all the land animals came to be.*[224]

The crew, suddenly entranced in silent stares with mouths opened in awe, watched and listened to the minstrel and lost all thought of strife. Merrily, they continued their course.

On the return journey, the crew succumbed to the eerie enchantment of the sweet-voiced Sirens. These seductive, deadly sea nymphs lived on a rocky island and lured the sailors of passing ships. Their irresistible song drew many men into dangerous shoals and sent them and their ships to a watery grave.

Fate proved even worse for those who made landfall among the *femmes fatales*. In their loving, lethal embrace, men languished and slowly died.

Even the Argonauts could not resist their charms. *Already they were about to cast the cables from their ship onto the beach*. But *Orpheus... strung his Bistonian Lyre in his hands and rung out the rapid beat of a lively song, so that at the same time the men's ears might ring with the sound of his strumming*. The Lyre promptly overpowered the song of the Sirens, and *the Zephyr and the resounding waves, rising astern, bore the ship onward*, and far away to safety.[225]

At journey's end, Orpheus returned to his native land. There, a throng of impassioned women fell in love with the famous bard, as often befalls musicians and poets. When he performed and *beat the ground rapidly with his shining sandal to the accompaniment of his beautifully strummed Lyre and song*, they swooned and became flushed in frenzy.[226] Finally, a mob of spellbound women, in jealous rage for his affections, tugged on him until they tore him limb from limb.

Orpheus figured foremost among men as the first of mortal musicians, and a gifted poet and prophet. Having received his inspiration directly from the Muses and his instrument as a gift from the gods, no human was ever able to match his musical skill. Zeus honored Orpheus—his grandson through his daughter Calliope—by granting the LYRE a prominent place in the sky, marked by one of the brightest of stars. For, as Homer truly said so long ago: *among all men that are upon the earth minstrels win honor and reverence*.[227]

One of Orpheus' shipmates, Asclepius, served as physician and surgeon on the *Argo*. During the long and perilous voyage, he preserved the health and welfare of the men. Asclepius had learned the medicinal use of plants from Chiron and carried his own herbarium aboard.[228] To this he added flora found in foreign lands along the route whenever their botanical properties proved of worth.

He also applied the means of healing that he had learned in Hellas. As a youth, he watched the mysterious methods of slithering snakes and studied their amazing restorative traits. For ages, the wise and wily creatures had devised incredible cures, such as shedding their skins for annual rejuvenation. But they kept their knowledge closely concealed from prying eyes.

Asclepius came to respect and befriend them, and often observed their ways. He even adopted, as his medical symbol, a serpent coiled around a staff.[229] Other mortals also esteemed the wisdom of snakes and entrusted them as guardians of sacred temples, shrines, and springs. The Athenians kept a sizable snake on the crest of the Acropolis for this purpose and fed it a monthly fare of honey cake.[230]

Asclepius became so absorbed in the healing arts that he overstepped his human bounds. After his return from Colchis, he heard that Theseus' son, Hippolytus, had died without warning. To console the tragedy-stricken father, Asclepius rallied all of his awesome powers and brought them to bear on Hippolytus' lifeless body. With firm focus and patient persistence, he brought the lad back to the land of the living.

But Zeus was angry. How dare Asclepius delve into the realm of the gods! In one impetuous moment, Zeus' thunderbolt darted down to earth and dashed away the life of the famed physician.

Then, in a fit of remorse, the flighty god commemorated Asclepius' astounding service to humankind by placing him and his favorite serpent in the sky. Asclepius appears in starry splendor as the SNAKE HOLDER and gently grasps the SNAKE in his caring hands. In this way, the symbol of medicine is forever portrayed at night. And to this day, physicians with healing hands take the Hippocratic Oath in the name of Asclepius.

Two more Argonauts, known as the twins—Castor and Polydeuces—earned a place in heaven for their lasting love for one another and for other mortals and gods. Out on the open ocean, the Twins amazed the crew with their uncanny skills of navigation. They often assisted Tiphys and Lynceus in finding a favorable route.

The Argonauts also admired the Twins' devotion to the divine and called on them as intercessors for safety at sea. During one especially fierce and frightening storm, as the disheartened men fell on the deck in despair, the Twins *stood up and raised their hands to the immortals and prayed*. Slowly, the tempest subsided and the reassured crew returned to their duties.[231]

Castor and Polydeuces served the Argonauts with such devotion that Zeus *entrusted them with ships of future sailors as well*.[232] Thus, seafarers through the ages, when seeking reassurance, have looked to the constellation of the Twins, with its two bright stars that mark their heads.[233] For added protection in open waters, mariners paint or carve icons of the two men on the bows of their ships. And when two fiery balls of light blaze on the masthead toward the end of a storm at sea, reverent seamen thank the Twins for their sign of assurance that all is well.[234]

The Twins helped the Argonauts find their way back home to Hellas through the same intuition that had helped them find each other as children.

Whenever the toddlers wandered apart, they searched with tearful eyes until, at a distance, one saw the other and hurried to a happy embrace.

As adults, they remained the best of friends and grew old together. But one day, many years after returning from Colchis, Castor failed to wake up in the morning. His soul had left his aged body and slipped away in the night.

Polydeuces was lost in loneliness and grief. His vision blurred and his hearing became muffled. His mind wandered in aimless confusion as if in a fog on a trackless sea. For days, months, and years he mourned and prayed to the gods to restore his brother or take his life.

At last, Polydeuces' soul ascended and reunited with Castor in perfect peace. Among the stars they stand side-by-side, together forever as constant companions with arms around each other's shoulders. Polydeuces stands slightly behind and to the right of Castor, while Castor extends his left arm out as if pointing the way through a narrow passage at sea.

As a constellation, the TWINS reflect the love and devotion they held for each other, and for mortals and immortals alike. Among the stars, they personify *arete,* and all that Hellenes hold dear.

Ram (Aries) depicted on the *Farnese Atlas* Celestial Globe. See Appendix 3. National Archeological Museum, Magna Graecia, Naples, Italy. Photo by author.

Argo (Argo Navis) depicted on the *Farnese Atlas* Celestial Globe. See Appendix 3. National Archeological Museum, Magna Graecia, Naples, Italy. Photo by author.

# Chapter 20. THE LONG ROAD HOME

MY GRANDSON, PAIS, had long since fallen asleep by the campfire as I reminisced aloud through the night and recalled Pappos' timeless tales. Dawn was now at hand with a hint of purple on the eastern horizon, and the phantoms in the shadows had fled. For a moment, I pondered how the anxieties of life are like phantom wolves that haunt the dark recesses of the mind, snarling and snapping, and forcing fears from the past into the present. Then I realized how readily our loving thoughts and memories can put phantoms to flight.

My heart welled within as I felt the enduring love that bound me to my little family, and my grandparents and brother who awaited me in spirit. But a deep sense of melancholy remained. I felt that something was left undone; that some unfinished business beckoned to me in my old age and weighed heavily on my heart.

With a growing, undefined sense of urgency, I called to Pais, threw dirt on the dying coals, and made an opening in the brushy pen to free the flock. Together, we drove the lead billy goat toward home with the others following close behind. Pais cheerfully piped his flute along the way and made the return trip seem shorter than the hurried hike of yesterday.

Tempe threw open the door and ran to us with tearful relief as soon as she heard the flute and the bleating flock. To her surprise, as soon as we penned the goats and sheep, I placed Pais safely in her arms and replenished my provisions of food and water. With a brief explanation, I assured her of my return in a day or two, then headed toward my old homeplace, fifty-one stades away. Her face revealed bewilderment at the sorrow she saw in my eyes, and at my haste to reach the very place I had refused to visit for fifty-five years.

Thoughts of Pappos hurried my shuffling feet along the path. He had always emphasized the oneness of family and how we should honor and remember each other. I had failed him in so many ways.

Unable to bear the grief, I had often shut him out of my mind along with Ama and Bronte. But now I thought of the homestead standing neglected, and the graves overgrown. The woods that enfolded our childhood paradise had not heard laughter for many years, and our family altar stood alone and forlorn.

As I pressed northwestward along the coastal road, old landmarks became familiar, though trees appeared larger, and the path diverted to avoid deepening ruts. By afternoon, I came upon the dilapidated remains of our home, and the scorched mud brick that still stood in lonely vigil over the path that led to the graves of Pappos and Ama.

Digging through brush and vines, I found the stone markers so tenderly placed there sixty-five years ago. As I lay beside my loved ones on a thick layer of leaves and closed my eyes, their reassuring voices returned to me as if they had only been gone a day. My heart was soothed by the beautiful memories and the peacefulness of the place.

At last, I awoke. I had fallen asleep as the sun slipped toward the western horizon. Pulling myself up, I dusted off and walked for more than a stade to the family altar.

The ancient oaks seemed darker and drearier than I recalled, and moss grew heavy on the altar stones. As I brushed away leaves and lifted a small slab, a feeling of disbelief swept over me. The little holm oak wreath that Pappos had made, and I had placed there so many years ago, still rested beneath the stone. Most of the leaves were gone and some of the twigs had broken free from their braids, but the wreath still held tight in a circle.

My trembling hand slowly reached for the precious wreath that had last been worn by Bronte. But my fingers withdrew for fear of disturbing its peaceful repose. Years of unspoken sorrow now welled within. I crumpled to my knees alongside the altar, shaking like a leaf in the breeze. Tears flowed hot on my cheeks as I wailed aloud for the loss of my brother, and my negligence of his memory.

But the words of Pappos came to my mind and made me long for the joyful reunion that would follow this woeful life on Earth. I now resolved to dismiss the tragic memories of the past and embrace the beautiful thoughts of my family at home, and the grandparents and brother I would someday see again. Soon, we would rejoice in eternal oneness.

As I wiped away tears and gently reached again for the hallowed wreath, a gnarled hand appeared alongside my own and lifted the circle of twigs from its resting place. I jumped with alarm and spun around to see who had slipped beside me in the lonely grove. My eyes blinked with wonder as I stared in shock at an image of my own likeness—with hazel eyes, a weathered brow, and snow-white hair flying free. Between heavy sobs I could only manage to utter the words: *Bronte, you are home.*

My knees collapsed as I fell into Bronte's arms. We embraced with all our remaining strength and refused to let go. Burrowing our faces into each other's shoulders, we wept for joy. Then we wept for the sorrow of so many lost years. Then we wept for joy again.

As the sun set, we slowly calmed our frayed emotions and rested beside the altar. In a soft and weary voice, Bronte revealed how he had been shackled as a child, thrust into the filthy hold of a ship, and sold as a slave in Pamphylia. He worked his life away laboring for another man's gain in the fields of a large estate. But the greatest distress came from the loss of his grandparents and brother, and the later death of his enslaved wife and child who had perished of fever many years ago.

Two years had now passed since his master died, and before the master's heartless son could seize control of the estate, Bronte fled. Slowly, he worked his way westward while following the setting sun and the star of evening called Hesperos—the one we call *the herdsmen's star* because it leads shepherds safely home.[235]

Bronte remained hidden by day and stealthily slipped through forested mountains in the darkness of night. He lived off the land or stole provisions to survive until he reached the Ionian colonies of Hellas. There, in old age, he worked on the docks for months before finding passage across the Aegean Sea to Attica.

Arriving at last in the bustling port of Piraeus, he remained at a loss to continue. He suffered from trauma that had haunted him since the age of ten. Sixty-five years in foreign lands speaking strange tongues had erased his mind of the place names of his native home. One day, a man took pity on him and listened intently to his tragic tale. He judged by Bronte's faint accent and vague descriptions of childhood that he came from the backcountry of northern Attica.

After loading his knapsack with food and a blanket, the kind-hearted man directed Bronte to his own friends in Oropus, hoping they could help him find his home. As Bronte wandered the coastal path toward town, landmarks seemed familiar. He followed them with improving recognition until he became confident of the rock formations and trails that led him home.

From the sad remains of the homestead, he found his way to the altar—the sacred spot he had often envisioned as a slave. Under Asian skies, he had gazed upon the same constellations. And through all the years of enslavement far across the sea, his mind still wandered home on quiet nights as he recalled Pappos' stories of the stars.

Bronte had remained near the homestead for more than a month, lost to the world and living off the land, until the day he heard loud lamentations coming from the altar in the old oak grove. Creeping warily through the woods, he finally found me.

We sat together as the night grew dark and watched the stars as they rose above the sparkling sea. We recalled Pappos' oft repeated words about how we must always stand by each other, and beyond that, our devotion should reach to family, friends, and strangers; to creatures of farm and forest; to the woodland nymphs and immortal gods, and the mysterious source of all creation. For, in spirit we are one, created to live in love.

At that moment, Bronte pointed a wavering finger at two bright stars that rose above the glittering Aegean Sea. As he framed them with the little wreath he softly whispered: *The Twins!*

¹ The Hellenes personified dawn as the goddess Eos. Homer often described her as *rosy-fingered Dawn* in the *Iliad* and *Odyssey*.

² Plato, *Timaeus*, in *The Dialogues of Plato*, translated by B. Jowett (New York: Random House, 1937), section 26.

³ One stade measured about 606 feet, so forty-eight stades measured 5.5 miles. See stade measurements in Appendix 1, Glossary.

⁴ Homer, *Iliad*, translated by A. T. Murray and William F. Wyatt (Cambridge: Harvard University Press, 1999), 8.555.

⁵ The forty-eight classical constellations and their associated stories depicted human and divine interaction that portrayed a code of ethics—a lesson for proper living. The code may be summarized from ancient Greek sources as follows: Honor and serve gods and fellow mortals to promote peace and harmony, and avoid arrogance and greed that breed divisiveness and strife.

⁶ Constellation, asterism, and star names are capitalized, and appear in all-capital letters when referring to their place in the sky.

⁷ *Arete* is the Greek word αρετη.

⁸ Homer said of the *great-hearted Erechtheus* that Athena *settled* him in her *own rich shrine*, which suggests some validity to the tradition that Erechtheus was buried at the temple on the Acropolis. [Homer, *Iliad*, 2.547.]

⁹ The *Charioteer of Delphi* once stood in the Temple of Apollo at Delphi. See illustration at *https://davidwestonmarshall.com/ancient-skies/*

¹⁰ Five of the Caryatids are now preserved in the Acropolis Museum while reproductions stand in their place at the Erechtheum. The sixth Caryatid stands alone in the British Museum, near the Elgin Marbles.

¹¹ The manger is marked by the open star cluster now called Praesepe, which is the Latin word for *manger*.

¹² Piscis Austrinus is marked by the bright star Fomalhaut.

¹³ Apollonius Rhodius, *The Argonautica*, translated by William H. Race (Cambridge: Harvard University Press, 2008), 4.933.

¹⁴ Homer, *Iliad*, 20.233.

¹⁵ See illustration at *https://davidwestonmarshall.com/ancient-skies/*

¹⁶ Homer, *Iliad*, 9.496.

¹⁷ In ancient Greek, the word *lightning* is αστραπη and *thunder* is βροντη.

¹⁸ Gorgo was the monster Medusa. Her hideous head appeared on the Aegis, and on the bronze shields of Athenian soldiers.

¹⁹ Apollonius Rhodius, *Argonautica*, 3.117.

[20] Democritus believed that humans learned the art of building mud and straw homes from swallows. He said: *We are pupils of the animals in the most important things.* The barn swallow (*Hirundo rustica*) is a species of ancient origin. It is also global, inhabiting six continents. It is frequently mentioned in archaic and classical Greek literature, and continues to draw admiration with its graceful acrobatics. [Democritus, quoted by Plutarch, translated by Kathleen Freeman, *Ancilla to the Pre-Socratic Philosophers* (Cambridge: Harvard University Press, 1962), p. 106, fragment 154; Hermann Diels, *Die Fragmente der Vorsokratiker* (Berlin: Weidmann, 1964), vol. 2, p. 173.]

[21] Homer, *Odyssey*, translated by A. T. Murray and George E. Dimock (Cambridge: Harvard University Press, 1995), 5.488.

[22] Hesiod, *Works and Days*, in *Theogony; Works and Days; Testimonia*, translated by Glenn W. Most (Cambridge: Harvard University Press, 2006), 336.

[23] Homer, *Odyssey*, 14.414.

[24] Hesiod, *Works and Days*, 724, 737, 740.

[25] Apollonius Rhodius, *Argonautica*, 4.264.

[26] Plato, *Timaeus*, section 77.

[27] Hesiod, *Works and Days*, 461.

[28] Hesperos, the evening star, looked like Phosphoros, the morning star, but they never shone in the sky on the same day. In the sixth century BC, Pythagoras recognized that the two were one and the same—the planet Aphrodite (now called Venus). Venus orbits relatively close to the sun and may appear either in the morning or evening. The planet is the third-brightest object in the sky, after the sun and moon, and can cast shadows on Earth on a moonless night. It is little wonder, then, that the ancient Hellenes revered the morning and evening celestial lights.

[29] Sappho, *Fragments*, in *Greek Lyric I*, translated by David Campbell (Cambridge: Harvard University Press, 1982), fragment 104.

[30] Hesiod, *Works and Days*, 623.

[31] Hesiod admitted that sailing a boat for trade sometimes proved necessary. Otherwise, he disapproved of seagoing commerce, saying: *Do not put all your means of life in hollow boats.* He frowned upon those who burdened their boats with trade goods out of greed for material possessions, even at the risk of drowning. He said that, to them, *property is life.* [Hesiod, *Works and Days*, 633, 689.]

[32] The Athenian polis, or city-state, included the city of Athens and the surrounding countryside of Attica.

[33] Homer, *Iliad*, 18.249.

[34] Hesiod, the rustic shepherd and farmer, gained wide acclaim as a poet and philosopher. The place where he received inspiration, on the slopes of Mount Helicon, also became famous. The location was known through the ages as the home of the Muses, where throngs of devoted pilgrims erected altars, porticos, theaters, and sculptures. The site became known as the Mouseion—the original Museum. [Hesiod, *Theogony*, in *Theogony; Works and Days; Testimonia*, translated by Glenn W. Most (Cambridge: Harvard University Press, 2006), 22; Albert Schachter, *Cults of Boiotia* (London: University of London, Institute of Classical Studies. 1986), vol. 2.]

[35] Plato, *Timaeus*, sections 47, 80.

[36] Apollonius Rhodius, *Argonautica*, 1.1132.

[37] Sappho, *Fragments*, 50.

[38] Pausanias, *Description of Greece*, translated by W. H. S. Jones (Cambridge: Harvard University Press, 1955), 10.24.

[39] Sappho, *Fragments*, 44.

[40] Ibid, 2, 44.

[41] Shepherds typically grazed their flocks in the uplands and mountains for six months, *from spring to the rising of Arcturus* on about September 17. After that, they brought them down for winter. [Sophocles, *Oedipus Tyrannus*, in *Ajax; Electra; Oedipus Tyrannus*, translated by Hugh Lloyd-Jones (Cambridge: Harvard University Press, 1994), 1137.]

[42] Hesiod, *Works and Days*, 225.

[43] Hesiod, *Theogony*, 378.

[44] Aratus, *Phaenomena*, in *Callimachus; Lycophron; Aratus*, translated by G. R. Mair (Cambridge: Harvard University Press, 1955), 107.

[45] In ancient Hellas, the heliacal rising of Vindemiatrix marked the beginning of the grape harvest on approximately September 13.

[46] The nine Muses—daughters of Zeus and Mnemosyne (Memory)—included Calliope (Muse of epic poetry), Clio (history), Erato (lyric and love poetry), Euterpe (instrumental music, and inventor of the flute and woodwinds), Melpomene (tragic drama), Polyhymnia (singing and oratory), Terpsichore (dance), Thalia (comedic drama), and Urania (astronomy). These represent the enlightened accomplishments of humans that transcend the tangible and mundane. History and astronomy are aptly included, as they represent a broadened human perspective in time and space, and like the arts, open the mind to a more meaningful existence.

[47] Pegasus had also danced in mirth and ecstasy in company with the Muses on Mount Helicon. During an especially robust prance, he pierced the ground

from which arose a sparkling stream, known thereafter as the Hippocrene. The name literally translates as fountain of the horse. The fountain served as a source of sustenance and poetic inspiration for the Muses and Hesiod.

48 Apollonius Rhodius, *Argonautica*, 1.553.

49 Heracles is also known by the Roman name Hercules.

50 Aratus, *Phaenomena*, 130.

51 Homer, *Iliad*, 11.152.

52 During the Bronze Age and Archaic past, Hellas maintained amicable trade relations with Phoenicia and other Asian provinces. This prolonged contact allowed Hellas to adopt many beneficial aspects of Asian culture, especially after the Hellenic colonization of the eastern Aegean, Mediterranean, and Black Sea islands and coastlines. The ensuing cultural amalgamation contributed to the height of Hellenic Classical civilization, although Hellas and Persia fought bitterly in the sixth, fifth, and fourth centuries BC.

53 Homer, *Iliad*, 1.3.

54 Aesop, *Fables,* in *Babrius and Phaedrus*, compiled by Babrius, translated by Ben Edwin Perry (Cambridge: Harvard University Press, 1965), Fable 79: The Dog and the Shadow.

55 Herodotus, *The Histories*, translated by Robin Waterfield (Oxford: Oxford University Press, 1998), 1: sections 1–4.

56 Homer, *Odyssey*, 1.1.

57 Centuries later, sailors renamed the island Sicily.

58 Zeus had designated *fertile Sicily to be the best of the fruitful earth*. [Pindar, *Nemean Odes*, in *Nemean Odes; Isthmian Odes; Fragments*, translated by William Race (Cambridge: Harvard University Press, 1997), 1.15.]

59 Apollonius Rhodius, *Argonautica*, 4.964.

60 The Persian Empire is also known as the Achaemenid Empire.

61 Herodotus, *Histories*, 1: section 4.

62 Ibid, 5: sections 97-102.

63 Mardonius was also Darius' nephew.

64 Herodotus, *Histories*, 6: sections 43-45.

65 Eleven years later, the Euboeans, thirsting for revenge, were able to assemble an army of six hundred hoplite warriors to fight against the Persians at Plataea.

66 Herodotus, *Histories*, 6: sections 94-117.

67 Ibid, 7: section 150.

68 Ibid, 7: section 82.

[69] Today, the pass is about five miles wider due to a lower sea level and sedimentary deposits from the mountains and hot springs.

[70] Herodotus, *Histories*, 7: sections 89, 97.

[71] [Herodotus, *Histories*, 7: sections 175-233.] Lacedaemon was the ancestor of the Spartans.

[72] Salamis Bay, with its narrow and winding entrances at both ends, is the present-day Bay of Elefsina.

[73] Herodotus, *Histories*, 8: sections 1-96.

[74] Ibid, 9: sections 25-75.

[75] Thucydides, *History*, translated by B. Jowett (Oxford: Clarendon Press, 1881), 7: section 28.

[76] Ibid, 2: sections 49-53.

[77] *Homeric Hymns; Homeric Apocrypha; Lives of Homer*, translated by Martin L. West (Cambridge: Harvard University Press, 2003), section 19.7.

[78] The Arctic region takes its name from this constellation, known in Greek as Αρκτοσ, meaning *Bear*.

[79] Eratosthenes credited Hesiod with this story. [Eratosthenes, *Catasterismi*, in *Star Myths of the Greeks and Romans*, compiled by Pseudo-Eratosthenes, translated by Theony Condos, *Star Myths of the Greeks and Romans* (Grand Rapids: Phanes Press, 1997), p. 197.]

[80] The name Bootes derives from *boetes*, which is Greek for *shouter*. [Richard Allen, *Star Names: Their Lore and Meaning* (New York: Dover Publications, 1963), 93.]

[81] The Bear and the Little Bear are the modern constellations Ursa Major and Ursa Minor, but they are commonly known by the names of their asterisms: the Big Dipper and Little Dipper. Aratus called Ursa Minor the Dog-tailed Bear. [Aratus, *Phaenomena*, 182, 227.]

[82] Aratus, *Phaenomena*, 276.

[83] Manilius, *Astronomica*, translated by G. P. Gould (Cambridge: Harvard University Press, 1977), 4.521.

[84] Apollonius Rhodius provided this tribute to Ariadne: *Once upon a time Ariadne, Minos' maiden daughter, rescued Theseus... from terrible trials through her kindness. Thereafter, she boarded his ship with him and left her country; and even the immortals themselves loved her, and in the midst of the sky her sign, a crown of stars they call Ariadne's, turns all night among the heavenly constellations.* [Apollonius Rhodius, *Argonautica*, 3.997.]

[85] Thucydides, *History*, 7: section 27.

[86] [Hesiod, *Works and Days*, 663.] The fifty-day period beginning with summer solstice lasted from about June 29 to August 17.

[87] [Hesiod, *Works and Days*, 618.] Hesiod refers here to the Pleiades' apparent cosmical setting on about November 3, when the asterism sets on the western horizon just before dawn. Hellenes marked the seasons by noting the positions of stars, asterisms and constellations on the eastern and western horizons at dawn and dusk. At early dawn, while the stars still shine, the heliacal rising of a star denotes its first appearance in the east just ahead of the rising sun. Every morning thereafter, the same star appears higher in the sky at dawn, that is, farther ahead of the sun. Months later, the same star finally sets on the western horizon at dawn. This is called the apparent cosmical setting. Hellenes noted similar positions at dusk. For further information on star, asterism, and constellation risings and settings, as well as diagrams and other factual and technical information, see [David Marshall, *Ancient Skies: Constellation Mythology of the Greeks* (New York: W. W. Norton & Company), 2018.]

[88] [Apollonius Rhodius, *Argonautica*, 1.120.] The Hellenes likely used the bright star Betelgeuse to mark Orion's risings and settings because it is the first bright star in the constellation to rise and the last to set. Thus, Orion's apparent cosmical setting, during the age of Hesiod, occurred on about November 20.

[89] Aratus, *Phaenomena*, 758.

[90] Homer, *Odyssey*, 12.310. The third watch lasts from about 2am to dawn.

[91] [Aratus, *Phaenomena*, 167.] Winter Solstice occurred on about December 26.

[92] Aratus, *Phaenomena*, 408.

[93] Theophrastus, *Concerning Weather Signs*, in *Enquiry into Plants*, translated by Arthur Hort (Cambridge: Harvard University Press, 1949), 1: sections 10, 14, 15, 38-40, 46, 47.

[94] Aratus, *Phaenomena*, 408.

[95] Homer, *Iliad*, 4.74.

[96] Apollonius Rhodius, *Argonautica*, 4.294.

[97] Ibid, 4.202.

[98] [Homer, *Iliad*, 5.1, 22.29; Aratus, *Phaenomena*, 330.] Sirius was known as the Dog Star, because it is the brightest star in the Dog constellation. The name Sirius comes from the Greek word *seirius*, which means *scorching*.

[99] Apollonius Rhodius, *Argonautica*, 2.41.

[100] Ibid, 2.712, note 63.

[101] Sappho, *Fragments*, 81.

[102] Homer, *Odyssey*, 6.182.

[103] Sappho, *Fragments*, 130.

104 Hesiod, *Works and Days*, 704.

105 Ibid, 311, 412.

106 Homer, *Odyssey*, 24.143.

107 Aratus, *Phaenomena*, 5.

108 Ibid, 740.

109 In the fifth century BC, the sun passed through the constellations Goat Horn (Capricornus), Water Bearer (Aquarius), and Fishes (Pisces), during the rainy season, from about December 26 to March 27.

110 [Hesiod, *Works and Days*, 564.] During Hesiod's time, Arcturus' apparent achronycal rising occurred on about February 24. Over the millennia, the precession of the Earth has caused seasonal harbingers, like Arcturus, the Pleiades, Orion, and Sirius, to make their heliacal risings a little later each year.

111 The pruning hook consisted of a sickle-shaped iron blade and wooden handle — a smaller version of the reaping sickle used for the grain harvest. [Hesiod, *Works and Days*, 569; A. W. Mair, "Agricultural Implements," in *Hesiod: The Poems and Fragments* (Oxford: Clarendon Press, 1908), p. 153.]

112 Xenophon, *Oeconomicus*, in *Memorabilia and Oeconomicus*, translated by E. C. Marchant (Cambridge: Harvard University Press, 1938), 17.12.

113 *When the Atlas-born Pleiades rise, start the harvest — the plowing, when they set. They are concealed for forty nights and days, but when the year has revolved they appear once more, when the iron is being sharpened.* [Hesiod, *Works and Days*, 383, 571.]

114 Xenophon, *Oeconomicus*, 18.1.

115 [Hesiod, *Works and Days*, 597.] Hesiod suggested winnowing the wheat when Orion made his heliacal rising, which in Hesiod's day occurred on about June 29.

116 In Hesiod's time, Sirius made its heliacal rising on about July 28.

117 [Hesiod, *Works and Days*, 414; Apollonius Rhodius, *Argonautica*, 2.524.] The Etesian winds occurred from about July 28 to September 6.

118 Hesiod, *Works and Days*, 393, 582, 588.

119 In Hesiod's day, Herald of the Vintage (Vindemiatrix) and Bear Guard (Arcturus) made their heliacal risings on about September 14 and 17, respectively.

120 Hesiod, *Works and Days*, 609.

121 [Hesiod, *Works and Days*, 383, 571, 615.] In Hesiod's time, the apparent cosmical setting of the Pleiades, the Hyades, and Orion occurred on about November 3, November 11, and November 20, respectively.

122 Hesiod, *Works and Days*, 427, 469.

[123] Aristophanes, *Acharnians*, in *Acharnians; Knights*, translated by Jeffrey Henderson (Cambridge: Harvard University Press, 1998), 96.

[124] Hesiod, *Works and Days*, 427.

[125] Xenophon, *Oeconomicus*, 17.2-4.

[126] Hesiod, *Works and Days*, 458, 479.

[127] Ibid, 551, 576.

[128] Ibid, 508, 537.

[129] Ibid, 713.

[130] Plato, *Timaeus*, section 60.

[131] The town of Oropus hosted an annual festival at the nearby Temple of Amphiaraus. The temple and sanctuary was named for a famed diviner beloved of Zeus and Apollo. Homer called Amphiaraus the greatest of seers among mortals, whom the gods *heartily loved*. [Homer, *Odyssey*, 15.244-253.] He had served as king of Argos, and gained further fame for his strength and agility as a champion of the long jump and discus throw. He participated with other heroes in the *Calydonian Boar Hunt,* and wounded the beast by shooting it in the eye with an arrow. When Polynices launched a campaign to regain the throne of Thebes, Amphiaraus marched beside him as one of the *Seven Against Thebes*. As a diviner, he foresaw the failure of the campaign and predicted his own demise, but still participated and fought bravely. As the Thebans gained the upper hand and forced Amphiaraus and the others to flee, Zeus could not bear to watch his enemies cut him down, so he cast a thunderbolt to open the earth and swallow Amphiaraus, chariot and all. In his honor, the people of Oropus built his sanctuary at a sacred spring. For centuries, pilgrims journeyed to the site to consult the spirit of Amphiaraus—the oracle and healer. After presenting an offering, they slept nearby in hopes of receiving favorable answers and insights in their dreams. Those in poor health also bathed in the waters of the sacred, healing spring. [Apollodorus, *The Library*, translated by James George Frazer (Cambridge: Harvard University Press, 1939), I.8: section 2, III.6: sections 1-8; Pausanias, *Description of Greece*, 1.34, sections 1-5.]

[132] Homer, *Odyssey*, 11.309, 572.

[133] Xenophon, *On Hunting*, in *Scripta Minora*, translated by E. C. Marchant (Cambridge: Harvard University Press, 1925), 1.18.

[134] Ibid, 4.1–2, 7–8; 5.1–5; 6.2–4, 11, 13.

[135] Ibid, 4.4–5; 5.10, 16–17; 6.11, 13.

[136] The parents, Atlas and Pleione, are now included in the asterism of the Pleiades, making a total of nine stars. But only six are easily visible.

[137] Aesop, *Fables*, Fable 5: The Fighting Cocks.

[138] Aratus, *Phaenomena*, 402, 643.

[139] Ancient Hellenic astronomers consistently viewed this constellation as the Claws of the Scorpion. But later Roman astronomers began to refer to the constellation as a set of balancing scales. Libra first appeared as such in the Julian Calendar of 46 BC. The Roman astronomer Manilius wrote that when the sun is in Libra (which marks the autumnal equinox), *then the Balance, having matched daylight with the length of night, draws on the Scorpion*. [Manilius, *Astronomica*, 1.266.] In time, the *Balance* was defined as Virgo's scales of justice. But, Arabic astronomers, several centuries later, retained the Hellenic designation of the constellation as the Claws. They called two of the stars: Zubenelgenubi—the southern claw, and Zubeneschamali—the northern claw. These remain their modern names.

[140] Aratus, *Phaenomena*, 323.

[141] Homer, *Iliad*, 18.487.

[142] Hellenes referred to Canis Major as a spotted dog. Perhaps this is because some of his bright stars appear like spots on the rump. Some have suggested that the spots refer to his position in the speckled Milky Way, or are due to Sirius' strong variability as it rises in the atmosphere. [Allen, *Star Names*, pp. 119, 127].

[143] The Greek term *Procyon* literally means *Herald of the Dog*, and at one time was applied to both the constellation and its brightest star.

[144] [Hesiod, *Theogony*, 338.] Phoebus means bright, and is a common forename for Apollo.

[145] Ovid, *Metaphorphoses*, translated by Frank J. Miller (Cambridge: Harvard University Press, 1984), 2.319.

[146] Aratus, *Phaenomena*, 359; Apollonius Rhodius, *Argonautica*, 4.603.

[147] Homer, *Iliad*, 6.182.

[148] Pindar, *Isthmian Odes*, in *Nemean Odes; Isthmian Odes; Fragments*, translated by William Race (Cambridge: Harvard University Press, 1997), 7.44–47.

[149] Homer, *Iliad*, 6.200.

[150] The orders, or styles, of temple architecture from this period included features that would be used on public buildings for more than 2400 years, up to the present. Fluted columns created a sense of heightened verticality and contrasts of light and shadow. They were topped by horizontal friezes and triangular pediments, which usually showcased architectural motifs and sculptures. The three orders included: the Doric—with massive features, broad columns and fluting, flat capitals on saucer-shaped bases, and friezes of alternating triglyphs; the Ionic—with elegant features, narrow columns and fluting,

scrolled or volute capitals, and solid friezes; and the Corinthian—with features similar to that of the Ionic order, but more elaborate with acanthus leaf capitals.

[151] Hesiod, *Works and Days*, 373.

[152] Ibid, 366.

[153] Ibid, 236.

[154] [Plato, *The Republic*, translated by Paul Shorey (Cambridge: Harvard University Press, 1970), sections 514-518.] Many of Plato's writings follow the form of fictional dialogues that accurately express his thoughts and truths.

[155] Sappho, *Fragments*, 31.

[156] [Plato, *Republic*, sections 514-518.] Plato refers to the *Good* by using the Greek word *agathou*, which is the singular form of the masculine/neuter noun. Since the word is singular, it is more specifically translated as the *one Good*.

[157] The list also includes Anaxagoras, Melissus, Empedocles, Philolaus, and Diogenes. Thales believed that all things in motion are alive; that all living things have souls; and that *everything is full of gods*. [Aristotle, *On the Soul*, in *De Anima*, translated by R. D. Hicks (Cambridge, UK: Cambridge University Press, 1907), pp 42-43.] Anaximander declared that: *the Infinite... eternal and ageless... is the cause and first element of things... from which arise all the heavens and the worlds within them*. [Anaximander, *Fragments*, in *Early Greek Philosophy*, quoted by Theophrastus and Simplicius, translated by John Burnet (London: Adam and Charles Black, 1930), p. 52.]

[158] Plato, *Laws*, in *The Dialogues of Plato*, translated by B. Jowett (New York: Random House, 1937), section 716.

[159] Plato, *Timaeus*, section 34.

[160] Ibid, sections 36-37.

[161] Ibid, section 92.

[162] Ibid, sections 40, 69.

[163] Ibid, sections 29-30, 40, 73, 90.

[164] Ibid, section 90.

[165] Plato, *Republic*, section 518.

[166] Homer, *Iliad*, 20.245.

[167] Plato, *Protagoras*, in *The Dialogues of Plato*, translated by B. Jowett (New York: Random House, 1937), section 329.

[168] Hesiod, *Works and Days*, 264.

[169] Ibid, 356.

[170] Sappho, *Fragments*, 158.

[171] Homer, *Iliad*, 20.245; Hesiod, *Works and Days*, 720, 760.

172 Homer, *Iliad*, 10.249.

173 Plato, *Timaeus*, section 81.

174 Theophrastus, *Concerning Weather Signs*, 1: sections 38, 48.

175 Homer, *Odyssey*, 5.269. If Odysseus sailed east with the Bear (Ursa Major) on his left at the time of the summer solstice, then the Pleiades would have risen in the east a few hours before the sun, and Arcturus, the bright star of Bootes, would have set an hour later in the northwest, thus matching Homer's description.

176 Eratosthenes, *Catasterismi*, p. 201.

177 [Aratus, *Phaenomena*, 37.] Thales of Miletus (c. 624-546 BC) is credited with pointing out the Little Bear (Ursa Minor) and convincing Hellenic navigators to follow the more accurate Phoenician method. Today, the tip of Ursa Minor's tail is marked by Polaris—the North Star. [Callimachus, *Iambi*, in *Aetia; Iambi; Lyric Poems*, translated by C. A. Trypanis (Cambridge: Harvard University Press, 1958), 1.52.] Phoenician sailors had a widespread reputation as excellent mariners. Xenophon, an Athenian historian and philosopher, expressed amazement at the impeccable outfitting of their merchant ships: *I have never seen tackle so excellently and accurately arranged.* Each item rested in its own compact storage receptacle, ready for immediate use. This included the full array of rigging, as well as a worthy assortment of weapons for fighting pirates. It also consisted of utensils for cooking and eating, and all the cargo carried for trade: *Each kind of thing was so neatly stowed away that there was no confusion, no work for a searcher, nothing out of place, no troublesome untying to cause delay when anything was needed for immediate use.* The captain's first mate routinely checked the quantity and arrangement of equipment and supplies. In the tight confines of their seafaring home, order remained essential: *People aboard a merchant vessel, even if it's a little one, find room for things and keep order, though tossed violently to and fro, and find what they want to get, though terror stricken.* [Xenophon, *Oeconomicus*, 8.11–17.]

178 Anaximander (c. 610-c. 546 BC) is credited with introducing the gnomon to Hellas. This simple vertical stick was used in his time to cast the sun's shadow and determine noon. The length of the noon shadow also marked the solstices. [Robert Hannah, *Time in Antiquity* (London: Routledge, 2009), p. 69.]

179 By similar use of a vertical stick, the Hellenistic mathematician, Eratosthenes (276-194 BC), measured the angle of the sun's shadow and used that information to calculate the Earth's circumference within 99.2 percent accuracy—an amazing feat. He based his calculation on the theory of a spherical Earth—a theory that dated back at least three centuries earlier to Pythagoras.

Eratosthenes also operated on the valid premise that the sun is at such an extreme distance that it emits virtually parallel rays on the Earth's surface. When he received reports of sunlight reaching the bottom of deep wells at Syene (present Aswan) at noon on summer solstice, he realized that the sun must be directly overhead on that day at that latitude. But farther north in Alexandria, where he lived, the sun at noon on summer solstice cast a shadow from a vertical stick at an angle of one-fiftieth of a circle (7.2 degrees). From this he correctly surmised that the distance from Syene to Alexandria must equal one-fiftieth of the Earth's circumference. Based on a camel trip between these two cities, he estimated the distance at 5040 Egyptian stades (one Egyptian stade equaled 157.5 meters). Fifty times 5040 stades gave the circumference of the Earth at 252,000 stades, or 39,690 kilometers. The north-south circumference of the Earth is actually 40,008 kilometers. His calculation was off by only 0.8 percent. In addition to his talents as a mathematician, Eratosthenes was an astronomer, geographer, historian, music theorist, poet, and athlete. He coined the term *geography* and founded the discipline. He created a map of the known world with latitude and longitude. He proved the Earth's spherical shape, calculated its circumference, and determined its approximate axis tilt. As an astronomer, he invented the armillary sphere and compiled a star catalog. As a historian, he recorded a chronology from the fall of Troy to his own time. As a humanitarian, he condemned Aristotle's division of humans into Hellenes and barbarians. He also produced a work on ethics. He served as the third head librarian at Alexandria, succeeding Apollonius Rhodius. His close friend was the famed mathematician and inventor, Archimedes.

[180] Polaris—the North Star.

[181] [Aratus, *Phaenomena*, 727.] This observation precedes all others in the human record in alluding to the use of time to measure the distance of a sea voyage. More than two thousand years later, the concept was used to solve the perplexing problem of calculating longitude.

[182] Homer, *Odyssey*, 12.310, 14.482.

[183] Sappho, *Fragments*, 168.B.

[184] Pegasus is depicted in the heavens as he emerges newborn from the sea foam, in the same manner that Taurus and Aries appear half-submerged in the sea.

[185] Euripides, *Fragments: Aegeus to Meleager*, translated by Christopher Collard and Martin Cropp (Cambridge: Harvard University Press, 2008), Andromeda section 124.

[186] Ovid, *Metamorphoses*, 4.625.

[187] Ibid, 4.673.

[188] Poseidon's wife, Amphitrite, was a nereid.

[189] Euripides, *Fragments*, Andromeda section 145.

[190] The Arabs later called the star Al-gol, meaning *the ghoul*.

[191] Herodotus, *Histories*, 7: section 61.

[192] Aratus, *Phaenomena*, 653.

[193] Hesiod, *Theogony*, 278.

[194] Heracles is also known by the Roman name Hercules.

[195] Since ancient times, the people of Kleones, in the province of Nemea, have handed down tales of the Nemean Lion whose cave is still visible near their village. The story relates how the long and winding cavern had front and back entrances more than three hundred meters apart. This allowed the maneater to launch forays from different directions and stealthily return to his lair. But when Heracles arrived, he blocked the back entrance with heavy stones to prevent an escape, and crept inside through the main opening.

[196] Hesiod, *Theogony*, 306.

[197] Hesiod related the story of Hydra and Heracles: *They say that Typhon, terrible, outrageous, lawless, sired the evil-minded Hydra of Lerna*, which Hera sent against Heracles. [Hesiod, *Theogony*, 306.]

[198] The Hesperides are the three daughters of Atlas and Hesperis. They lived in the westernmost region of the known world, on the shores of the Strait of Gibraltar.

[199] Serpents are often depicted as trusted guardians, typically keeping watch over springs, homes, and temples. The Erechtheum on the Acropolis had its own guardian serpent, tended by temple maidens.

[200] Apollodorus provided a concise account of the voyage, based upon Apollonius Rhodius. [Apollodorus, *The Library*, I.9: sections 16–28.]

[201] Apollonius Rhodius, *Argonautica*, 4.1192.

[202] Ibid, 2.160.

[203] Ibid, 3.189, note 10.

[204] Ibid, 2.1145.

[205] Ibid, 4.123.

[206] Standard shipbuilding tools of ancient Hellas included an axe and an adze for cutting and shaping timbers and mortises, an auger for drilling holes for pegs, a mallet for joining the timbers by means of pegs and mortises, and a chalk line to shape the timbers straight and true. [For descriptions and illustrations of tools used for constructing boats and dwellings, see Anthony Rich, *The Illustrated Companion to the Latin Dictionary and Greek Lexicon* (London:

Longman, Brown, Green, and Longmans, 1849); W. M. Flinders-Petrie, *Tools and Weapons* (London: British School of Archaeology in Egypt, 1917); Henry Mercer, *Ancient Carpenters' Tools* (Doylestown, PA: Horizon Press, 1975).] Homer described the tools that Calypso provided to Odysseus so he could build a raft: *She gave him a big axe, well fitted to his hands, an axe of bronze, sharpened on both sides; and in it was a beautiful handle of olive wood, securely fastened; and thereafter she gave him a polished adze…. Twenty trees in all did he fell, and trimmed them with the axe; then he cunningly smoothed them all and trued them to the line. Meanwhile Calypso, the beautiful goddess, brought him augers; and he bored all the pieces and fitted them to one another, and with pegs and mortising he hammered it together…. And he set in place the decks, bolting them to the close-set ribs, as he continued the work; and he finished the raft with long gunwales. In it he set a mast and a yardarm fitted to it, and furthermore made him a steering oar…. Meanwhile Calypso, the beautiful goddess, brought him cloth to make him a sail, and he fashioned that too with skill. And he made fast in the raft braces and halyards and sheets, and then with levers worked it down into the bright sea.* [Homer, *Odyssey*, 5.233.]

[207] [Apollonius Rhodius, *Argonautica*, 1.106, 4.1466.] The helmsman served as the primary navigator. He was the onboard expert in noting celestial signs both day and night. He interpreted the winds, ripples, currents, and flocks of migrating birds. His mind held a storehouse of information about coastal landmarks, dangerous obstacles, and the local aggregate of the seafloor. He also steered the ship and adjusted the sail by means of brail lines. As such, he remained indispensable. [Samuel Mark, *Homeric Seafaring* (College Station: Texas A&M Press, 2005), p. 148.]

[208] Apollonius Rhodius, *Argonautica*, 1.1182.

[209] [Apollonius Rhodius, *Argonautica*, 1.562.] The steep and lofty Tisaean Headland lies west of Aphetae.

[210] Pindar, *Pythian Odes*, in *Olympian Odes; Pythian Odes*, translated by William Race (Cambridge: Harvard University Press, 1997), 4.202–203.

[211] Apollonius Rhodius, *Argonautica*, 1.1272.

[212] [Apollonius Rhodius, *Argonautica*, 1.1084.] A halcyon was likely a kingfisher.

[213] Apollonius Rhodius, *Argonautica*, 1.1118, note 118.

[214] The Black Sea was known as the Pontus. The Sea of Marmara was the Propontis, which means *Before Pontus*.

[215] Apollonius Rhodius, *Argonautica*, 3.957.

[216] Ibid, 3.744.

[217] Ibid, 3.1348.

[218] Ibid, 3.1372.

[219] Pindar said the serpent *exceeded in breadth and length a ship of fifty-oars*. [Pindar, *Pythian Odes*, 4.244–245.]

[220] The Aries motif appeared in archaic Hellenic art, most notably in images of Hermes Kriophoros (the ram-bearer), and remained popular into late antiquity. The Ram looking back over his flank, like the constellation image, became a common pose that also appeared in early Christian depictions of the Good Shepherd. These may still be seen in sculptures of the first centuries AD, and in stuccos at the Catacomb of Priscilla in Rome, and elsewhere. See illustration at *https://davidwestonmarshall.com/ancient-skies/*

[221] Homer revered the ship of the Argonauts as *that Argo famed of all*. [Homer, *Odyssey*, 12.70.] Because of its size in the heavens, Argo Navis was divided in modern times into four constellations: Carina, Vela, Pyxis, and Puppis. It also contained one star that is now part of the modern constellation Columba.

[222] Pindar, *Pythian Odes*, 4.176–177.

[223] Apollonius Rhodius, *Argonautica*, 1.26.

[224] Ibid, 1.496.

[225] Ibid, 4.904.

[226] Ibid, 4.1193.

[227] Homer, *Odyssey*, 8.478.

[228] Pindar said, Chiron *raised Jason in his rocky dwelling and then Asklepios, whom he taught the gentle-handed province of medicines.* [Pindar, *Nemean Odes*, 3.53–55.]

[229] For one of many modern depictions of the Rod of Asclepius, see the flag of the United Nations World Health Organization.

[230] Herodotus, *Histories*, 8: section 41.

[231] Apollonius Rhodius, *Argonautica*, 4.592.

[232] Ibid, 4.652.

[233] The star that marks Polydeuces' head is known in modern times by his Latin name, Pollux.

[234] Ancient sources refer to these appearances of St. Elmo's Fire on several occasions.

[235] Apollonius Rhodius, *Argonautica*, 4.1629.

# WORKS CITED

PRIMARY SOURCES

Aesop. *Fables*. In *Babrius and Phaedrus*. Compiled by Babrius. Translated by Ben Edwin Perry. Cambridge: Harvard University Press, 1965.

Anaximander. *Fragments*. In *Early Greek Philosophy*. Translated by John Burnet. London: Adam and Charles Black, 1930.

Apollodorus. *The Library*. Translated by James George Frazer. Cambridge: Harvard University Press, 1939.

Apollonius Rhodius. *The Argonautica*. Translated by William H. Race. Cambridge: Harvard University Press, 2008.

Aratus. *Phaenomena*. In *Callimachus; Lycophron; Aratus*. Translated by G. R. Mair. Cambridge: Harvard University Press, 1955.

Aristophanes. *Acharnians*. In *Acharnians; Knights*. Translated by Jeffrey Henderson. Cambridge: Harvard University Press, 1998.

Aristotle. *On the Soul*. In *De Anima*. Translated by R. D. Hicks. Cambridge, UK: Cambridge University Press, 1907.

Callimachus. *Iambi*. In *Aetia; Iambi; Lyric Poems*. Translated by C. A. Trypanis. Cambridge: Harvard University Press, 1958.

Democritus. *Fragment* 154. In *Ancilla to the Pre-Socratic Philosophers*. Translated by Kathleen Freeman. Cambridge: Harvard University Press, 1962.

Eratosthenes. *Catasterismi*. In *Star Myths of the Greeks and Romans*. Compiled by Pseudo-Eratosthenes. Translated by Theony Condos. Grand Rapids: Phanes Press, 1997.

Euripides. *Fragments: Aegeus to Meleager*. Translated by Christopher Collard and Martin Cropp. Cambridge: Harvard University Press, 2008.

Herodotus. *The Histories*. Translated by Robin Waterfield. Oxford: Oxford University Press, 1998.

Hesiod. *Theogony*. In *Theogony; Works and Days; Testimonia*. Translated by Glenn W. Most. Cambridge: Harvard University Press, 2006.

Hesiod. *Works and Days*. In *Theogony; Works and Days; Testimonia*. Translated by Glenn W. Most. Cambridge: Harvard University Press, 2006.

Homer. *Iliad*. Translated by A. T. Murray and William F. Wyatt. Cambridge: Harvard University Press, 1999.

Homer. *Odyssey*. Translated by A. T. Murray and George E. Dimock. Cambridge: Harvard University Press, 1995.

*Homeric Hymns; Homeric Apocrypha; Lives of Homer*. Translated by Martin L. West. Cambridge: Harvard University Press, 2003.

Hyginus. *Poetic Astronomy*. In *Star Myths of the Greeks and Romans*. Translated by Theony Condos. Grand Rapids: Phanes Press, 1997.

Manilius. *Astronomica*. Translated by G. P. Goold. Cambridge: Harvard University Press, 1977.

Ovid. *Metaphorphoses*. Translated by Frank J. Miller. Cambridge: Harvard University Press, 1984.

Pausanias. *Description of Greece*. Translated by W. H. S. Jones. Cambridge: Harvard University Press, 1955.

Pindar. *Isthmian Odes*. In *Nemean Odes; Isthmian Odes; Fragments*. Translated by William Race. Cambridge: Harvard University Press, 1997.

Pindar. *Nemean Odes*. In *Nemean Odes; Isthmian Odes; Fragments*. Translated by William Race. Cambridge: Harvard University Press, 1997.

Pindar. *Pythian Odes*. In *Olympian Odes; Pythian Odes*. Translated by William Race. Cambridge: Harvard University Press, 1997.

Plato. *Laws*. In *The Dialogues of Plato*. Translated by B. Jowett. New York: Random House, 1937.

Plato. *Protagorus*. In *The Dialogues of Plato*. Translated by B. Jowett. New York: Random House, 1937.

Plato. *The Republic*. Translated by Paul Shorey. Cambridge: Harvard University Press, 1970.

Plato. *Timaeus*. In *The Dialogues of Plato*. Translated by B. Jowett. New York: Random House, 1937.

Ptolemy. *Almagest*. In *Syntaxis Mathematica*. Translated by J. L. Heiberg. Leipzig: B. G. Teubneri, 1898.

Ptolemy. *Almagest*. In *Ptolemy's Almagest*. Translated by G. J. Toomer. Princeton: Princeton University Press, 1998.

Sappho. *Fragments*. In *Greek Lyric: Sappho; Alcaeus*. Translated by David Campbell. Cambridge: Harvard University Press, 1982.

Sophocles. *Oedipus Tyrannus*. In *Ajax; Electra; Oedipus Tyrannus*. Translated by Hugh Lloyd-Jones. Cambridge: Harvard University Press, 1994.

Theophrastus. *Concerning Weather Signs*. In *Enquiry into Plants*. Translated by Arthur Hort. Cambridge: Harvard University Press, 1949.

Thucydides. *History*. Translated by B. Jowett. Oxford: Clarendon Press, 1881.

Xenophon. *Oeconomicus*. In *Memorabilia and Oeconomicus*. Translated by E. C. Marchant. Cambridge: Harvard University Press, 1938.

Xenophon. *On Hunting*. In *Scripta Minora*. Translated by E. C. Marchant. Cambridge: Harvard University Press, 1925.

SECONDARY SOURCES

Allen, Richard. *Star Names: Their Lore and Meaning*. New York: Dover Publications, 1963.

Condos, Theony. *Star Myths of the Greeks and Romans*. Grand Rapids: Phanes Press, 1997.

Diels, Hermann. *Die Fragmente der Vorsokratiker*. Berlin: Weidmann, 1964.

Flinders-Petrie, W. M. *Tools and Weapons*. London: British School of Archaeology in Egypt, 1917.

Freeman, Kathleen. *Ancilla to the Pre-Socratic Philosophers*. Cambridge: Harvard University Press, 1962.

Hannah, Robert. *Time in Antiquity*. London: Routledge, 2009.

Mair, A. W. "Agricultural Implements." In *Hesiod: The Poems and Fragments*. Oxford: Clarendon Press, 1908.

Mark, Samuel. *Homeric Seafaring*. College Station: Texas A&M Press, 2005.

Marshall, David. *Ancient Skies: Constellation Mythology of the Greeks*. New York: W. W. Norton & Company, 2018.

Mercer, Henry. *Ancient Carpenters' Tools*. Doylestown, PA: Horizon Press, 1975.

Rich, Anthony. *The Illustrated Companion to the Latin Dictionary and Greek Lexicon*. London: Longman, Brown, Green, and Longmans, 1849.

Schachter, Albert. *Cults of Boiotia*. London: University of London, Institute of Classical Studies, 1986.

Homer, c. 750 BC.

Hesiod, c. 700 BC.

# ABOUT THE AUTHOR

David W. Marshall, PhD, is a historian and Professor Emeritus at Texas Tech University. For four decades, he has researched the history of Archaic and Classical Greece in libraries, archives, and museums throughout Europe and North America, and at more than two hundred Hellenic archeological and historic sites in Greece and adjoining countries. His broader studies of ancient and primitive cultures have led him to remote villages and related sites in seventy-seven countries and seven continents. In addition to academic publications, he is the author of *Ancient Skies: Constellation Mythology of the Greeks* (Countryman Press, W. W. Norton, 2018), and *Mountain Man: John Colter, the Lewis & Clark Expedition, and the Call of the American West* (Countryman Press, W. W. Norton, 2017).

# Appendix 1.   GLOSSARY

amphora (pl. amphorae): large jugs with narrow necks and double handles used to store and ship water, wine, and olive oil.

aulos: a flute-like woodwind instrument.

cithara: a lyre. The word is ancestral to *guitar*.

drachma: a standard silver coin used in classical Greece. At the time of the Persian wars its value was equivalent to that of one day's wage for skilled labor.

dryad: nymphs that inhabit oak trees.

hecatomb: the sacrifice of one hundred cattle to the gods.

hoplite: a heavily armed and armored infantryman.

naiad: nymphs that inhabit freshwater sources.

obol: a standard coin. Six obols equaled a drachma. At the time of the Persian wars its value was equivalent to that of one day's wage for unskilled labor.

oread: nymphs that inhabit mountains.

pentathlon: a highly regarded athletic contest consisting of five events: the sprint, long jump, wrestling, discus throw, and javelin throw.

penteconter: a fifty-oared galley that served as a merchant vessel or warship.

phalanx: a tight formation of hoplites with shields overlapping and spears thrust forward.

phratry: a kinship clan that accepted boys as members when they came of age, typically at fourteen years.

polis (pl. poleis): a city-state, with citizens that inhabited a capital city and its outlying villages and countryside. Athens was a polis that included the capital city and surrounding area of Attica. An acropolis was a high point within a polis, which served as a temple site and stronghold.

rhombus: an oblong object twirled on the end of a long cord to produce a whirring sound. It was often used to communicate with spirits or deities.

satyr: woodland spirits with horse-like ears and tails. They often accompany Dionysus and Pan.

sophist: a teacher of philosophy, rhetoric, music, mathematics, and other subjects designed to provide a broad education for students. Some sophists were condemned for focusing on the art of persuasion and exploitation, and for charging their eager students inflated tuitions.

stade: a unit of measure that varied from country to country. In Attica, one stade was equivalent to 606 feet. Stade measurements in this book include 2 stades (just under a quarter mile), 4 stades (just under a half mile), 20 stades (2.3 miles), 24 stades (2.8 miles), 29 stades (3.3 miles), 44 stades (5 miles), 48 stades (5.5 miles), 51 stades (5.8 miles), 100 stades (11.5 miles), and 230 stades (26.4 miles). An area that was one-half stade by one stade was equivalent to four acres.

titans: twelve immortals that preceded and sired the gods.

trireme: a warship which typically held 170 oars arranged in three banks, and a crew of about two hundred men.

tympanum: a shallow-framed skin drum struck with the hand.

# Appendix 2.   TIMELINE OF APPROXIMATE DATES, BC.

*Fictional events are italicized.*

1200    Trojan War

750     Homer writes the <u>Iliad</u> and <u>Odyssey</u>.

700     Hesiod writes <u>Works and Days</u> and <u>Theogony</u>.

624     Thales of Miletus is born. He lives until 546.

547     Cyrus, King of Persia, conquers Hellenic colonies in Ionia.

499     The Ionian Revolt begins as Hellenes rebel against Persian rule.

495     *Astrape's grandfather, Pappos, is born.*

492     The Persian invasion of mainland Hellas, led by Mardonius, falls
        victim to a storm off the coast of Mt. Athos.

490     Darius, King of Persia, sends an invading force against Eretria and
        Athens. It is defeated at Marathon and withdraws.

480     Xerxes, King of Persia, invades Hellas. His massive army defeats a
        Hellenic coalition led by Leonidas and three hundred Spartans at
        Thermopylae. Persians ravage the countryside and destroy the
        Athenian Acropolis. The Hellenic fleet defeats the Persian fleet at
        Salamis. Xerxes withdraws but leaves a large army in Hellas.

479     At the Battle of Plataea, a Hellenic coalition led by Spartans and
        Athenians defeats the Persian army, forcing it to withdraw from
        Hellas. Athens emerges as a maritime power and takes the offensive
        against Persians in Ionia. The Classical Age begins.

478     The Delian League is founded as a maritime alliance, but becomes an
        Athenian Empire. About three hundred poleis ultimately join.

470     Athens forces Naxos to remain in the Delian League.

449     The last Ionian cities are freed from Persian rule.

447     Pericles begins rebuilding the Acropolis following its destruction by Persians in 480. Work begins on the Parthenon, which will be completed in 438.

440     Socrates begins teaching in Athens.

431     The Peloponnesian War commences when Sparta challenges Athenian military dominance and begins a series of annual invasions.

430     Plague breaks out in Athens.

428     Plato is born. He dies in 348.

426     The Athenian plague subsides after one-fourth of the population perishes, including Pericles.

425     *Astrape and Bronte are born. Their mother dies in childbirth.*

421     A truce halts the Peloponnesian War, but both sides violate terms. The Erechtheum is begun, and completed in 406.

420     *Astrape and Bronte listen to Pappos' stories of the constellations.*

416     Athens conquers neutral Milos, killing or enslaving the inhabitants.

415     Athens launches a fleet to capture Syracuse. *Sea raiders from Pamphylia ravage the unprotected Attic coast.*

413     The Athenian fleet is defeated at Syracuse. Spartans establish a fortress in Attica at Decelea and free Athenian slaves from mines.

407     *Astrape enters military training.*

405     The naval battle of Aegospotami results in Spartan victory over the Athenian fleet. *Astrape begins military service.*

404     Athens is blockaded and surrenders her fleet and fortifications to Sparta. Athens is placed under the rule of the Thirty Tyrants which promptly executes hundreds of political rivals.

| | |
|---|---|
| 403 | The Thirty Tyrants are deposed and replaced by a democracy. |
| 400 | *Astrape and Tempe are married.* |
| 399 | Socrates is executed. |
| 395 | The Corinthian War commences in opposition to Spartan dominance. The alliance consists of Athens, Thebes, Corinth, Argos and other poleis. The war continues intermittently until 371. |
| 390 | The Athenian army under Iphicrates defeats the Spartans. *Astrape participates.* |
| 380 | Plato writes <u>The Republic</u>. |
| 375 | *Astrape voyages to Joppa.* |
| 371 | Thebans defeat Spartans at the Battle of Leuctra. |
| 350 | *Astrape rescues Pais, and reflects on his life during one winter night.* |
| 338 | Philip of Macedonia's victory over Athens and Thebes at Chaeronea makes him overlord of Hellas. He creates a federation and plans an invasion of Asia. |
| 334 | Alexander the Great, Philip's son, launches an invasion of Persia. |
| 323 | Alexander dies. The Hellenistic Age begins. |

# Appendix 3.   FARNESE ATLAS CELESTIAL GLOBE

The oldest surviving images of the Greek constellations are depicted on the *Farnese Atlas*—a Roman sculpture copied from a Greek original of the second century BC. The marble sculpture portrays the titan Atlas holding a large celestial globe on his shoulders. The globe depicts all but a few of the forty-eight classical constellations. Hipparchus, the famed astronomer (c. 190-120 BC), likely contributed to the creation of the Greek celestial globe in the second century BC. The later Roman copy is in the Farnese Collection, National Archeological Museum, Magna Graecia, Naples, Italy.

Note: When observing a celestial globe, one must remember that the sphere represents the sky, with the Earth inside at the center. It is as if the viewer is standing in outer space, beyond the constellations, and is looking back toward Earth. That is why celestial images appear in reverse, and some have their backs to the viewer as they fix their gaze on Earth.

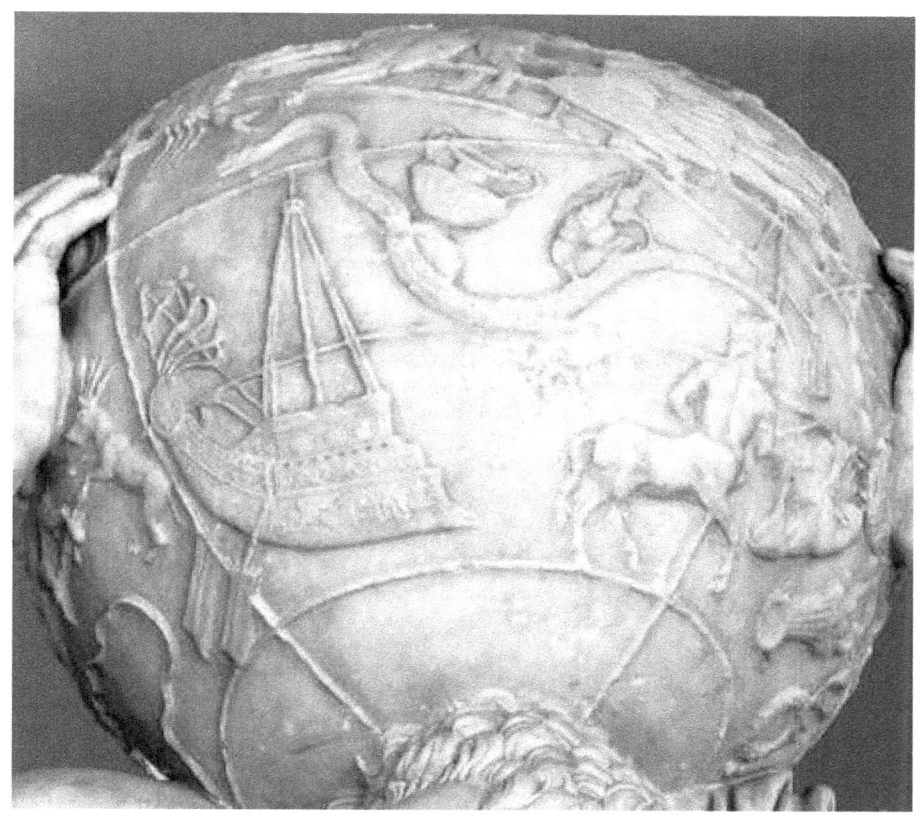

Constellations (left to right; top to bottom): Crab (Cancer), Lion (Leo), Maiden (Virgo), Hydra, Crater, Crow (Corvus), Dog (Canis Major), Argo (Argo Navis), Centaur (Centaurus), Wild Animal (Lupus), Scorpion (Scorpius), River (Eridanus), Incense Altar (Ara), Southern Wreath (Corona Australis). National Archeological Museum, Magna Graecia, Naples, Italy.

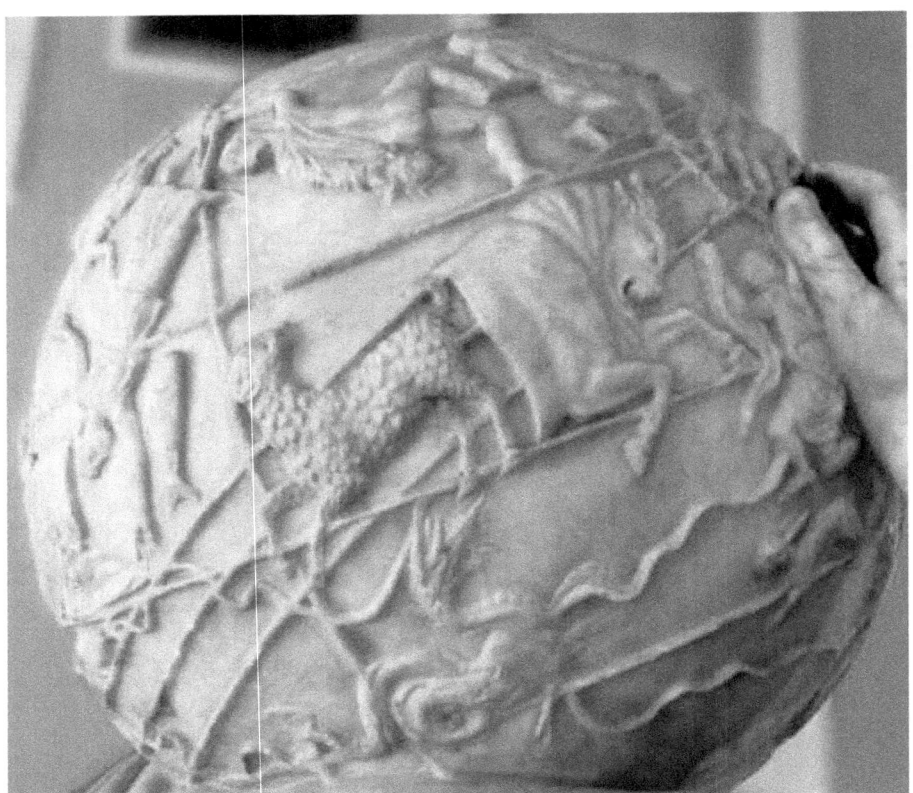

Constellations (left to right; top to bottom): Perseus, Charioteer (Auriga), Twins (Gemini), Cassiopeia, Andromeda, Fishes (Pisces), Ram (Aries), Bull (Taurus), Orion, Sea Monster (Cetus), River (Eridanus), Hare (Lepus). National Archeological Museum, Magna Graecia, Naples, Italy.

Constellations (left to right; top to bottom): Dragon (Draco), Cepheus, Bird (Cygnus), Cassiopeia, Andromeda, Perseus, Eagle (Aquila), Dolphin (Delphinus), Fishes (Pisces, upper fish), Horse (Pegasus), Ram (Aries), Goat Horn (Capricornus), Water Bearer (Aquarius), Fishes (Pisces, lower fish). National Archeological Museum, Magna Graecia, Naples, Italy.

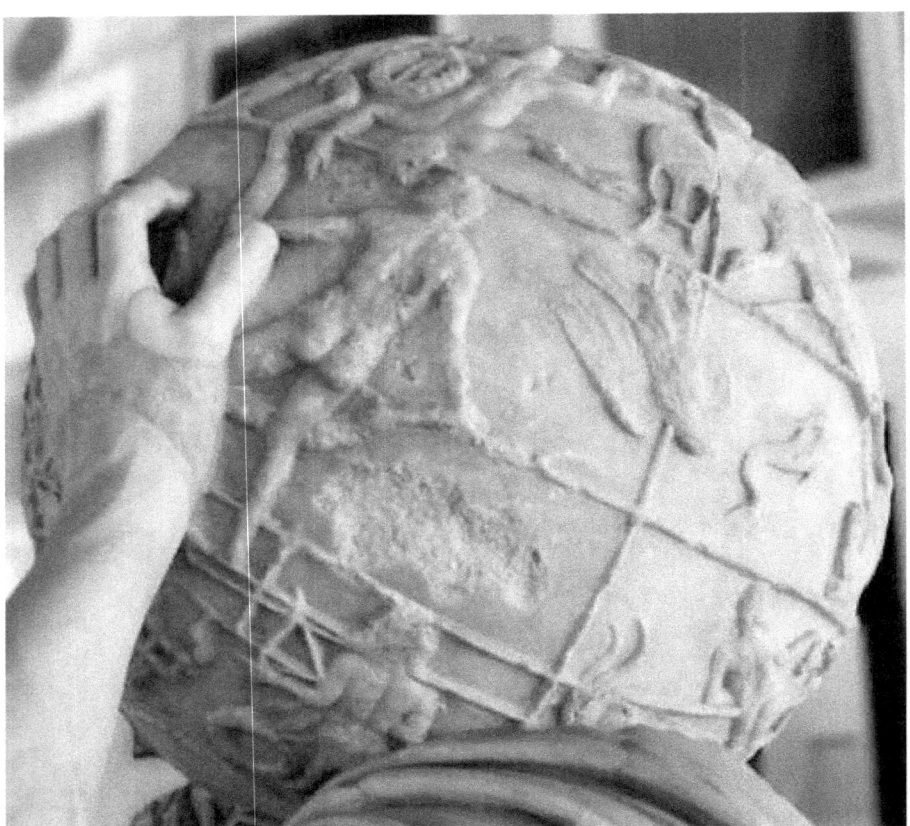

Constellations (left to right; top to bottom): Bootes, Snake (Serpens), Northern Wreath (Corona Borealis), Kneeler (Hercules), Dragon (Draco), Lyre (Lyra), Bird (Cygnus), Snake Holder (Ophiuchus), Eagle (Aquila), Dolphin (Delphinus), Horse (Pegasus), Incense Altar (Ara), Scorpion (Scorpius, stinger), Southern Wreath (Corona Australis), Archer (Sagittarius), Goat Horn (Capricornus), Water Bearer (Aquarius). National Archeological Museum, Magna Graecia, Naples, Italy.

# Appendix 4.  GREEK CONSTELLATION, ASTERISM, AND STAR NAMES

| Translated Greek Name terism/Star | Greek Name | Latin/Modern As- |
|---|---|---|
| Andromeda | Ανδρομεδα | Andromeda |
| Archer | Τοξοτησ | Sagittarius |
| Argo | Αργω | Argo Navis |
|     Canopus | Κανωβοσ | Canopus |
| Arrow | Οιστοσ | Sagitta |
| Bear | Αρκτοσ | Ursa Major |
| Bird | Ορνισ | Cygnus |
| Bootes | Βοωτησ | Bootes |
|     Bear Guard | Αρκτουροσ | Arcturus |
| Bull | Ταυροσ | Taurus |
|     Pleiades | Πληιαδεσ | Pleiades |
|     Hyades | Ὑαδεσ | Hyades |
| Cassiopeia | Κασσιεπεια | Cassiopeia |
| Centaur | Κενταυροσ | Centaurus |
| Cepheus | Κηφευσ | Cepheus |
| Charioteer | Ἡνιοχοσ | Auriga |
|     Goat | Αιξ | Capella |
|     Kids | Εριφοι | Haedi |
| Claws | Χηλαι | Libra |
| Crab | Καρκινοσ | Cancer |
|     Donkeys | Ονοι | Aselli |
|     Manger | Φατνη | Praesepe |
| Crater | Κρατηρ | Crater |
| Crow | Κοραξ | Corvus |
| Dog | Κυων | Canis Major |
|     Dog Star | Κυων | Sirius |
| Dolphin | Δελφιν | Delphinus |
| Dragon | Δρακων | Draco |
| Eagle | Αετοσ | Aquila |
|     Eagle | Αετοσ | Altair |
|     Ganymede | Γανυμηδησ | Antinous |

| | | |
|---|---|---|
| Fishes | Ιχθυεσ | Pisces |
| Goat Horn | Αιγοκερωσ | Capricornus |
| Hare | Λαγωοσ | Lepus |
| Herald of the Dog | Προκυων | Canis Minor |
|     Herald of the Dog | Προκυων | Procyon |
| Horse | Ἱπποσ | Pegasus |
| Horse Head | Ἱπποσ Προτομησ | Equuleus |
| Hydra | Ὑδρα | Hydra |
| Incense Altar | Θυμιατηριον | Ara |
| Kneeler | Εν γονασιν | Hercules |
| Lion | Λεων | Leo |
|     Prince | Βασιλισκοσ | Regulus |
| Little Bear | Αρκτοσ μικρα | Ursa Minor |
| Lyre | Λυρα | Lyra |
|     Lyre | Λυρα | Vega |
| Maiden | Παρθενοσ | Virgo |
|     Ear of Grain | Σταχυσ | Spica |
|     Herald of Vintage | Προτρυγητηρ | Vindemiatrix |
| Northern Wreath | Στεφανοσ βορειοσ | Corona Borealis |
| Orion | Ωριων | Orion |
| Perseus | Περσευσ | Perseus |
|     Gorgon | Γοργω | Algol |
| Ram | Κριοσ | Aries |
| River | Ποταμοσ | Eridanus |
| Scorpion | Σκορπιοσ | Scorpius |
|     Ares Counterpart | Ανταρησ | Antares |
| Sea Monster | Κητοσ | Cetus |
| Snake | Οφισ | Serpens |
| Snake Holder | Οφιουχοσ | Ophiuchus |
| Southern Fish | Ιχθυσ νοτιοσ | Piscis Austrinus |
| Southern Wreath | Στεφανοσ νοτιοσ | Corona Australis |
| Triangle | Τριγωνον | Triangulum |
| Twins | Διδυμοι | Gemini |
| Water Bearer | Ὑδροχοοσ | Aquarius |
| Wild Animal | Θηριον | Lupus |

# Appendix 5.  MODERN CONSTELLATION NAMES

| Latin/Modern Name | Translated from Latin | Translated from Greek |
|---|---|---|
| Andromeda | Andromeda | Andromeda |
| Antlia | Pump | |
| Apus | Bird of Paradise | |
| Aquarius | Water Bearer | Water Bearer |
| Aquila | Eagle | Eagle |
| Ara | Altar | Incense Altar |
| Argo Navis* | The Ship Argo | Argo |
| Aries | Ram | Ram |
| Auriga | Charioteer | Charioteer |
| Bootes | Bootes | Bootes |
| Caelum | Chisel | |
| Camelopardalis | Giraffe | |
| Cancer | Crab | Crab |
| Canes Venatici | Hunting Dogs | |
| Canis Major | Big Dog | Dog |
| Canis Minor | Little Dog | Herald of the Dog |
| Capricornus | Goat Horn | Goat Horn |
| Carina | Ship's Keel | |
| Cassiopeia | Cassiopeia | Cassiopeia |
| Centaurus | Centaur | Centaur |
| Cepheus | Cepheus | Cepheus |
| Chamaeleon | Chameleon | |
| Cetus | Sea Monster | Sea Monster |
| Circinus | Compass for Drawing | |
| Columba | Dove | |
| Coma Berenices | Berenice's Hair | |
| Corona Australis | Southern Wreath | Southern Wreath |
| Corona Borealis | Northern Wreath | Northern Wreath |
| Corvus | Crow | Crow |
| Crater | Wine Mixing Bowl | Crater |
| Crux | Cross | |
| Cygnus | Swan | Bird |
| Delphinus | Dolphin | Dolphin |

207

| Dorado | Swordfish | |
| Draco | Dragon | Dragon |
| Equuleus | Little Horse | Horse Head |
| Eridanus | Eridanus | River |
| Fornax | Furnace | |
| Gemini | Twins | Twins |
| Grus | Crane | |
| Hercules | Hercules | Kneeler |
| Horologium | Clock | |
| Hydra | Hydra | Hydra |
| Hydrus | Water Snake | |
| Indus | Indian | |
| Lacerta | Lizard | |
| Leo | Lion | Lion |
| Leo Minor | Little Lion | |
| Lepus | Hare | Hare |
| Libra | Scales | Claws |
| Lupus | Wolf | Wild Animal |
| Lynx | Lynx | |
| Lyra | Lyre | Lyre |
| Mensa | Table | |
| Microscopium | Microscope | |
| Monoceros | Unicorn | |
| Musca | Fly | |
| Norma | Level | |
| Octans | Octant | |
| Ophiuchus | Snake Holder | Snake Holder |
| Orion | Orion | Orion |
| Pavo | Peacock | |
| Pegasus | Pegasus | Horse |
| Perseus | Perseus | Perseus |
| Phoenix | Phoenix | |
| Pictor | Painter's Easel | |
| Pisces | Fishes | Fishes |
| Piscis Austrinus | Southern Fish | Southern Fish |
| Puppis | Ship's Stern | |
| Pyxis | Ship's Compass | |
| Reticulum | Net | |

| | | |
|---|---|---|
| Sagitta | Arrow | Arrow |
| Sagittarius | Archer | Archer |
| Scorpius | Scorpion | Scorpion |
| Sculptor | Sculptor | |
| Scutum | Shield | |
| Serpens | Snake | Snake |
| Sextans | Sextant | |
| Taurus | Bull | Bull |
| Telescopium | Telescope | |
| Triangulum | Triangle | Triangle |
| Triangulum Australe | Southern Triangle | |
| Tucana | Toucan | |
| Ursa Major | Big Bear | Bear |
| Ursa Minor | Little Bear | Little Bear |
| Vela | Ship's Sail | |
| Virgo | Virgin | Maiden |
| Volans | Flying Fish | |
| Vulpecula | Little Fox | |

*Argo Navis is one the forty-eight classical Greek constellations. But it is not one of the eighty-eight modern constellations because, in the eighteenth century, it was divided into the modern constellations of Vela, Carina, Pyxis, Puppis, and the star, Eta Columbae.

# INDEX

*Abbreviations: st=star, cs=constellation*

212

215

www.ingramcontent.com/pod-product-compliance
Lightning Source LLC
Chambersburg PA
CBHW051432170626
46809CB00006B/2428